Robbie's Story

Robbie's Story

Published by The Conrad Press in the United Kingdom 2018

Tel: +44(0)1227 472 874
www.theconradpress.com
info@theconradpress.com

ISBN 978-1-911546-43-6

Typesetting and Cover Design by:
Charlotte Mouncey, www.bookstyle.co.uk

The Conrad Press logo was designed by Maria Priestley.

Printed and bound in Great Britain
by Clays Ltd, Elcograf S.p.A.

Robbie's Story

stuart carey

For Leo and Liam

Part One: The Town

1

It was a cold and blustery day in early January, 1983, and I was twenty-two.

I caught the three-thirty afternoon train from Manchester Piccadilly and headed back to Munford By-Water, my home town. I had my appointment letter in the top pocket of my jacket, offering me the post of probationary English teacher at a comprehensive school for eleven- to eighteen-year-olds, situated on the outskirts of town. In many ways it was the safe bet, but then I'd been playing it safe all of my life. I'd be staying with my mum and dad until I could find myself a more permanent place to live.

University had proved to be a missed opportunity, so had my year at a teacher training college in Chester. I'd promised myself that I would indulge in all kinds of queer sex, come out and return home triumphant with a permanent boyfriend in-toe. I had bungled the whole affair. Although I was no longer quite the vestal-virgin, I was scarcely more than a demi-verge.

Goldsmiths College in London, where I had been an undergraduate studying for my degree in English for three years, had offered plenty of opportunities. I had known I was gay for most of my life. Indeed, I'd never had so much as the slightest interest in the opposite sex, romantic or sexual. At the age of nine, I fancied one or two boys in my class, to whom I gave more than a passing glance. By the time puberty had arrived and with all of those sweet hormones singing through my veins, I was fancying every boy in my class.

I'd been terribly religious too. Since the age of twelve, I'd attended St John the Evangelist church and regarded myself as a born-again Christian since the age of fourteen. Neither my mum nor my dad was in the least bit religious and neither was my older sister, Natalie. They tended to see my religious devotion as something of a hoot, along with my passion for classical music, vintage hi-fi and all the poetry and literature I could cram into my head.

'Such a very curious child,' my dad had always said of me.

Like me, our Natalie had decided to go into teaching. She taught Geography at a comprehensive school up in Edinburgh. Chris, her husband, had moved there with his work as a motor insurance underwriter. They had a little boy, Ryan, my nephew who was now five and had just started school.

At Goldsmiths College I had been appointed president of the student Christian union during my second term. And between my studies and my added administrative responsibilities as president, I had successfully hidden myself away from queer temptation and life. And then one wet Saturday morning, in October, walking down Oxford Street, at the beginning of my third year, I suddenly realized I didn't believe a word of it. I thought it was all a pile of tosh and arrant nonsense.

If C.S. Lewis had once been surprised by joy and called to faith, I found I'd been surprised by reason and common sense. I also realised that what I'd been doing was using religion to hide away from myself and not face up to the queer soul I really was. I'd most effectively played the greatest of literary conceits, and I'd almost been fooled.

The kind of young men I had allowed myself a romantic dalliance with were altogether the wrong kind. They were terribly middle-class, educated, rather effete and not unlike the protagonist in T.S. Eliot's satiric poem: 'The Love Song of Alfred J. Prufrock.'

I remember one young lad, a second year student, reading Theology. He'd been eying me up, in church, of all places. His name was Adrian. He was somewhat tall and lanky. He wore glasses. I recognised him in the student's bar, a couple of days later. He noticed me, and disengaging himself from his other friends, he came across.

'So, what gives?' he said. He offered to buy me a pint.

'I saw you looking over at me, right in the middle of "The Magnificate", of all things,' I said.

'Well, I thought you were rather magnificent too,' he said.

We went back to my room in halls. He'd come ready prepared. He had condoms in his left pocket of his jacket, and tubes of lubricant, in the other. He wore jeans and a T-shirt, all freshly ironed. Indeed, there was still the faint trace of washing powder, about them. He undressed, rather like anyone would get undressed, before going to bed, or submitting themselves to an irksome medical examination. I found myself undressing with the same disinterest.

He smelled of soap. His hair smelled of shampoo. He also combed it, regularly. His hands looked like they'd never done any hard graft, and I wondered if his nails had ever been anything less that perfectly clean and well kept. He lay on the bed, smiling at me. I got on the bed, but lay beside him, as opposed to jumping on top of him. We kissed. Our tongues met in the almost dry space. There was some perfunctory stroking; he played gently with my nipples. He told me I had a nice cock and that he couldn't wait to feel it inside of him.

It was an easy fit, too easy! It all felt like fixing shelves in the kitchen, attending to the laundry or doing the shopping. I wondered, not for the first time, if this was how straight people, especially when married; experienced sex. I knew he would want me to screw him, but I was not feeling anywhere excited enough to reach the moment. Fortunately, the lights were out, and despite the campus flood-lights, it was still dark enough for me to imagine.

I remembered a working class black lad, from the wrong end of Brixton. He had been sitting with his friends on the tube, back to halls, a couple of days before. I thought about him. I thought about pulling his grubby jeans down around his ankles, eating his face with my hungry kisses, fighting for his love, the endless tussle down some seedy backstreet, and at last, turning him towards a wall, with his face pressed up against the bricks, and screwing him like crazy! With these uncensored thoughts, I found I was able to perform my conjugal duties. He seemed pleased enough. He grunted and moaned in all the right places. We finished and he climbed slowly off the bed and got dressed.

'That was good,' he said, rather like he was telling me that the sky happened to be blue and the Pope just happened to be a catholic, 'no doubt I'll see you around.' And then he was gone.

The type of young man I actually was attracted to was decidedly working-class, with no more than a basic education, with dirt under his finger-nails and grit in his soul. As yet, I'd not allowed myself to have what I really wanted.

Dad owned a grocer's shop in partnership with Uncle Harry.

It was situated down a back street in the centre of town: a thriving concern and to my eyes more like a deli and up-market emporium. The shop cured its own ham and bacon and produced its own tea and coffee. It also offered house-to-house deliveries. Their selection of cheeses was perhaps the finest outside of Manchester. Stebson and Sons was what it said on the sign above the door. It had an almost yesteryear 1950s feel and atmosphere about it. Indeed, going into my dad's shop was like stepping back in time.

Until five years before, we'd lived in a between-the-wars semi. I'd loved the place. Since then Dad had bought a much more impressive house: red-bricked, detached, with an Edwardian walled-garden.

'We might be in trade,' said Dad, 'but that doesn't mean we can't have a good address.' For me, well, our old house seemed a perfectly good address to me.

It was at our old address that I'd become friends with Matthew Penley and David Symcox. We'd hung about together, playing knock-about on the streets since we were nine. We'd gone to the same primary school and had progressed to the local comprehensive, sharing our triumphs and our woes as well as all of our academic successes. Matthew had gone to Lancaster University where he had graduated in Maths. He'd come back to re-settle in Munford and was now working in a bank on their fast promotion track for graduates. David, every bit as clever as Matthew and I, had not wanted to go into further education. His dad had a plumbing business and after getting three good A' Levels, in the end, he'd decided to go into that line of work with his dad.

'There's money in toilets,' he was prone to say. He was right, for he was never short of a bob or two.

The main reason I'd decided to move back to Munford, was Matthew and David. We hated being apart and during the time Matthew and I were at university, the three of us still spent most of our weekends together. And then I was looking forward to joining them on our lads' night out, a ritual we carried out religiously every Saturday evening, at our local real ale pub. The taciturn Welsh landlord, Selwyn Jones, happened to serve the best pint of the local brew.

The previous Saturday at eight in the morning, David had turned up to drive all my stuff back to Munford. He'd brought his dad's vehicle. It was a large white van with the motif: *Symcox Family Plumbers*. And then there was the somewhat cheeky slogan: *Toilets Are Our Business*. He'd said he was bringing the much smaller van. David's idea of a joke, no doubt intended to shock my landlady. I went down the long narrow and rather dark hall of my digs, to his loud ringing of the front door bell. I opened the door to his cheery face.

'Robbie, the man,' he said.

We hugged and bashed each other on the back. The landlady was standing, hands on hips with an amused expression on her face, wondering what all the commotion was about.

'Meet, Ivy Dukes,' I said, 'the best landlady in Chester.'

'Have you eaten?' she asked him. He told her he could do with a spare bite if she was willing. A few minutes later he was tucking into a full English breakfast and a steaming mug of roast coffee.

I'd taken on a temporary teaching post, covering for maternity leave. The job didn't finish until the end of the week, so David was taking most of my stuff home before me, including

my pride and joy, the vintage hi-fi as well as over six hu
records.

When I got off the train in Munford I was tempted to ge
a taxi. I only had one small suitcase and I therefore decided
to walk the mile to our house. It was a frosty January late
afternoon, with deep shadows creeping along the sides of the
shops, all along the busy high street, the gentle, poised prelude
to a winter's evening.

Mum and Gran, that is my maternal grandmother, were
fussing away like crazy as soon as I rang the front door.

'What's that gorgeous smell?' I said as I entered the house.

'Naturally, I've gone and killed the fatted calf,' said Mum.

She had actually cooked my favourite dish of steak and
potato pie with all the trimmings. And Gran had cooked her
own speciality of apple-suite pudding.

'Where's, Dad?' I said.

'Oh, he's still busy making his first million with your Uncle
Harry,' she said, 'before he is fifty.' This roughly translated
meant he was still at work.

'I dare say you'll be off to the pub tonight?' she said. I told
her it was a matter of tradition.

Gran thought that Fiona and Rhona, Matthew and David's
girlfriends, might have other ideas, and she told me so. She
also informed me that Matthew and Fiona were hoping to get
married in the spring.

'And I shouldn't wonder if that, David,' she said, 'isn't
running up that isle behind them.'

'I wish it was your wedding we were going to,' said Gran.

I always hated it when they brought up the subject of
marriage and why I hadn't got a girlfriend. I'd lied that I'd met

15

one or two girls at college, but it hadn't come to anything, and that was why I'd not brought them back home on a visit.

Gary, my twelve-year-old brother then came in, along with Jack our boisterous four-year-old Labrador.

'Cool,' said Gary catching sight of me. It was his favourite word of the moment. But then Jack was jumping up all over me, pinning me down to the ground and giving me a serious licking, much to the amusement of everyone else.

When I stepped into the pub later that evening, Matthew and David were already there. A pint of best bitter was on the table, along with a shot of my favourite single malt. They were shouting and hollering my name as I entered.

'Here,' said David, 'let's have a moment of due reverence whilst you sink your lips into that ale.' I took my first sip.

'Nectar of the ruddy gods,' I said, causing the other two to laugh.

'Welcome home,' they both said in unison with great smiles plastered all over their faces.

I'd not even been up to my room, so I hadn't noticed that my hi-fi wasn't there. They informed me that they were getting it overhauled and reconditioned with new vales in the amplifier, all the bearings oiled in my turntable and my pickup re-tipped.

'Call it our welcome home present,' said David. I was tear-fully grateful.

'You guys are the best mates in the entire world,' I said.

They agreed with me and we were all off laughing and getting gloriously drunk on all of that fabulous ale. They also informed me that they had been putting feelers out for a place for me to rent.

'The landlord can keep it back for another week,' said

Matthew, 'but I think you'll approve. It's mid-terrace and it's only round the ruddy corner from this place. It's got two bedrooms, a bathroom you could put the London Symphony Orchestra in and there'd still be room. There's also a gorgeous kitchen I dare say you'll want to live in.'

'And the best bit is the landlord is a personal mate of dad. They go to The Rotary Club together, so he's only wanting £120 a month and no bond or deposit,' said David.

'I'll drink to that,' I said.

The pub had a pool table. We rarely played. At weekends, some of the younger lads, from the nearby council estate, popped in for a couple of games and a pint or two of lager. They were aged between eighteen and twenty. Two of them were skin-heads. They didn't cause any bother, but could be a bit rowdy at times. One of the skin-heads, very much under the thumb of 'his lass,' always took my fancy. He was such a cocky little bugger too! In the gents, he would stand back from the urinal and having held onto it all, he would piss in a great celebratory fountain, all the while beaming and saying to anyone who was close at hand, 'it's better out than in.'

Later in the evening David said:

'Guess what, they've gone and opened a gay bar off the town centre!' He told me it was called The Manhattan Bar.

'Well if I want my shirt lifting,' I said, 'I'll know where to go.'

Whenever the subject got round to anything gay, we always thought of something fatuous to say. I had to prove to them my own straight credentials and so I would think of something crude and homophobic to add to the conversation.

Secretly, I was deeply curious about the place. I also wondered how far from the town centre it was, and whether or not I would be able to sneak myself there one evening, without anyone being any of the wiser.

I'd been interviewed by a couple of the school governors, as well as the deputy head mistress. She looked like she was approaching retirement. She was black. They called her Clarissa Knight. I found her a bit scary. The actual head, Mr Henry Wilson and my department head, Norman Jackstone, I was still to meet. I got to meet Mr Wilson towards the end of the first day.

'It's a busy school with a good reputation. We get the results. School uniform is to be worn correctly at all times and any homework assignments not handed in on time, warrants an immediate detention.

'Three detentions in the same term and that pupil must be suspended. There is no exceptions to this rule and no mitigating circumstances, so good day to you sir,' he said.

Mr Jackstone was there from the beginning of the week. It took him until the end of that first week before he honoured me with an audience.

'So you're what they've sent us from teacher training college?' he began.

'And I also have a good 2.1 from Goldsmiths, one of the finest institutions in the UK for English,' I said. I was trying to level the playing field. He looked me up and down and sniffed.

'Well we'll have to see how you make out,' he said.

'Oh and by-the-way, I'll be scrupulously going through all your lesson plans with a fine tooth comb. And God help you if I should find anything amiss. Now return to your class,' he said dismissively. By the end of my second week, I signed up with a union. I thought I might need them.

It was still the dreadful dark ages, where most schools used corporal punishment. I was pleased to learn at my interview, that the school had adopted a policy where such punishments were only ever administered, in the direst of cases. I'd always considered the use of the cane as a form of legalised child-abuse.

My teaching plans were indeed gone through. They seemed to pass muster.

'I suppose they'll do,' he said. 'I bet you are full of lots of daft new-fangled notions. Believe it or not, I used to be an idealist when I was your age,' he said.

'There's no sense in that. Kids need drilling. Most of them have straw for brains and it's only through constant repetition that anything sticks.'

So much for all my grand ideas of actually getting the kids turned on to learning and falling in love with both literature and the English language, I thought.

When I was a child of eight, a teacher read to us 'The Tiger' by William Blake. It was the first time I'd heard the poem. Somehow it sounded all wrong, but I didn't know why. 'I bet I could read it better and I bet one day I could be the best English teacher in the whole big wild world.' I had said to myself.

It was a few months later that my mum read me the poem again. This time, along with a group of my fellow urchins, our faces covered in face paint, we all listened; we all danced to the rhythm of his verse, thrilled in our hearts, awakened to the firelight incantation of his poetry. By the time I was twelve, *Songs of Innocence and Experience* was part of my DNA, and all the poets from the Romantic era woven up with the strange and crazy tapestry of my soul. When I went to face my very first class, there was no stage fright. You see I had been rehearsing the part since I was eight, along with my teddy-bears. I knew exactly how it would be.

As for keeping order and maintaining discipline, it was just never an issue. The kids loved me and I loved them. It was a mutual appreciation society from the first, in every class, with all ages, abilities, backgrounds and ethnicities. I got to know the parents and other guardians and careers too, and they quickly came to know me. We were all in it together and I watched timid children blossoming before my wonder-struck eyes, into confident and happy young people. Teaching wasn't a job, it wasn't even a vocation or a profession, and it was my very own special and magical gift from the gods; a sacred trust.

So the actual teaching part of my job was as enjoyable as it had always been. And as for lesson plans, I meticulously wrote them all out, and never followed one in my entire teaching career. As of writing, this is still the case. I believed then, that life consisted of two types of people: the grey ones, with a deeply disturbing puritan agenda and the souls of light, with a spontaneous, maverick, 'let's try and find out' way of going about things.

West Munford Comprehensive fortunately had a great deal of the latter, and only a very few of the former. Unfortunately, the head master and my head of department, were very much part of the former. It came as a refreshing surprise to learn that the deputy, who also taught English to the lower school, was not only one of the latter, but its leading light.

Clarissa Knight, sixty, feisty, who off school campus chain-smoked, loved single malt whisky and adored the music of Al Jolson, who she would only listen to, on her old seventy eight gramophone records; was both an inspiration and a stalwart support to me in those early days.

'You're quite the natural, my dear,' she said to me over coffee in the staff room one lunch time. 'Mind you, that's why I appointed you in the first place. I knew you cared about the kids and I could detect that delightful gleam of pure and delicious madness in your eyes, without which you simply can't teach.'

On the subject of madness, the kids were of the same opinion, especially with the way I got so stirred up about things, from literature, the gorgeous joys of the English language and getting the kids to stop what they were doing, to join me at the classroom window and observe the rain, the suddenness of the falling snow, or sunlight peeking through the gap in the trees along the playing fields.

'Are you just a little bit mad, Sir?' said one of the girls in my class full of fourteen-year-olds.

'Oh, I expect so. I reckon to keep your sanity in this crazy world of ours, you have to be a bit mad,' I said to her. She smiled back at me and the rest of the class began to laugh.

My kid brother insisted on helping out with my move into my new rented house. Matthew and David were fond of him and spoiled and indulged him at every turn.

'I don't want you trying to lift anything heavy,' I said to him.

He told me I had of late become quite the teacher, and that I was all bossy and a complete spoil-sport. Matthew and David laughed at this.

'Don't encourage him,' I said, to no avail.

After four hours of considerable graft, I was fully settled into my new abode, with one or two little things to sort out.

'I never can remember,' said Gary, 'does *Nicholas Nickleby* come before or after *Barnaby Rudge*?'

Matthew, ever the practical one, was making us all a brew

in the kitchen. He'd finally found the kettle and David had nipped out for the milk. My hi-fi had been delivered to David's house. He went back to collect it and then carried out the ritualistic re-installing of it. I let Gary choose a record. He chose a favourite folk rock album.

'That child has excellent taste,' said Matthew. It sounded rather wonderful, and then we were laughing and whooping and hollering out our delight.

And so I was now fending for myself, even though my mum still did all my washing for me and popped it round at my house every Wednesday afternoon. I could always tell when she had been, because the place tended to look a bit more clean and tidy. I was a bit of a house slob, like most young men. I still went round home for Sunday lunch and now and again, popped round for tea on Saturday.

Uncle Bob and Aunt Beverley were regular guests. When I was a child, they had always been my favourite relatives outside of our immediate family. Life had been hard on my aunt in many ways, and sometimes she could be fractious and cantankerous, especially as she'd got older. They had two grown-up children, now both in their early forties. They were her brood and as long as things were going well with them, her mood was fairly jolly. But of late, her daughter's first marriage was on the rocks. And there was my mum boasting away about me and how well I was doing in my new job.

'His deputy says he's a born teacher,' she said.

I could see my aunt visibly begin to bristle.

'What I want to know is this,' she said, 'why is it that a right good-looking lad like your, Robbie,' she said, 'never has a ruddy girlfriend? Why, when I was his age, I had the first one born and the second one on the way. There's not summit up with him is there?' she said.

Everyone round the table went quiet. Gary looked puzzled, my dad looked almost sorrowful. My uncle looked embarrassed, with an expression which seemed to say he wished his wife knew when to hold her tongue. The look on both my mum's and my gran's faces was altogether something else. It was one of horror. It was like they had suddenly been presented with something they had never wanted to see or to admit to. I was queer.

'Come on our, Beverley,' said my dad, 'help yourself to some more grub, your plate's nearly empty.'

It was then that mercifully, the subject passed onto something else. I wanted to get up and leave the table and take myself home. To have done so, would have only brought the whole ghastly episode, into sharper relief. I was meeting up with Matthew and David along with their girlfriends that night at our local. I quickly gave my apologies for having to leave early, making the excuse I still had some homework to mark before I went out. My dad followed me out into the driveway.

'You all right, son?' he said. I told him I was fine. 'You don't want to take any notice to what your aunt says,' he said. I smiled nervously at him, but was anxious to be off. 'Take care, son,' he said as I started to walk up the road, 'and have a good night.'

As I walked the mile home to my place, I was aware that I was shaking with both fear and anger. It was however mostly fear. I'd been rattled. I told myself that I had wanted to come out, whilst also remonstrating, but not like this. By the time I joined the others later that evening, I was almost back to my usual calm equanimity. I was aware however, I was contributing little to the conversation most of the night, and that I was knocking back the shorts much more than was my habit.

Getting into bed at last, I suddenly experienced a fit of the shakes. I put it down to the cold winter weather. In my heart, I didn't believe this for a moment. In a kind of desperation, I asked out one of the secretaries from the typing pool at school. She was twenty-eight and her name was Sandra Telford. We frequented a new wine bar in the centre of town. The décor, all kitsch continental was quite dreadful, the wine was even worse. Sandra loved the place and thought it was full of sophisticated ambience.

'Just think,' she said, sipping her sweet white German wine, 'it's been a whole month that we've been together, a whole month!' And for me that month was already beginning to feel like a lifetime.

She came from a small market town called Addlesworth, about twenty miles south west of Munford. Coal mining was its main industry. She rented a place a short walk from the school, house-sharing with the landlady. They disliked each other. Mrs Hossle, the landlady, was a cheery chain-smoking old cockney. I was rather fond of her. She liked to reminisce about the east end during the fifties. I loved to keep her talking as long as possible. Eventually, however, she would put down her knitting needles, stump out her cigarette and get up to go to bed.

'I better leave you two love-birds alone,' she would say.

And I would have done anything just to keep her there. For after she left, the hideous routine was always the same. Sandra would kick off her shoes, remove her jumper, undo her bra and then settle herself, 'all cosy,' on the sofa, whilst I fondled her breasts. Women's breasts absolutely repulsed me!

Although I had always been a dreadful Maths scholar at school, barely passing my O' Level in the subject when I was sixteen, I now found that I was getting rather good at mental arithmetic. It was impossible for me actually to exist in the present moment. And I thought if she ever asked me to go the full way with her, I could take up a new career as a quantum physicist.

'You certainly know how to please a girl,' she would say afterwards. And there she would be, smiling up at me, making me feel like a total bastard.

She made several visits to see Mum and Dad. Dad was always polite with her and tried to make her feel at home. Mum was barely civil.

'What the hell are you ruddy playing at?' she said to me one evening after Sandra had left.

'I'm not playing at ought,' I said, 'I happen to love her.'

'Love,' tutted my mum, 'you don't even know the meaning of the word.'

The bad feeling between me and my mum got worse, because she could plainly see that I neither loved her nor even liked her. And therefore I needed all the more to prove that I did.

Every Wednesday evening, we went to a working men's club at the bottom of her street. I hated the place. The beer was undrinkable; the turns were usually stand-up comedians, whose stock-in-trade jokes were usually racist, misogynistic and homophobic. Sandra loved them, the cruder the better. I inwardly cringed.

The school had recently employed an assistant caretaker. He was Irish, twenty-years-old, with a mop of red curly hair, quite an attitude on him, rough as hell and as cute as they come. They called him Tyrone Kelly. I also thought he might be gay. He would come into the classroom to deliver something, like some stationary I had ordered, or to fix one of the windows that wouldn't shut properly. He would always give me a sort of cheeky smile. It was as if he knew. I quickly realised he also often frequented the same club Sandra was so very fond of, as did a group of other young men, who were all delightfully rough.

I remember one night, going to the gents and seeing young Tyrone, very much the worse for wear. He had obviously been drinking too much most of the evening. He was nearly falling into the urinal. He had spittle trailing from his gorgeous young mouth and I noticed a large dark wet patch on his jeans, where he had pissed himself and missed the urinal. He was turning me on like crazy. I wanted to gather him up, spittle and all and kiss him hungrily. Instead, I left the gents quickly and walked slowly back to Sandra. The smell of her perfume was abhorrent to me, whereas the aroma of the gents seemed like a kind of heavenly incense in comparison.

Gran had been right, Matthew and Fiona were about to get married. He approached both me and David, saying one of us would have to be his best man. David said he was much too nervous to actually get up in front of all of those people and make a speech. He also thought, as I was a teacher, I must have the gift of the gab. And so I found myself saying I would do the honours.

2

Ned Farrows was head of games. He was in his early thirties. At first I was not sure about him. He would bounce into the staff room and bounce out again. He was Oxford educated; I was informed by Clarissa, with a brilliant first in the classics. He talked with one of those terribly annoying, cut-glass accents, and I thought he was pompous and bumptious. Clarissa tended to agree with my initial assessment of him, but then added,

'Yes my dear, I'm very much afraid he is all of those things, but he also happens to have a heart of pure gold. The kids love him.'

On my very first day, he had bounded over to me in the staff room.

'Great to have you on board, old man,' he said, shaking my hand so hard, that I wondered if he had dislocated my right shoulder. By the end of my first month, we had become close friends and allies.

'You and, Sandra,' he said, 'must come along and have a spot of dinner.'

He had caught me for a quick word in the corridor between classes.

'Thanks,' I said, 'I'd love to.'

His house was old, ramshackle and full of Edwardian charm. His wife, Hilary, was delightful as were their four boisterous children, all boys.

'I hear on the grape-vine that you're looking for a new car, a vintage Morris Minor if I've heard right,' he said, pouring me a generous measure of his best brandy.

'And where did you hear that?' I said.

'Oh, the kids, they talk. I overheard two girls saying that although you haven't got a car at the moment, if you did, it would have to be a moggie.'

I told him, that the kids were curious as to why I always walked into work and was it because they didn't pay me enough?

'We could always have a whip-round, Sir,' they had said.

Ned and Hilary laughed at their cheek. Sandra remained stony-faced. She thought I was much too familiar with the kids, and no good would come of it.

'But your spies have well-informed you,' I said. 'The last car I had in Chester, was one of those seventies Leyland rust buckets. It failed its M.O.T spectacularly a few months before I came back to Munford.'

'Well, old chap,' he said, 'it just so happens I may know where you can get one,' said Ned.

He then told me that he had an uncle, now in his late seventies and getting a bit past it, who had a 1954 Morris Minor sitting in his garage. It was in mint condition, as it was the old fellow's pride and joy.

'He wants it to go to a good home. The problem is he lives in Cheltenham. I could always drive you there, if you are not doing anything this Saturday?' he said. I asked Sandra if she wanted to come along.

'No, I'll leave you two together, honestly boys and their toys.'

Secretly I was glad she didn't want to come. I did invite

David along, because as well as being a plumber he also knew quite a bit about engines.

It was on the journey down, that I asked Ned why he had decided to teach games in an inner-city comprehensive, instead of the classics at Eton, or somewhere equally grand.

'The classics were Dad's idea. I'm afraid they always bored the absolute tripes out of me. So I went and did a post grad diploma at Loughborough in sports science, and then my teaching certificate. Mind you, the old man didn't talk to me for a twelve month, and he cut my allowance down to half.'

I had told him I'd always hated sport at school, except swimming, though I'd never won any competitions with it.

'You must avail yourself of the pool after hours. It's one of the perks of the job,' he said. I said I would probably take him up on his offer.

'That new assistant caretaker attends to it all. I'll tell him you may be popping down after class for a splash-about,' he said.

His uncle's place was rather baronial, as expected. He was an old bachelor, who wore a lavender cravat, chain-smoked and adored opera and good claret. I took to him instantly. They called him Henry Danbury. After lunch he took us all out to the garage. There was still a thin frost all along the lawn and a cold blue February sky, with yellow wisps of sunshine peeking through the clouds. The car was under-wraps.

'She's rather sensitive to the cold weather, don't you know,' he said with a smile.

It looked like it had just come out of the showroom. It had a split-windscreen and side-indicators. David and I took it for a spin. The engine purred like a delightful kitten. It was a love affair from the first. It was a dark brown colour. I would have it re-sprayed in racing green. By late afternoon, the deal was done.

I then decided to have a bit of a competition with the kids, who would get to name her. They drew the suggested names out of a hat, during Wednesday lunchtime, with Ned adjudicating the solemn proceedings in the sports hall. The chosen name was Clara. I loved it and Clara she became.

Matthew was getting ready for his wedding day, scheduled for a couple of weeks' time. Fiona insisted that the stag night, should be held the Saturday before the wedding, and not on the previous evening. Matthew told me that his cousin Billy Hardcastle would be coming along to the stag night and he was going to be one of the ushers. I had first met his cousin when we were both nine- year-old schoolboys during the summer of 1970. We had become close, spending a great deal of that summer, as I seem to remember, hiding up in the tree-house in our garden. On one of these occasions he had said to me,

'I wish you were a girl.' I'd asked him why.

'Cos then I could kiss you,' he had said.

'So why don't you?' I'd said.

'Little boys aren't supposed to kiss little boys,' he had said, becoming rather flustered, 'me dad says so.'

I asked him what they were supposed to do.

'They shake hands,' he said and then we had both burst out laughing at the sheer absurdity of it all.

A few days later we were back up in the tree-house. He reached across and kissed me. It was very chaste, indeed, the merest peck.

'Now it's your turn,' he said.

I kissed him back.

'Do you think we're wicked?' he said.

'Yeh, I suppose so,' I said. And then we were both off laughing.

In the ten days since we had first met, I had grown to love so much about him. As a nine-year-old, his voice was kind of croaky. His long, mousey hair was like an unkempt haystack. He never combed it. And then there was his lop-sided grin, usually followed by his laugher, a giggle that was irrepressible and always had me in fits of laughter too! I loved his ears, which poked through his tangle of hair. I don't know what it was about them, I just loved them. I even loved the shape of his knuckles, and the way when we were playing football, in which he hunkered down; waiting for a pass.

A group of us had been racing our bikes up a steep hill, that same summer. I'd been showing off, really trying to get Billy's attention. I'd taken the bend too quickly and I'd come flying off my bike, fracturing my wrist, ending up in a plaster cast for the remainder of the school holidays. He had taken control of things that day, coming down to casualty with me, and telling the others to take my bike home and to tell my mum what had happened.

That evening, he had ridden back round to our house, on his bike to see how I was doing. Mum had ruffled his hair, and given him a large slice of her homemade chocolate cake and a glass of lemonade, for all of his troubles and good sense that day. He had looked puzzled with all of her praise. He'd turned to her and said,

'We're mates and you'll do anything for your best mate, anything in the world.'

And when he'd said this, I felt a warm, delicious feeling stealing all over me.

I remember that night. I lay awake for quite some time, just thinking about him. And as I did so, I felt a strange kind of ache that I couldn't explain. Outside were the sounds of a late summer's evening, a blackbird was singing in the hedgerow and someone in a neighbouring garden was mowing the lawn. I couldn't understand how it was, that an ache could both hurt and still feel kind of wonderful, all at the same time. I was thirteen when I experienced my very first wet dream. The first erotic dream, however, was that night. We were back up there in the tree-house together, and we were naked. I was aching all over, but it was a delightful ache, I'd never felt before. The echoing resonance of this dream, stayed with me for days afterwards.

We had met up again twice more. The first time was on a holiday at the coast. We had both been fourteen and had shared a bedroom together. It had been Matthew's younger brother's birthday and Matthew and his brother had pigged themselves out.

The following day, Billy and I had the whole day to ourselves. We had gone up to the sand dunes, and after our packed-lunch, made up from the previous evening's party food; we had started to horse-play and then tentatively sexually experiment with each other; for the very first time. He had climbed down into one of the sand-dunes. He beckoned me to join him. We kissed, sticking our tongues in each other's mouths experimentally for the first time.

'Yuk!' he said.

I didn't know whether he was pretending he didn't like it. He was the first boy I'd kissed properly. I loved the feeling, the wetness inside his mouth, the strange warmth of it and the aftertaste of the raspberry pop we had both been drinking, all mingled with his spit, which had an after smell of vinegar. It was the autumn school holidays, so there was no way either of us was going to remove all our clothes. We lay next to each other at the bottom of the dune, and Billy, tentatively reached his hand underneath my thick, woollen jumper. He slowly began to move his hand further up, feeling my nipples and sticking his forefinger in my navel. I was beginning to shiver, but I was not sure, whether it was coming from the cold, or this new sensation, riding a force, that I could not quite control yet.

That night, when everyone was asleep, I felt his hand reaching towards me. He had removed his pyjamas, and was leaning on the bed, gazing down on me. This time we kissed again; we both felt surer. He was stroking me and discovering me, and slowly removing my own pyjamas. Never had my own nakedness seemed more thrilling. His nakedness seemed then, to be the most beautiful thing I had yet beheld. It had been our secret delight for the remainder of the holiday.

We had met up once more, when we were both seventeen. He had joined us on a camping holiday, in the middle of August, to The Lake District. Billy and I had shared a tent together. At first I thought he had out grown it all; as the first night he kept to his own sleeping bag.

The following evening, there was a torrential downpour and Billy climbed into my sleeping bag with me. Moments later, his hands were moving towards me. And then we were both kissing. We kissed, with hunger. He was in my mouth and kissing my face, my cheeks, licking inside my ears and grabbing hold of my hair, and kissing that too! That was to be the first night I screwed him, indeed it was the first night I screwed anybody. We tried it with spit. 'God it hurts like hell,' he said.

33

I decided to use some dubbing, meant for water-protection for our fell boots. It had the consistency of goose-lard, and smelt like car oil. It felt like dipping my finger into ice. He yelped with the cold. The tent smelt of our trainers and dirty socks. Its pungency was turning me on like crazy. I entered him with slow grace. I could feel him beginning to relax.

He chose to face me, with his legs slightly raised. I adored his smooth legs and his naked feet, which I kissed and licked with a wanton pleasure. 'God, you've got gorgeous feet,' I said. This made him laugh. Afterwards, we shared a cigarette by the light of his torch, and then cuddled up in each other arms, enfolding ourselves, like we could not get enough of each other. And after that we had been happy, secret lovers for the rest of the week.

And yet there were other memories; much older than these. They too were gay, and yet happened before I ever perceived the aching beauty of my own sex. Those memories were my real baptism; my queer epiphany. It was during that time, when Oedipus is supposed to enter the lives of little boys; causing them to fall out with their fathers, and want to run off with and marry their mothers. Other voices, much more powerful; were calling to me then.

Stonewall and all those gay men taking to the streets in New York; was still a year or so away. Homosexuality was still a crime. I suddenly found myself captivated and strangely enchanted by another dream.

Mum had gone off for the day with two of her older women friends; Gladys and Clara. Clara it was who was driving the car; taking us back into town. There had been no baby-sitters available that day; so Mum had to take me along as well. I was well into my night's sleep; as the car rattled through the early evening, ploughing into the deep countryside; with the fields and hedge-rows in blackened silhouette, underneath a burnished sunset sky; illuminated by an autumn Moon: big, terrible and magnificent.

An early evening request programme; was playing away on the car radio. I would wake up spasmodically; the ancient suspension of the car, tracing every bend and bump in the road. A song came on the radio. It would be a few years later, when I heard that particular song again, and recognised it as 'The Trolley Song,' sung by Judy Garland.

As the song played, a kind of disembodied voice inside my head, that was me and yet somehow was not me; began to speak to me. It was as if it was telling me to listen, and to give all of my attention to that song. Indeed, that song, during that early autumn evening; was somehow the most important thing in my world. The curious voice said to me, 'This is you. This is who you are.'

At that moment, I somehow felt connected up with a part of me that was unborn and deathless. It was timeless and an all-encompassing force, that was here and yet everywhere at the same moment. A kind of inexpressible joy overcame me then; like silent laughter, whirring up and eddying deep inside me.

I gradually passed into a gentle, blissful slumber. When I awoke, I was at home, in my own bed and it was morning. And I forgot. The memory was re-awoken some years later; on hearing that song again. It was the evening of the day, when I had fallen off my bike and broken my wrist; and Billy had called round. They were playing that song on the radio, in the kitchen; whilst my mum was busy washing the dishes. It was all one; giggling childhood and spirit; woven out of the same strange matter.

There had been a parent's evening, the Saturday of Matthew's stag night, which I was eager to attend. So it was past nine, when I joined the rest of the gang in our local, later that evening. The others were well into the party mood. And there was Billy, smiling up at me as I came across to the table. It had been five years since we'd last met. Five years since our happy loving beneath the canvas.

'God, Robbie,' he said, 'it's great to see you again.'

I smiled without answering him. I was thinking that he looked more gorgeous than ever. His features seemed more honed somehow, like a master sculptor had crafted in all the finer details. And yet he still had that lop-sided grin, filled with boyish mischief. We all got outrageously drunk, but Billy more so than the rest of us. We went on to a nightclub, where we indulged in more beer and whisky slammers. And then Billy was throwing up in the gents. I decided to call for a taxi and I got in beside him, to make sure he got safely home.

He had been living in Sheffield, until a couple of months ago. He had decided to move to Munford. He was working as a car mechanic and had a council flat, in a rather notorious part of town. He was slumped up against me in the taxi, babbling a lot of drunken nonsense. I could smell his stale odour along with the vomit. Some of it had trailed onto his shirt. I was feeling so turned on by him, and the way he was looking so vulnerable, was making me even hungrier for the touch of him. I wanted him so.

I managed to see him up the precarious stairs of his flat, and got him safely onto his sofa, removing his shoes and tie and placing a cushion under his head. I found his bedroom all cluttered up with discarded clothes, dirty socks and trainers, at last finding a grubby blanket, which I went and threw over him to keep him warm. He was now fast asleep, looking entirely beautiful as he lay there. I reached across and gently placed a kiss on his forehead before leaving. I had stolen a pair of his grubby boxer shorts. They were covered in the sweat from his groin. They looked like he had worn them for several days. I went to bed that night woven up in the wonderful scent of him.

Billy and Matthew's brother, Phillip were going to be ushers. I slipped out during lunchtime from school, to get measured up for my morning suit. Billy and I ended up sharing a changing room. There we both were, in nothing but our boxer shorts and socks; gawping at each other in a love-sick crazy way.

'I haven't forgotten all those years ago in Keswick, on that camping holiday you know,' he said, breaking into his best mischievous grin.

'Me neither,' I said.

'I still fancy the ruddy pants off you as well,' he said.

A couple of days before the wedding, I had gone back to that dreary wine bar with Sandra. If we talked about the school, she liked to make me sound like the fount of all knowledge. It irritated me in the extreme, because it was false, a mere feline wile to draw me in, the lethal touch of the spider. We went back to her digs. Her landlady was already in bed. And so we got down to the usual routine, whilst I brushed up on my square roots. But to my horror she wanted more.

'I want you to finger me down there,' she said.

This was the one place I refused to go. If I found her breasts mildly distasteful, I found her genitals too horrid to even begin to contemplate. I got up to leave, but she stood in my way at the front door.

'You've just made me feel cheap,' she said.

'You've done that all by yourself without any help from me,' I said. I then left.

It was raining heavily as I stepped out of the door. With a sudden sense of fire at my heels I began to run, not sure where I was running to. All I knew was that I had to get away from her. I was running down the road and through the many alleyways between the rows of terrace houses; when I finally reached the wall to someone's backyard. Here I stopped to catch my breath, and then I proceeded to vomit up my insides. Having done this, I was overcome by a sudden fit of sobbing.

The next day we chanced to cross paths in the admin building, on my way to class. She took me aside. She was all apologetic.

'I'm sorry about last night, I got all carried away. I guess I was too fast for you. You're such a gentleman,' she said.

Billy and Phillip were already at the church, when Matthew and I arrived. Matthew looked like he was about to pass out. The rest of us found this highly amusing. The wedding guests had started to drift in. Billy and Phillip showed them to their seats. The vicar asked Billy and me, if we would be so good as to pop into the vestry, to collect the remainder of the order of services. And so we were alone together, for a few brief moments, whilst the vicar was having a word with the organist.

'I want you to screw me stupid before this day's out. And I won't take no for an answer,' he said.

I was feeling delighted and scandalized all at the same time.

'You've got no ruddy reverence you haven't,' I said, keeping my voice to a stage whisper.

'For this place, with all of its ruddy cant and Bible clap-trap, no you're right,' he said, 'but for me and you,' he said, 'well that's quite a different matter.'

There were over a hundred guests as I stood up at the wedding breakfast to make my best man's speech. I was feeling so very nervous, and all the witty things I'd wanted to say, seemed to fly right out of my head. And then I saw Billy, sitting at the next table down from me with his girlfriend, Shona. He was smiling up at me, and suddenly my confidence returned. I could've been standing up in class. The words came easily, along with all my best jokes and anecdotes. And it felt like there was no one else in that large reception room. There was only Billy and I. We were the only people in the whole damn world!

Most of the guests went round to the bride's family, to see the presents. Matthew stayed back at the hotel, for a quick pint at the bar, before going back to the in-laws. There was to be a disco at the hotel later that evening.

When I arrived back at the hotel, it was difficult to get a moment alone with Billy, as Shona, his girlfriend, kept hogging him. Fortunately, Sandra and Shona really seemed to hit it off. They were both secretaries. Talk about fonts and carbon paper, seemed to fascinate them. Meanwhile, Billy came to the bar to help me with the drinks.

'So then, big boy,' I said, 'how are you going to pull it all off?'

'You leave that to me, sunshine,' he said. He was smiling enigmatically and making me laugh.

I was caught up with all the boring talk, with people I'd never met and wondering where Billy had disappeared to. And suddenly he was there, beckoning me over to the bar.

'I've managed it,' he said. He then triumphantly produced a set of keys for the bridal suite from out of his jacket pocket.

We made the excuse to Sandra and Shona that we wanted to go up to the bridal suite, to cause a bit of mayhem for the happy couple. They both thought this was a hoot and let us go. I was surprised how easy it had been.

The hotel had six floors and needless to say, the bridal suite had to be on the top floor. Billy kept dropping the keys with nerves, before we finally stumbled into the room. We were giggling like a couple of school kids. No sooner had we closed and bolted the door, than we were kissing each other hungrily. And then, we just needed to be naked. I turned on the bedside lamp, and we stood and kissed, stroking each other with a kind of reverent joy. Billy was blushing. I asked him why.

'It's because you look so gorgeous!' he said.

I pulled him onto the bed, and then we were caught up in a wild, mad tussle, wrestling for each other's love. We were pinning each other down and then we were biting and clawing, and pulling each other's hair, and kissing with needy desire.

I knew I had to enter him quickly. Inside him felt warm, and a pulsating place of the most incredible pleasure. He was causing the most ecstatic ache to rush up the backs of my legs; awaking some strange fire in my loins and shooting through my entire body. The hot, fevered moment caught me within the wild ecstasy, the discovery, the joy of something, singing, something laughing; deep inside of me. And oh, the delicious ache, riding and racing through every sense and every fibre of me, and yet ever wanting him and still more of him; with the fire-flame of my love.

We lay there on the bed, nestled in each other's arms. I nuzzled my nose in amongst his wet hair, which smelt like a rose garden after summer rain. And so we fell asleep. It was an hour later when we finally woke.

When we came back into the function room, everyone suddenly went quiet. My mum and gran were giving us both poisonous looks. Again, for some strange reason, Dad looked sorrowful. My brother was laughing and pointing at me, so much as to say, 'my God, are you well and truly for it now!' It was the DJ, who then said,

'Well now that the best man has chosen to honour us with his presence, we can finally start the ruddy disco.' And then everyone was off laughing, all except my mum and my gran.

'Where the hell have you been?' said Sandra, during that first dance.

'We got held up,' I said.

I refused to say anything more. And then I could see Billy. He was making faces at me, and all kinds of rude gestures from behind the pillars, that surrounded the dance floor. And I was trying not to laugh. The whole thing was impossible, but delightfully so and I was off laughing, feeling high, despite a murderous look from Sandra. At midnight I saw her into a taxi and gave her a chaste kiss. She wanted to know why I wasn't coming back with her.

'I've still things to see to, all part of my best man's duties,' I told her, lying outrageously.

Most of the other guests, including Billy and Shona had left sometime before. I noticed the bar was still open. They must have managed to get an extended license for the day. And so I went into the bar and ordered myself a large whisky. I sat down to savour it, and to mull over in my mind, all the strange and wonderful events of the day. And along with the whisky and the mellow lights of the bar, a warm glow was stealing over me; as a glad smile lighted up my face. And all I could think about was the warm deep, dark space he had offered up to me so freely.

3

I stayed over with my mum and dad. Getting gingerly out of bed and going to the bathroom that morning, I looked at my naked reflection in the bathroom mirror. I was covered in cuts and bruises and I was aching all over. 'All this queer loving isn't for the faint-hearted,' I said to myself. It was whilst shaving, that I suddenly noticed a great angry love-bite on the right-hand side of my neck. When I got back to my bedroom, I decided I better cover it up. So I put on a rather thick polo-necked jumper, despite it being a mild spring day.

'So, he's finally surfaced,' said my mum, addressing me in the third person, something she always did when she was in the mood for a bit of bitter ironic sarcasm. Meanwhile, I went and helped myself to some cornflakes. Gary, still in his pyjamas was smirking at me.

'And what time did you finally role in last night?' said Mum.

'Oh give over, Mum,' I said, 'it was a wedding for God's sake,' I said.

'The rest of us,' she said, 'all left at a reasonable hour, why couldn't you have done the same?'

'I'd things to do,' I said.

'I'll bet,' said my mum. 'And why on earth are you wearing a great thick sweater on a mild day like this?' she said.

I told her I was feeling the cold. She saw through this rouse immediately and came across and pulled down the collar of my jumper.

'Honestly did that, ruddy lass,' she said, 'not get enough to eat yesterday, without taking a great bite out of your neck?'

Gary was off laughing and obviously enjoying the entertainment. He was usually being told off for something or other, it made a nice change for it to be someone else.

'It weren't her,' I said. It was a sudden fit of honesty and I wished I'd kept my mouth shut.

'Aye up,' said Dad looking up from his paper, 'don't tell me that lad has got a bit of gumption about him after all?' And then Mum, Dad and my brother were in howls of laughter.

We had our lads' night out as usual. Marriage did not seem to have changed that.

'You want to ask that, Sandra,' said David.

'Ask her what?' I said.

He said, I should ask her to marry me, for he thought she seemed a nice enough lass.

'It won't be long before me and, Rhona,' he said, 'are getting hitched.'

'It can't come quick enough, even if we have been sleeping together for the last three years,' he said.

A couple of days later, I'd gone up for tea to my gran's place. She was hardly civil to me. I asked her what was up.

'What do you think's up,' she said. 'My God, the pair of you, the way you both came waltzing in without a care in the world, looking like a couple of ruddy lovers. And him with his long hair just like a ruddy lass. Eeh, I didn't know where to put me self for shame,' she said.

'Don't be daft, Gran,' I said. I was feeling flustered. 'We went for a game of pool in the other bar and we forgot the time that was all.'

'How long have you been rehearsing that one? I don't know, I'm beginning to think your, aunt Bev,' she said, 'was right, that there's summit up with you. Eeh, talk about ruddy history repeating itself.'

'What history?' I said.

'It's nothing, finish your tea. I've said too much,' she said.

That night I was unable to sleep. My queer secret was all but discovered. What was causing me to feel so frightened was all I stood to lose. If they knew, would they still love me, or would all my family and all my friends turn their back on me? Would they begin to hate me? With thoughts like these, I was beginning to feel desperate and desperate situations called for desperate measures. I decided I would ask Sandra to marry me.

Whilst I was still contemplating how I'd go about this, things were troubling me at school. I was unable to put my finger on the cause. I felt something was brewing away, somewhere in the background, rather like the necromancer in *The Hobbit*, who actually turned out to be Sauron, the dark lord of Middle-Earth himself.

Milly Armstrong was twelve years old, always surrounded by a group of boys, some a lot older than her. Nevertheless, she was the undisputed leader of the gang. I used to think in another age and another place, she would probably have been a shield-maiden, fighting side-by-side with her men-folk, the Boadicea of West Munford comprehensive. She was also a young carer for her mum, Beatrice, who had arthritis, which caused her to be wheelchair bound for most of the time. Beatrice was a single mum, surviving on benefit. She was also passionate about her daughter getting for herself, the best possible education. I often called round to their house, for an informal cup of tea and a chat.

In later life, Milly would eventually go on to work on the international stage, in women's rights. Her mother would have been so proud of her, but unfortunately she passed away shortly after Milly went to university to read women's studies in the October of 1990.

I had noticed of late that Milly seemed withdrawn. Her homework remained of the same very high standard. No doubt her mother saw to that. She always had so much to contribute to the lessons. Now she would just sit there and say nothing. Her mother was as equally baffled by her changed behaviour, for she seemed every bit as withdrawn at home.

'She doesn't even play her music. I'm always telling her to turn it down as a rule,' said her mother.

Then there was fourteen-year-old William Henderson, another bright kid. He was a popular boy with lots of friends and was good at sport. Ned described him as,

'A bit of a prodigy actually. Damn good footballer. All instinctive you know, and a bloody good team player to boot!'

Ned had been concerned that he'd suddenly pulled out of Friday evening five-a-side practice.

'Good God, man,' he said, 'he's the ruddy leading light of the whole show.'

He too had seemed for the most part withdrawn. And then one day, he had not done the homework I'd set the class. I took him to task over it.

'I've not done it so there,' he had said. 'Put me in detention if you like, see if I care.' I now knew there was something decidedly wrong.

I tried talking it over with Sandra. 'Do you know your

trouble?' she said, 'you get too close to the kids. Teenagers are always having moods. I was always having tantrums, when I was there age. You think too much about them and you care too much.'

'How can you ever care too much?' I said to her.

'Most kids just want to get through school with as little fuss as possible and then get on with their lives. You see it as young blossoming souls and all of that clap-trap. I guess you're just a hopeless romantic,' she said. I didn't answer her, but I hoped I'd always remain so. And this was the woman I was going to ask to marry me and share my life. We were so different in every conceivable way.

Even though the music was loud, it might as well have been coming from another room. All the voices were distorted. It was all unreal and dream-like. I was caught up in the phantasmagoria of it all. Ghoulish faces leered at me and everyone seemed to be laughing. A group of young bloods were lifting me shoulder high and carrying me around the main function room of the working men's club. I could hear from the brash PA system the strains of, 'For He's a Jolly Good Fellow'. And somewhere amongst my befuddled thoughts was the distant memory of Sandra saying to me,

'You've just made me the happiest girl in Munford.' But already the memory was beginning to fade, for it seemed like it had happened to someone else long ago.

'You great daft appeth,' said my mum.

She was screaming and hitting me across the head and any part of me she could slap. It was the next day, Saturday lunchtime and I'd called round to break the news. Dad rushed into the kitchen, wondering what all the commotion was about.

'Your big daft, son,' she said, 'has only gone and asked that scheming hussy to marry him.'

'Oh, son,' he said, 'why on earth did you go and do that?'

I couldn't answer him. At that moment I felt about six. All I wanted to do was burst into tears and run into his arms for comfort. Instead, I decided to get some fresh air by taking the dog for a walk. And out there on the park, with all the springtime flowers coming into bloom and the birds singing from the swirling trees, the happy sounds of nature, which now seemed discordant and out-of-tune with my present mood, I suddenly was struck by the enormity of what I'd done the previous evening. How could I go through with it? How could I not? There was no way out. I was trapped.

A male cousin on my mum's side of the family was also getting married. He had got a police woman pregnant and against his parents' wishes, had decided to marry her. The wedding was in Addlesworth at the local Methodist Church. Despite the warm spring day and the bluest of skies first thing that morning, as everyone gathered at the church, it began to rain heavily and a strong easterly wind was blowing through the churchyard. It felt more like the depths of winter. At the reception, neither side of the respective families were speaking to each other. Indeed, it felt colder in doors. And coming back from the reception, Gran wanted to phone one of her relatives in Scotland to tell her all about it.

'And don't forget to tell her about me and, Sandra,' I said.

Gran started to tut at me. She looked disgusted.

'What's Gran's problem?' I said to my mum.

'Don't you mean what's your problem?' she said.

I followed her into the kitchen determined to have it out with her.

'Are you going to be like this even when we're married?' I said.

'Marriage,' she said, indeed she spat out the word. 'You don't even like her. In fact you ruddy well hate her.'

'How can you say such a thing?' I said but she cut me off in mid-sentence.

'I don't know what it is with you these days,' she began, 'it's like everything you do is just an act, a pose, a pretence, and you are standing back to judge the ruddy effect you're having on your audience.

'There's nothing real about you anymore. You know what, you've become a hollow man, all stick and straw and there's nought left inside,' she said.

'Oh, Mum,' I said stung by her harsh words.

Later that evening, I took the bus out to a pub where I wasn't known. I wanted to get very drunk, to drown out my mum's words. And yet the more I drank, the more her words seemed to pierce right through me. Before midnight, somehow remarkably sober, I wandered myself back home. And yet as soon as I'd got into bed I was overwhelmed by a fit of sobbing that lasted far into the night.

From that point on, things went from bad to worse. This started off with the inevitable visit to her parents. They lived on one of the better council estates in Addlesworth. Her dad was a miner; her mother ran the local branch of the women's institute. She opened the door to us both with a face that could have shelled nuts at ten paces.

'So you've arrived then?' she said.

Sandra didn't seem in the leastways put out by her mum's cold attitude. I offered her my hand. She took it dispassionately and there was no pressure in the handshake.

49

'No doubt you'll both want summit to eat? You better come in,' she said.

Her dad was watching sport on television. He looked up briefly in acknowledgement, only to quickly return to his sport. Meanwhile, Sandra went and helped her mum set the table and get tea ready. I was left sitting on the settee, with her dad glued to the box in his armchair by the fire. There was some motor-racing event on. He seemed content to all but ignore me, except for now and again making some comment about the events unfolding on screen. And the more he ignored me, the more uncomfortable I began to feel. I also thought he was bad mannered. I had always been brought up with the admonition that when guests arrived, the television was always turned off.

The table was gradually being laid. Her dad didn't join us at the table. Instead he was given a large plate of food, which he ate on his lap, in front of the telly. The rest of us: her mum, Sandra, her ten year old sister Maggie and me, sat down to eat.

'I hope you like salad?' said her mum, 'not that it much matters whether you do or you don't, for there's nowt else.'

I told her it was fine. She then turned to Sandra talking about local gossip, excluding me from the conversation.

'Our, Sandra,' said her younger sister 'says you are a teacher?' So what do you teach?'

I told her I taught English.

'Oh,' she said. She didn't sound impressed and then after that, I found it difficult to re-engage her.

Sandra was showing off her engagement ring. 'So what do you think, our mum?' she said.

'It'll have cost a pretty penny I'll bet?' said her mum.

'She's worth it,' I said.

Her mum didn't reply, but gave me one of her inscrutable looks. It would have iced over an erupting volcano.

After tea, we went round to visit her brother Ivan and his wife Tracey. They were warm and pleasant enough. At least they tried to put me at my ease. Ivan even offered me a can of beer.

'How's, Mum?' said Ivan.

'Oh you know,' said Sandra, 'same as usual.'

'I don't think she likes me,' I said.

Ivan burst out laughing at this.

'I wouldn't worry about that. She's always like that with folk she doesn't rightly know,' he said.

We argued on the bus back to Munford, especially about her mum's cold attitude towards me.

'Honestly, you can't expect them to put out the red carpet just for you,' she said.

This angered me more.

'Your mum is nowt but a cold hearted bitch and she has got a stone where her ruddy heart should be,' I said. She slapped my face hard and got off the bus, a couple of stops early. And I thought to myself, this is the girl who two weeks ago I asked to marry me.

'You can't stay in that rented place of yours,' said my dad to me one day when I'd popped round.

'We'll find you somewhere nice you can buy, and I'll give you the deposit for the mortgage as a wedding present.'

There was an area of Munford called Sparrows Walk. It was full of terrace houses, all nicely kept and renovated. It was an up and coming area of the town, where the house prices were still reasonable. Dad had looked out a place around there.

'You could certainly do a lot worse,' he said.

'Why are you encouraging him with all of this ruddy nonsense?' said my mum.

'Now Kathy, he has to have somewhere to live.'

'He already has somewhere, and this place to fall back on, not living with that bloody hussy,' she said. She left the room in tears.

So my dad came along with Sandra and me to look at a house. It was the kind of place as a single man; I would have loved to live in. It had bags of character. The thought of sharing it with Sandra seemed too hideous to even contemplate.

'And there's plenty of room for when the kids arrive,' said the estate agent.

He had one of those man-of-the-world leering smiles. It made me shudder.

'Aye, it's a right love nest for sure,' said my dad. I wanted to be sick.

When we left, Sandra wanted me to go back and spend the rest of the day with her at her digs. I made the excuse; I still had lots of marking to do, and lessons to prepare. I just needed to get away from her and to think.

I suppose most of us have our own particular ways of trying to cheer ourselves up. For some, it's a dose of their favourite comfort food, whilst for others it's a shopping spree. For me, it was either buying records or books. And that afternoon, I was feeling in somewhat of a literary mood. And there was only one place to assuage that thirst. There was a bookshop down an alley, in the centre of town. It was a paperback book chain. All they sold were new paperback books. The shop was narrow, squeezed in between an estate agent and a solicitor. It had three floors, filled with glorious books. I browsed my way through some of the more contemporary fiction, held on the ground floor. After about half an hour of this, I took myself up to the next floor, where all the classics were to be found. It was here I bumped into Billy about to buy a science fiction classic.

'I didn't know you read,' I said.

'Just because you're an English teacher doesn't mean the rest of us can't read,' he said.

He was pretending to be affronted, but his eyes told me that he seemed not only pleased, but delighted to see me. He bought his book, and I purchased a new copy of a favourite Henry James novel. There was a park close by. We decided to take a walk there. I thought he was looking particularly gorgeous, in his faded jeans and scruffy red T-shirt. It began to rain heavily and so we quickly tried to find somewhere to take shelter.

There was an old disused gent's toilet. It had brambles growing in the doorway. Billy eased open the creaking wooden door. We crept inside. It stank of dank moss, mildew and ancient piss, probably from some bygone age. And judging from the graffiti on one of the walls which read: *Georgie is the best;* I don't think the place had been used since the sixties. And yet to me, it felt like a trespasser's sanctuary.

'Eeh, Robbie,' said Billy with a look of tender concern furrowing his brow, 'you look like you're carrying the whole ruddy world on your shoulders. Come here,' he said, taking me gently into his arms. And then, I began to sob like my heart was breaking.

'Come on, our kid,' he said, 'get it all out. You won't feel better till you do.'

At last my grief subsided. Billy brushed away a stray tear with his for-finger. He then sucked it in a most suggestive manner, which finally brought a smile to my face. I could hear the rain dancing off the flat reinforced glass roof. Shadows moved along the walls, in a dappled, kaleidoscopic maze. Billy pressed me up hard against the wall. I felt his closeness and the sudden touch of his nakedness, as I reached my hand tentatively beneath his T-shirt.

He threw off his T-shirt quickly, and it fell somewhere out of sight on the dirty floor. And even in the half-light, I could see his naval and the strange curve of his belly, and they were a wonder to me. And there in the hushed silence of the hallowed space, our soft, initial kisses came almost like a whispered prayer, before growing more insistent and more desperate.

I needed to be inside him. I needed to possess him. I knew he wanted to be taken, utterly and completely. I turned him round, so that he was facing the wall of ancient tiles. I then began to unfasten the button on his jeans. They fell slowly down his muscular thighs. He was wearing red boxer shorts; I pulled them down until they were practically around his ankles. I then pulled my own trousers and underpants down. I enveloped my arms around him and his torso. I was kissing the nape of his neck. The smell of him came up to me, full and strong. There was wild honey, musk, deep resin and nutmeg in that scent, the aroma of a boy being had and wanting to be had.

He turned his face towards me, darting his desperate tongue, full into my mouth, as I entered him fully. He gave a little yelp, which then turned into a groan of pleasure. And still I pulled him ever more towards me and held him tighter in my grip, like I could never quite get enough of him, or of his wild honey and nutmeg smell. Standing there, our bodies and our legs were entangled inside each other, kissing and fighting for each other's love, woven up in the deep shadows. And somewhere within the touch, my heart seemed boundless, galloping with the wild horses, caught up with the wind-tide eagle and one with all the strange creatures of the forest. Then too, it was the sea, the fire and the wind, and then all too suddenly the plunder-down descent of all our desire.

We kissed one last time, before stepping back outside into the world of ordinary things; the hum-drum debris of all that was left. We walked off back along the park in the pouring rain. Eventually, he took the turning for home and I had to let him go. I watched him trudging through the rain and I ached and I yearned for him, I loved him so.

4

I went out for a meal with Sandra to officially mark our engagement. And over our second glass of wine, she told me she had a very special surprise waiting for me back at her digs. Her landlady was away for the weekend, visiting her son and daughter-in-law in London. We therefore had the whole place to ourselves. This was the surprise and I was horrified.

'I think it's high time I test-drove the goods,' she said. She smiled at me suggestively, turning my stomach. 'You wait here, whilst I get myself into something more alluring. I'll call you when I'm ready.'

I found myself chain-smoking in the front room and guzzling on her landlady's best sherry. The actual thought of sexual intercourse with any woman, let alone Sandra, grossed me out entirely. When I kissed her, and stuck my tongue in her mouth, it repulsed me with every fibre of my being. And yet I still did it, wanting it all to end as quickly as possible. The gag reflex was never far away and I was always swallowing back what was a natural instinct, protecting me from foreign bodies. To have any kind of sex with any woman, was to go counter to my body, my mind, my heart and my soul. It was wrong, just plain wrong, in every way. And so I smoked and so I drank.

'Oh, Robbie,' I could eventually hear her calling to me, from the top of the stairs.

And so I ascended those stairs, like a condemned man facing

the gallows. As I entered her bedroom, the curtains were closed and she was burning scented candles. She was laid on the bed, naked except for a bright, orange chiffon vale. She also had painted her toe-nails in a lurid red. I loved young men's feet and everything about them. I hated women's feet and especially painted toe-nails! And there it was, her genitals, like some black beast staring up at me, a thing quite separate. It seemed to have a life and a conscious reality, different from her. The whole thing was a complete impossibility to me. To have gone through with it, would have felt like the most sacrilegious act, to my authentic self. And anything seemed preferable, than this abomination I was being asked to perform. I found my voice at last.

'I can't go through with this. I'm sorry. I don't love you and I don't think I ever have. I can't marry you. If I was to do so, both our lives would be a complete misery.'

I slowly walked out of her bedroom and started to descend the stairs. When I'd reached the bottom, she raged at me from the top of the stairs.

'You're a puff, a rotten, stinking puff and I hate you! I hope you rot in hell!'

I made no reply but quickly strode out of the house.

I told my mum and dad over Sunday lunch that our engagement was now over. Mum jumped up from the table.

'Glory be!' she said, coming across and hugging me.

Billy phoned me later that day. He wanted to cook us both a meal for that Friday evening.

'I didn't know you could cook,' I said.

'I ruddy can't,' he said, 'but I'll have a damn good try.'

At twenty-two, I'd not as yet fully discovered the finer joys of life, like how to choose a good red wine. So Friday evening finally came off, and neither of us seemed at all bothered by the burnt steaks and the cheap red wine, that tasted like cat's piss and smelt like it too.

We made love on his unmade bed, in a bedroom of shabby neglect and discarded clothes. I loved the smell of his dirty sheets, in a bed that had probably not been changed for weeks. I believed he probably washed but once a day, and tended to change his clothes once every three days or so. And so there was something always days-old and stale about his aroma, and this coupled with the unwashed clothes, socks and ancient trainers in his room, was for me, the ultimate turn on smell! I could never quite get enough of it! How I loved to fill his mouth with my hungry kisses. And yet there was a kind of nostalgia I felt, for times that had been that could never come again. Ecstasy and tears were all caught up in the forbidden trespass of this night. We fell asleep cuddled up in each other's arms, surfeit, and content. It was enough.

The following morning he was already up, sitting in his boxer-shorts and rolling a cigarette on the coffee table beside the sofa. I loved him like this. I even loved the nicotine stains on his fingers. It was then that he told me.

'I've got, Shona, pregnant,' he said, 'I got drunk and some-how it happened. We'd not had sex for months. Well it wouldn't be fair of me to let her go through it all on her own. I'm going to do the decent thing by her and marry her,' he said.

'But you love me,' I said. I could not help the tone of desper-ation, now creeping into my voice.

'Aye, I love you, more than I could ever say. I'll never have feelings for, Shona,' he said, 'or for any woman for that matter like I've got for you. Just hold me.'

I took him in my arms and we both cried, kissing each other with desperation and a tender longing that felt like torture. I finally found the courage to let go of him. I walked back through Munford town centre, with the early morning sun just beginning to squeeze itself through the buildings, from a watery sky overhead, and rising from the rooftops. The shops were beginning to pull up their shutters. I could hear the drowse of traffic from the main road. Everyday life was still going on around me, unconcerned, indifferent and without as much as a passing care for two young men and two broken hearts.

5

I now intended to come out. I felt I could no longer live my life, having to keep lying to myself and others. However, I decided it would have to be a carefully thought-out strategy. Rather than a few weeks, I believed it would be something that would probably take many months. I would choose people I felt I could trust, and tell them first. I would in this way, gradually build up a network of support. This was not to be. I was exposed. It was Sandra's doing, the last deathly sting from the tail of the scorpion. She'd told her friends in the typing pool first, and one or two members of staff she was on speaking terms with. Within a couple of days, it was all round the teaching staff of the school. She had left me no place to hide.

The first I was aware of it, was one morning leaving class, and bumping into a couple of members of female staff. They were busy chatting away to each other. I wished them good morning, as I passed. I then heard them begin to snigger. I reasoned with myself, they could not be sniggering about me. They were merely talking about something amusing. I told myself I was just being paranoid. And then later on the same day, two male staff from the science department were both standing chatting in the corridor.

'Oh, and how are we, dearie?' one of them said in a camp voice.

His meaning was obvious. And then when I got into my car to leave work, another male teacher, this time from my own department quipped, 'and I'd go easy on the Vaseline if I was you.' I then knew I'd been exposed. My hands were shaking as I tried to start the car. Indeed, I wondered if in my present emotional state, I was in any fit state to drive. I don't really remember getting home.

I was in the kitchen, making myself something for my evening meal. No sooner had I cooked it and placed it on the kitchen table in front of me, than I realised I wasn't hungry. I tried listening to music; to help calm myself down, but even Mozart was jangling my nerves. When I went to bed that night, I was overcome by a fit of the shivers.

When I did finally drop off into a very fitful sleep, I was pursued by shadows and spectres and fearful things, which did not quite take form or recognisable substance. When I woke, I realised I'd gained no rest from my troubled slumbers. I felt tired and all my limbs were aching. Even a bowl of cornflakes, a bit of toast and a cup of coffee, seemed difficult to keep down. I wanted to throw-up. I also wanted to cry. There was to be yet another fit of shaking, before I was able to leave the house. I decided to take the bus to work and leave the car at home. It felt safer that way.

During my first class, full of thirteen- year- olds, I set them something to copy from the board. I rarely did this. It wasn't my style. The next class after that got some comprehension exercises to do. It was all I felt able to cope with. I was in no mood for putting on a performance for the kids. They'd just have to knuckle down and do a bit of grim ordinary school-work, the sort of stuff most of the other teachers were more than happy to dole out. And yet I knew I was being unfair to them. I was working on auto-pilot, treading water and giving, so much less than my best.

Ned had invited me round for a meal. I politely refused, telling him I'd got a lot of work on.

'Everything all right, old chap?' he said.

'Yes perfectly,' I said, 'why do you ask?'

'Oh, I don't know, you just seem a bit on edge that's all,' he said.

He was looking concerned. I felt there was the possibility if I told him everything; he might be the first friend I'd lose.

Indeed, I wondered if I would end up friendless and all alone. Would even my own family want to talk to me after this? And still the shakes persisted. They would come upon me at the oddest of times. So far it hadn't happened in class. Instead, I often got a feeling of light-headedness and dizziness. Sometimes I found it difficult to focus, and once or twice the stuff I'd written out on the blackboard, danced before my eyes. My throat seemed to be forever dry. I'd developed a nervous cough as if I was always trying to clear my throat. Even the kids began to notice all was not well.

'Are you all right, sir?' one of my fifteen-year-old boys had said. 'You are no fun anymore. You've become just like all the other teachers. It all feels like drudgery,' he said.

'Welcome to life,' I told him. I wished I hadn't said it. They deserved better than this.

I'd gone round home. Gary was being more annoying than usual. I found myself being overly sharp with him. He told me to sod off, but I could tell he was hurt by my off-hand manner.

'Do you have to speak to your brother like that?' said Mum over the tea table.

'Oh, don't you start as well,' I said.

The dog was barking and barking, and I didn't know what he was barking about. His high-pitched yelp was going right through me. I had to leave. I had to be away from them.

That Friday evening, I went as usual, with Matthew and David to our local. I knew I was putting on something of an Oscar winning performance. They were not taken in by it.

'There's something really up,' said David, 'I don't know what it is, but it's pretty major.' I told them both in the strongest terms I was completely fine and for them to back off.

'If you told us what's on your mind, maybe we could help,' said Matthew, 'after all we're your friends, your best friends. So come on, give out.'

'Will the pair of you just back off,' I said.

I put down my half-drunk pint of beer and stormed out of the pub. When I got home, no sooner was I inside the front door, than I was overtaken by another fit of the shivers. I realised I couldn't go on like this. Somehow, I had to turn things round. And then the following day, late in the afternoon, I bumped into Ned.

'The pub, eight o'clock prompt tonight, and no excuses,' he said hurrying off down the corridor. He was there before me, with a pint of bitter and a whisky chaser there in front of me.

'Now sink your lips into that lot and then we'll talk,' he said. He was smiling his usual good-natured smile. And yet I knew what was coming. I decided to pre-empt him.

'No doubt you've heard all the gossip?' I said.

'I'm afraid so, old man,' he said. 'Poor you'.

'So I suppose this is a farewell drink, to tell me in so many words that you want nothing more to do with me?' I said.

'Steady-on, old man,' he said. 'What do you take me for;

don't forget I read the classics. For all those Greeks at the time, well it seemed to be obligatory. And as for Eton, well enough said.'

For the first time in many days, I found myself laughing.

'Now that's much better. I haven't seen you laugh in ever so long,' he said. 'It's that ex of yours, Sandra,' he said, 'she's been putting the word around, so to speak. She's a woman scorned and you know what they say about that?'

We sat and chatted about it for some time and then he said, 'don't get me wrong, old chap,' he said, 'but well I always had my suspicions.' I asked him how?

'Well there's my favourite, uncle,' he said, 'he practically invented it. When I used to visit him as a kid on the long summer vac, he had some very mysterious and curious coves round the place, I can tell you. You know, artists and writers and people of, how should I put it, a bohemian persuasion. When I was older, he made no secret of the fact. He was in some senior position in the civil service over in India for years. He once boasted he'd had most of the British infantry whilst he was out there. That car you drive, old Clara there, was actually a gift to him from a particularly appreciative squaddie. You know your problem, if you don't mind me saying, is that you behave more like a furtive fox as opposed to an inheritor.'

'Now what on earth do you mean by that?' I said.

'I mean just this, old man, in the vineyard of life, you have the furtive foxes nibbling away at the odd stray grape or two and then, running off in the dead of night. Then you have the owner of the vineyard. He takes freely of the grapes and drinks his full unhurried share of the wine.'

I had my first good night's sleep in many days. And I sat over the breakfast table the following morning, thinking to myself I had a right to as much happiness as anyone else. I told myself I could go through the rest of my life feeling like a victim, or start to really enjoy it. Most of that day at school, I found myself somewhat more cheerful because of my positive self-talk.

'Things are going to be different,' I told myself.

On Thursday afternoons, I had a couple of hours of free time. It always felt like a luxury. I would usually spend it, sitting in the staff room, marking books and dreaming up ever new and fantastical ways, to make the great classics of English literature, really live and jump right off the page. There were a couple of female teachers, still in their twenties. They were talking quite loudly and animatedly. I could not but help, overhearing what they were saying.

'That's right, Sandra,' she said, 'from the typing pool told me only yesterday. He'd practically lead her up the aisle and everything, and then she finds out he's a ruddy puff. I mean can you imagine it?' I felt if I did not boldly confront all of this, my life would continue to be a misery.

'I know you're talking about me,' I said.

'You bet,' said one of them.

'If I had a boy old enough to attend this school, I wouldn't let him anywhere near, you,' she said, 'that's for sure.'

Clarissa had overheard the entire conversation.

'You two,' she said, 'I want you both in my office at once. Oh, and by the time I'm finished with the pair of you, you'll both need union representation.'

All eyes were turned towards me. All of my courage seemed to evaporate.

That evening I was listening to some jazz on my vintage hi-fi and sipping some wine, when there was a knock on my door. It was Clarissa. I invited her in.

'Don't worry,' she said, 'I already thought you were gay? Your job is completely safe. Those two women are both on final written warnings. If they so much as sneeze the wrong way, they're out.'

I then found myself with an invite round to her flat for Saturday tea. This was my first of many visits to Clarissa's flat. The outside brash sixties façade, gave no hint of what lay inside. A visit to Clarissa's place was an altogether seductive experience for all the senses. She was a wonderful host. She put me at my ease as soon as I'd entered.

'Sit yourself down, kick off your shoes and make yourself at home,' she said, after giving me a warm hug. She had lit lots of scented candles. There was Brahms playing away on a system that made my own vintage system seem as if I'd just bought it yesterday. Another woman, also black, though who looked to be in her early fifties, came in to join us. Clarissa introduced us both. Her name was Maddie and she and Clarissa had been gay partners since the late 1950s. She worked as a carpenter making be-spoke furniture. Many of the items in the flat had been carefully crafted by her. Like Clarissa, she was warm and vivacious. And sitting over the best Caribbean food I had as yet tasted, we were all soon laughing away and chatting like we had all known each other over many life-times, and who knows but maybe we had.

Towards the end of the evening, Clarissa got out both the single malt and her prize collection of Al Jolson 78rpm records. 'I Only Have Eyes for You', had to be one of my favourite ballads of all time, especially sung by the greatest entertainer of them all. Maddie was picking her way through her large collection. She was then popping them onto another turntable and amplifier, especially set-up for 78s.

'You've got to decide, whether you're going to let the bigots win or not,' said Clarissa. 'When you're gay, well you can waste your whole damn life hiding away in the shadows, just because some people are too narrow-minded, to ever understand. It's much better to be who you really are, and as for the bigots, well to hell with them.'

When I got home, after what had been a most delightful evening, I thought over all she had said. I knew now regardless of anything, I was fully coming-out. My first thoughts were about young Tyrone Kelly and whether or-not he was really gay. I was thinking about his red curly hair, and the slight stigmatism in his right eye, which made him look even more gorgeous. I had already taken myself, quite a few times, for a swim after school in the school baths. On a couple of these occasions, I could have sworn, when I got out of the pool, that he was looking at me in an amorous way, with the eyes of hungry lust. I now hoped it was not just my fond imaginings.

Tyrone continued to surprise me even after six weeks. It was not that we were actually lovers, at least not in the true sense of the word. We were not an item. We were not dating or going out together, only having the most wonderfully, mouth-wateringly, extraordinarily and perfectly brilliant, casual sex with each other. He still had a girlfriend. Someone he informed me he was going steady with. She would turn up at his house, hopeful about something she could never really have.

'One day I'll marry her and we'll have a nice house, kids and everything. It's going to be perfect, just you wait and see,' he would say. I knew he had to find out the truth of things for himself. I did not feel it was my job to strip the sad delusion away.

I adored his grubby red curly hair and his sly mouth, which I loved to fill with my hungry tongue. Sometimes we made love standing up, his legs wrapped around my torso. And then there were his naked feet, and his heels and ankles, which sent me into paroxysms of ecstasy! He was as keen as I was. No sooner had I closed the front door to my house, than he was on to me, a boy very much on heat during the early summer of that year.

'You are such a dirty little slut,' I said to him, as he lay there in my arms, whilst we shared a cigarette. He just laughed at me in his cheeky, irreverent way.

'You wouldn't like it if I was all prim and proper,' he said, this wanton assistant caretaker, who liked to parade himself naked in front of my bedroom mirror, admiring his reflection.

'That you never will be, or a modest one either,' I said.

'Now I can't help it if I just happen to be gorgeous,' he said.

I had finally plucked up the courage to take myself to The Manhattan Bar in town. On the far wall facing me as I entered, was a mural of the Manhattan skyline.

They also served all kinds of fancy American cocktails at an expensive price. The music was eighties disco, something they called *High Energy*. It was peculiar to the gay night clubs of the time. I found it infectious. With that music, we were all dancers, smoky cowboys and hustlers, fire-side tale-weavers, married to chance. We were brazen prophets, wise jesters, marketplace minstrels, naked and pagan, caught up in strange winds. The base metal of our ordinary lives was transmuted into the alchemist's dream, for but a few brief moments, out there on the floor. It was indeed an infection, a fever, blood-racing, a shivering wave of enchantment, the jocund, festive trance that told us, we owned the world!

I sat down with a bottled beer, rather enjoying the sights and sounds of the place. It was full of lots of gorgeous-looking young guys, obviously out on the pull. And there holding court amongst them was Tyrone, dressed up in a pair of the tightest and the brightest red jeans I'd ever seen. He toned things down at work, but here he was being so deliciously camp! I knew most of it was an act, but I enjoyed the performance anyway. Eventually he saw me and came over.

'So all that stuff they've been saying about you at work is true. You're just a dirty little faggot like me?' he said.

'I guess so,' I said. He told me he'd fancied me for months now.

'I'm so glad the rumours are true. I'd love you to screw me,' he said. I told him he was being very forward.

'Oh, darling,' he said, 'wait until I've got a few gins inside me, that's just for starters.' He then planted a great wet kiss on my lips.

As the night progressed, there was a drag act on and then in the upstairs room, a fairly small space, they hosted a mid-week disco. We both went upstairs and smooched and danced for an hour, before sitting back down for another drink. And then we were kissing seriously. I asked him if he wanted to come back.

'I'll have to ring me, mum,' he said, 'she worries about me if I stay out and she doesn't know that I'm with someone.'

'Anyway, I'll say you're this dead respectable teacher from work. She'll be so impressed,' he said smiling mischievously at me. I was finding him irresistible. We caught a taxi back to my place. I put some music on at a low volume and made us some coffee. We sat on the sofa and began kissing again, like continuing a conversation where we had left off.

'You've got gorgeous ears,' I said. He burst out laughing.

'Well, no one has told me that before,' he said.

He was undressing me with his eyes, and I loved his accent, which was part southern Irish brogue and somehow part broad North Lancashire. His dialect, felt like the curious fingers of a lover. The sweet, laughing tone of it caressed me. He removed his black satin shirt. His nipples stood out, already aroused. His navel, protruded outwards. His soft belly was slightly rounded. I stroked his chest with my fore-finger. He gave what seemed to be a shudder of delight. I reached across and gently kissed the curve of his belly. I somehow knew that despite all his street-wise banter, he was probably a real romantic at heart.

This boy really wanted to be wooed, and not taken quickly. I removed his black patent leather shoes, carefully and slowly untying the laces to each shoe. I then removed each of his white socks. I wanted to gasp with the beauty of his naked feet. I knew I needed to undress all of him, nice and slow. He kept running his fingers through my hair, as I did so. His jeans were next. His legs were almost smooth, except for a wispy trace of golden down. His knees were kind of boyish. I could imagine them being scraped on many occasions, when he was a boy, out playing with his friends. His legs had the strange musculature of a young man. Finally, I removed his pink underpants, and taking a delight as I watched his cock, spring itself wonderfully free from its restraint. And there he was before me, completely naked and utterly beautiful!

'God,' I said, 'you are completely beautiful.'

As I said this, I noticed he was rather tearful. We changed

places. I got up from my knees, beside the settee, and I sat down, whilst he removed my own clothes with the same slow and deliberate love.

'And you're beautiful too!' he said. We both laughed.

We finished the conversation in the bedroom. And after that heated, incredibly passionate first night, I knew I adored him: totally, utterly and completely! I remember it was if our bodies seemed to have a will of their own. The touch of him seemed almost unbearably lovely. He was all sweaty and the smell of his youth was as sexy as it was strangely poignant. I entered him, after what seemed a long while of tender kissing and stroking. The space inside him felt warm. I knew he wanted to feel me in there. He wanted to face me, so we could kiss and screw at the same time.

'Sweet and glorious Jesus,' he kept saying, as I rode the wave of him. I smiled, thinking I was bringing out the Irish Catholic in him! And afterwards, as we lay together in each other's arms before falling to sleep, there was an afterglow, like the falling of summer rain, in the all too subtle air.

It was a Thursday morning. He left early to get ready for work. We kissed gently and smiled at each other fondly. And an hour later, when I stepped outside my own front door and got into the car, everything seemed clean and fresh, like the first day of a new world to me. The blackbirds were singing in the hedgerows and the early sun was still low in the sky, dazzling my eyes with its sudden, blazing light.

6

We would sometimes go across to Canal Street in Manchester and catch the last train back to Munford, which left just before midnight and got us back into town an hour later. There were times when Karen, his supposed girl-friend, hogged his attention. And one evening, he rang me to say something a bit serious had come up with her. He would be in touch, but had to call off at the last minute. 'Hundreds of apologies and thousands of kisses,' he said to me before he put the phone down.

And so I decided to take myself off to Manchester. I was outside one of the bars, sitting at a table overlooking the canal, sipping a glass of cool beer. Dusk was gathering into a smoky hue across the water. Groups of revellers milled up and down around me, with every so often an outrageous scream. Just then, Tyrone walked across to me.

'Hi there, stranger,' he said.

'I thought you were supposed to be doing something with, Karen?' I said.

'One of, Karen's, cousins,' he said, 'saw me going into the Manhattan Bar, the other week, and one night when we were waiting for a taxi home, he also caught me snogging away with you in a shop doorway. So I'm very much afraid the game is up. I'm busted. He went and told, Karen,' he said, 'so now she knows I'm a puff. She got really nasty and threatening and all of that. So I ended it there and then. I told her not only that I was a regular faggot but that I was glad to be so. She slapped my face and then she left. I caught the train to Manchester, hoping I'd bump into you,' he said.

'So does that mean we're now an item?' I said.

'Yeh, if you like, he said.

'This calls for champagne,' I said.

And so there we were sitting drinking champagne, our hands gently touching across the table, watching the beginning of the moonlight cast its first glow up against the old warehouses at the other side of the canal.

'Should we see if we can book a room for the night?' I said.

'Yeh,' he said, 'that would be nice. I better phone, Mum,' he said, 'to say I'm staying over in Manchester.'

For me, it was the strange touch of his nakedness. It made me gasp. And all the joy was dancing inside of me, whirring up like a fire-flame on the hot summer evening air. Then too there was the smell of him, even detectable through the aftershave, the latest scent that everyone was wearing at the moment that he wore like a badge of honour. It was raw, musky and so of the earth and so wild and natural.

I felt like I could curl up and wrap myself in it all forever. In the hotel room, as we lay on the bed, we could hear the traffic outside the open window. An amber street light cast its iridescent glow into the room. We kissed, feeling the warmth of the inside space of each other's mouths. I could still taste something of the quinine on his breath, from all the gin and tonics he had been sipping that night. His hair was moist with sweat. We had been dancing. I was nuzzling my nose and face in amongst it, the wild, wild honey of all those pheromones, shooting off amorous rockets to the stars.

'Screw me,' he said. He sounded almost pleading, almost tearful. He had already told me, being screwed, felt like an unbearable need, an ache that just wouldn't go away, or let him be, until it had been completely satisfied. I found myself being rather ungentle; he had stirred me up so. And yet, he was riding the wave right along there with me. His kissing grew more desperate, and he was ploughing his bitten nails into my back, or pulling at my hair. He cried out, like a mother giving birth, with the force of our shared orgasm, something which always reduced us both to tears, and threw us so far out of ourselves, it took us a few moments, to come back, as it were, inside our bodies. I lit us a cigarette, and he cuddled himself in, his head lying gently on my chest, the delightful honey smell of him, escaping from his hair.

When you're young, love cuts deep. Happiness is sung in a different key. It had rained for most of May that year. Early June offered little hope of better weather. And then the skies began to clear. Blackbirds and finches were singing in the hedgerows, the smell of flowers and the heady musk rose was upon the air and everywhere was filled up with a lush, vibrant green. At school I would be teaching a lesson, when I would think about him, and our love making the night before, and I would feel a sudden rush of delight; racing through my veins like a summer fever. And all my classes seemed inspired. I was living inside the days of grace.

He insisted on dragging me round to see his mother. 'She'll love you,' he said. And so the meeting came off. I was feeling nervous all day at school before-hand. She was a middle-aged Irish woman from County Mao with the same infectious smile as her one and only son. She welcomed me in, with a warm hug and a laugh.

Tyrone had told me that he was an only child, he had been brought up as a Roman Catholic and his dad had left, shortly after he was born. She worked at the Fulton Road working men's club as chief barmaid. They lived just up the road from the club, a mere two minutes' walk away. She had cooked us both a hearty meal. She also baked her own bread, which was entirely delicious. Tyrone, who could never sit still for long, gambolled about clearing things away and helping her with all of the dishes.

'He's a good lad,' she said. 'I've always known he was gay. I had to let him work it all out for himself,' she said. She spoke with a warm southern Irish brogue. I told her my own parents were still ignorant about it all.

'The longer you leave it, the more personal anguish you'll cause for yourself,' she said. I tended to agree with her.

He usually stayed over on Friday nights. I adored waking up with him on a Saturday morning. He loved to cook us both breakfast. He'd just discovered ground coffee and broadsheet newspapers. And he would wander about my house in an old T-shirt, a pair of scruffy jeans, bare-foot. He would sit crossed-legged on the floor, pawing his way through my vinyl collection. If his own taste until recently gravitated towards pop and disco, he was hungry for all the other genres still to discover and experience. Indeed, he was developing quite a taste for 1950s jazz. He would listen to something a couple of times and declare himself to be quite the leading authority on it. I loved when he did this, and so did his mum. His mum and I would have a quiet laugh about it all.

I took him with me one Saturday evening, to our local to meet Matthew and David. I introduced him as a friend from work. He was wearing something really toned down. He did not wish to embarrass me or let the cat out of the bag. He was doing his best to drink real ale. I could tell he hated the stuff. When we were at the bar together I told him to get himself a gin and tonic.

'But if I don't knock back forty pints of ale, they'll know I'm a woofter,' he said. I smiled and told him to just be himself.

And yet that whole evening had been a strain on both of us. I wanted to tell them, but somehow couldn't find the words. We left and Tyrone came back with me. He was pootling about in the kitchen for a while, doing the rest of the washing up from our early evening meal. I came up behind him, putting my arm around his waist. He turned round with a smile and we kissed.

'Leave all of that and let's go upstairs,' I said. The hunger was on us both again, and all of the yearning for the naked caress.

'Oh God, you beautiful boy, how I love you,' I found myself saying, whilst smothering every inch of him with my desperate kisses.

His nakedness, there in the half-light of the bedroom, somehow always seemed like a new thing to me, as if I was looking at him for the first time. I stroked the curves of his belly, wandering my finger in and amongst his navel. I remembered how at church, they talked of 'worship.' I now wondered if they even knew the true meaning of the word. What I had with Tyrone, naked and suppliant, there before me, was worship. I was aware that we were both crying and yet happy, blissfully happy at one and the same time. And then afterwards, how I loved the way he nestled into me and the after-love smell of him, like wild honey and roasted cinnamon. We were caught up in the delicious drowse of a strange heaven.

I would sometimes look at myself, naked, in the bathroom mirror, when he had gone. I would wonder what he saw in me. I was five foot four, with dark brown hair; I could never keep tidy with a cheeky, hopeful grin. What did he see in all of that? And then at other times, especially just after our loving, I would look again and see me as a naked being and I was beautiful. Our loving made me feel this way.

Tyrone had left school without any qualifications. His English teacher, when he was thirteen had told him, 'You know I think you're the dumbest kid I've ever taught. And that's really saying something, because I've taught some extremely dumb kids in my time.' He had never questioned this judgement. He'd hated school. He was just that little bit camp, and found it difficult to hide it, and so he had spent most of the time being one step ahead of the bullies. Since leaving school, he had had a series of dead-end jobs; his present employment was no different.

A year ago, he had gone out for a walk on a cold winter's day. He had passed by a waste bin in his local park. He noticed that someone had simply thrown away what appeared to be a paperback book. His curiosity was aroused. He delved into the bin and rummaged it out. There were bits of apple peeling, fag-ash and other detritus that had got smudged all over the cover. Also the book was torn. It was a paperback edition of *Oliver Twist*. One of the classics he had thought, and he told me his first instinct was to throw it back in the bin. Despite this, he put it in the inside pocket of his thick winter coat.

'I just might read it and prove my old English teacher wrong,' he had said to himself. And that evening he had repaired the front cover and snuggled up in bed, he had read it. Three hours later and little Oliver now rescued by the benevolent Mr Brownlow, he was hooked. Since then, he had bought every classic he could get his hands on, as well as using his own and his mum's spare library ticket. He loved to browse through my extensive collection, of four large book-cases, which took up an entire wall.

He was always borrowing some book or other. He'd even taken to reading some of my volumes on literary criticism, asking me for help on the passages he couldn't quite get his head around. And then there was all of my music. Jazz and progressive rock had been his initial favourites. I'd been able to tempt him further afield into the rich realms of classical music. He'd now discovered Beethoven and Brahms, and the heady delights of great interpretations of these awesome works.

There had been a rather glorious Saturday evening. I'd called off my usual meeting with Matthew and David at our local and gone down to The Manhattan Bar with Tyrone instead. The drag act that night was particularly crude, lude, outrageous and hilariously funny. We had gone upstairs to the intimate nightclub, dancing hot and wild to all of that gay disco music, as well as a few tracks we could smooch to. And then coming home with me, there had been yet another wonderful night of loving. The softness of his body, curled itself into me that night. He cried afterwards. . 'Did I hurt you baby?' I said.

'No, you just took me to strange places. Time and place, lose their meaning when I'm with you, and I feel you all deep and hungry inside of me. It feels so right, it feels so good, that it makes me cry,' he said.

The following morning we were sitting across the kitchen table from each other. The table was strewn with *The Sunday Times* and *The Observer*. Mozart was playing softly away on the turntable. I looked across at him, his hair still tousled with the morning. I loved him this way. He was absorbed with an article about D.H. Lawrence that he didn't agree with at all! He'd discovered *Sons and Lovers* the week previously, and now felt he could give even old F.R. Levis a run for his money. He looked up at me from his paper and smiled at me.

'Do you know,' he said, 'I think I could quite happily spend the rest of my life with you.' I told him not to be so daft.

'What's daft about it?' he said.

'Gay people don't settle down. We're all complete and wanton sluts,' I said.

'Yeh I know, but why does it have to be that way? Why can't we do the happy ever after thing?' he said.

'Before you met me, how many blokes had you slept with from Manhattan? I said.

'Loads I suppose, but that's hardly the point,' he said.

'Isn't it?' I said.

'Monogamy is for heterosexuals, not for the likes of us,' I said. 'And anyway once your paint starts to peel, I'll be trading you in for a new model,' I said. He threw the paper at me, but we were both laughing. I hoped the serious moment had passed along with the absurd idea.

In many ways, when I'd been growing up in Munford I'd always considered it to be a cultural wasteland. There were no theatres or concert halls and only one of the cinemas still survived. The rest had been turned into bingo halls. And yet if you were prepared to really look, there were still plenty of good things to go and see and listen to. It was called alternative. There was a local rep theatre company, amateur but rather good. They did four or five productions a year. There was also lots of folk and jazz happening in intimate settings, tucked away down cosy back-streets in the middle of town. We called them a find. We loved them.

One Saturday before the end of the summer term, we packed ourselves some lunch and drove off in Clara up to Borrowdale. All the trees seemed of that kind of green which is almost an impossibly lovely thing. There was a faint summer breeze, and we loved to watch as stray pieces of pollen were falling into the valley, like white confetti. The afternoon sunshine was woven into a hazy mist. Sheep were grazing in the high fields. And up by a dry-stone wall, Tyrone filled my mouth with his hungry kisses. And as we were caught up in our tender afternoon embrace, I started to wonder if there was any truth in what he had said about spending the rest of our lives together, and in time becoming an old married couple. It seemed an altogether outrageous idea, a mere fairy-tale. And yet I wanted to believe it anyway.

He went over to Ireland with his mother every year to visit family. 'No doubt you'll be too busy to want to come with your old, mother,' she said, 'this year?' Indeed he was reluctant to go. 'Go on, remember absence makes the heart grow fonder,' I said to him, which made his mother laugh at us both. However, in the end, he decided to go. And I thought what on earth was I going to do with myself for the next ten days?

I was rather dreading my interim report from Norman Jackstone. It turned out to be glowing. He had also taken the time to write plenty about me in the comment sections.

'I must say, you're a real natural with the pupils,' he'd said to me, gifting me with one of his rare smiles. 'There are a couple of pupils that if we're not careful, are going to slip through the net. I'm giving them extra stuff to do. You might want to help me. They resent me despite all I'm trying to do for them. They trust you, so if I had you on board as well, then they'd know it was all for their own good, so to speak. Anyway, not to worry, we'll talk more about it after the summer hols. I'll see you for the results days,' he said.

I didn't give it anymore thought. I was looking forward to seven wonderful week's holiday, most of it spent with Tyrone. And then on the first day of the holidays, the landlord popped round. He told me he had decided he wanted to sell the house. He gave me first refusal. He only wanted a reasonable price for it, and I'd grown to actually love the place. Dad gave me the deposit and I was able to get a mortgage. By the second week in August, the place was mine.

It was whilst Tyrone was still on holiday with his mum in Ireland, during the third week of a sweltering July, feeling at a loose end, I had decided to pop down to The Manhattan Bar. It was early in the week and not particularly busy. Two older queens were sitting at the bar drinking cocktails. I'd gone up to the bar to get myself another bottled beer. One of these men came and approached me.

'Excuse me but you don't happen to be, Jack Stebson's son?' he said.

I told him that I was.

'Well, well, well,' said his friend, 'the apple never falls far from the tree. Like father like son.'

I thought they meant me and my dad shared more than a

passing resemblance. Later on, one of them said,

'I suppose it must be in the genes or something.'

I was growing mildly annoyed with them, and what felt to be some suggested innuendo left hanging in the air like a bad smell. I asked them to say what they meant.

'Ok, to be blunt, I take it that you're gay?' I told them I was. 'And surely you must know that your, father,' he said, 'is as bent as a ruddy corkscrew. Always has been. Why, he is quite the deva of Howley sauna,' he said.

I went back to sit down with my drink. I knew my dad had always gone to Munford Turkish Baths every Wednesday afternoon. I thought nothing about it. Just as my Uncle Harry, who was in partnership with him, had every Thursday afternoon gone off to play golf. Howley Sauna however, on the outskirts of town, I knew to be a gay sauna with a reputation. It had been raided by the police on several occasions, and some of the local residence had tried to get it closed. I finished my drink and quickly left.

I went home to try out a new pair of headphones and a second-hand transistor amplifier, to serve as a back-up to my valve amp. It sounded really good. Nevertheless, my mind kept going over what had been said to me that night. I'd always thought Mum and Dad loved each other and that there were no difficulties in their marriage. How could I have been so blind?

Over the next few days, other things started to come together in my mind. Gran had always thought my dad was, 'far too handy with a duster.' There was often a tension in the air between them, I'd never been able to fathom out until now. And then after Matthew's wedding Gran had talked about history repeating itself and suddenly deciding she had said too much. And then too, Dad always insisted on ironing all his own clothes. He was obsessional about his shoes. He had loads of pairs. His handkerchiefs came especially from Bond Street. He was so very gentle and if he got angry over something, he also seemed visibly upset, more like a woman than a man. Had their marriage been a complete sham all those years? It felt too terrible to contemplate. I was shaking and becoming tearful. I was to spend a restless night with little sleep.

Tyrone came back. We hugged, we kissed and we went straight upstairs to make love. He said he found me distant and preoccupied. 'You've found someone else, that's it and you don't know how to break the news to me that we're history,' he said and then he was in floods of tears. 'I knew I shouldn't have gone away,' he said.

'Tyrone,' I said quite sharply, 'will you stop being such a drama queen and just listen.'

I then said that there was no one else, and I loved him just as much as ever. I wanted to tell him about all the gossip and malicious rumour about Dad, but felt I couldn't. This was the first of the secrets. I was keeping something back from the one person I loved, more than anyone else in the world.

'I don't care what you say, there's something up. You're not the same,' he said. And of course he was right.

We went to The Manhattan Bar. I tried to keep him occupied by asking him about his holiday. 'I've always wanted to visit Ireland,' I said, 'I bet it's really beautiful at this time of year?'

'You don't give a damn about Ireland or me for that matter,' he said, 'I'm leaving.' And then he got up and left the bar, barely holding back the tears. I knew I should have gone after him, and told him all that was on my mind. The thing was, sharing it felt like it was all too real. By keeping it to myself I could still try and fool myself that it was just all bitchy tittle-tattle. And then a red-headed older man, probably in his late forties, came across to me and asked if he could join me.

'Don't worry,' he said, 'I'm not trying to chat you up. I'm not really into Twinks and Chickens.' He wanted to know what I was drinking. Moments later he came back with a whisky for himself and another bottled beer for me.

'I better introduce myself,' he said offering me his hand.

'My name is, Arthur Devlin,' he said, 'your father and I used to be lovers.'

I felt myself reddening up. He told me that most of it had happened before my dad was married. He also said that, whether I believed it or not, my dad had always been honest with my mum. He told me that my dad was sixteen at the time and working as a junior reporter on *The Munford Gazette*. Arthur was eighteen and working as a printer, in the middle of his apprenticeship.

'We met in the staff canteen. I'd seen him ogling me for weeks. I fancied your dad like crazy. Believe me in those days, he was quite a catch. Well we got talking and we both found out that we were madly into films. That Saturday afternoon, we went to see a film at the old flee-pit on the outskirts of town. When we came out of the cinema, or the picture house, as we used to call them in those days, we passed some deserted ground. They had been bull-dosing some old houses.'

He told me that he had wanted my dad so much, that he had pinned him against a wall that was still standing amongst the rubble, and thrust his tongue into his mouth.

'He resisted and pushed me away. But I came back for more.

This time, he punched me, giving me a bloody lip. I told him to fuck off and then ran away. I was worried he might report me or something, I mean in them days it was all still completely illegal. We did our best to avoid each other in the canteen over the next few days. But unbeknown to me, well I'd woken something up in your dad.'

He said he found out that my dad came from a family of strict Methodists, and that my paternal grandmother was a right old Bible-Basher. 'So not only was he completely riddled with guilt, but up until then, he had not even allowed himself to indulge in such thoughts.'

I found myself warming to him. I felt somehow, I could trust him. I then told him how strange it was that I too, had tried to hide away from my true queer feelings, using religion to do so. He went on to tell me that my dad had sent him a hastily scribbled note, asking him to meet him outside the gas works that evening. It was a cold November night, full of mist.

'I hope you haven't called me back to give me another bust lip?' I'd said to your dad.

"No, of course not," said your dad. "You took me by surprise, that were all," he had said to me.

He said he had suggested to my dad, that they went back to his place and that as it was a Wednesday evening, his dad was working nights and his mum was out at her Co-Op meeting. He told me my dad seemed nervous and yet eager at the same time. He agreed to come back.

'There he was this respectable young lad, who had never done anything in the least bit daring in his whole life, being asked to come back with me to a very shady area of town. Nevertheless, he did come back with me. We ended up making love and then cuddling up together, sharing a cigarette in the half-light of my bedroom. After that we were secret, hungry lovers.' He told me that things went on for a few months, but that my dad was torn between his Christian believes, lying to his mother, who he adored, and their relationship.

'I remember him sitting at the side of the bed, barely holding the tears back. I popped a lighted cigarette into his mouth. "I just get so scared," I remember him saying. "What if we got really carried away and your mum came in and caught us both at it?" he had said. I tried to convince him that he was worrying about nowt. But in my heart, I knew I was losing him. Well, he went and handed in his notice. The editor was furious with him. He told him he was throwing away a good career. But your dad was determined. He ended it with me the next week. He had lots of dead-end jobs after that, until your grandad wanted to retire and hand over the business to your dad and uncle.' He said he had heard through the grape-vine that my dad was seeing my mum and also, he knew they had finally got engaged. She had called off one night. It was New Year's Eve.

'He came waltzing in to this Irish bar, dead rough an all that I used to drink in. Well, I hadn't seen him for best part of five years. But we got talking. I persuaded him to come back with me. I was a fully qualified printer now and I'd rented a small terrace house, just off the town centre. He burst into tears when we got back. He had been trying to keep strong, but sometimes he found it so hard. I told him to give himself up to it, just for one night. And so we ended up making love.'

He told me that the following morning, neither of them could hold back the tears, as they hugged for the last time. A month later, he told me that my dad had married my mum.

He said he was so utterly heart-broken, that after a couple of months, he packed in his job on *The Gazette* and got himself another printing job over in Dublin, where he remained for the next thirty years.

He told me he had only recently moved back to the area. His mum was still alive, though she was dying of cancer. She had passed away. So he had taken up his old job on *The Gazette*. He said that my dad didn't know he had come back, and he didn't want him too. He thought there was too much water under the bridge, to meet again.

'I just wanted you to know,' he said. We shook hands again and then he left.

7

I'd been putting off telling Mum and Dad. I went round during the week; saying very little about anything over the evening meal. 'Cat got you tongue or something?' said my mum.

'You're mother's right; you've hardly said two words,' said my dad.

'There's nowt up is there?' said Mum.

'Will you both just leave me alone; I'm fine,' I said.

I left shortly afterwards, using my usual excuse that I had lots of marking to attend to. I'd got half way up the road, when I turned back. I rang the front door bell. Dad answered it. 'Now what's up?' he said.

'Where's Gary?' I said.

'He's out playing with his mates,' said Dad.

The three of us went into the sitting room. Mum turned off the telly.

'I've something I need to tell you,' I said, 'I've wanted to tell you for ages; but somehow I didn't know how, and I couldn't find the right words.'

It was then that Mum looked at me with a steady, knowing gaze. 'You're not trying to tell us that you're a homosexual?' She said.

'Yes, I'm gay,' I said. I couldn't hold back the tears.

Dad came rushing towards me, jumping out of his seat. He flung his arms around me; whilst I sobbed like a small boy.

'It's alright, it's alright,' he said, 'we still love you just the same. You're still our son.'

I was feeling as vulnerable as a nine-year-old-school boy.

'Is there anyone?' said Dad.

'Yeh,' I said, raising my head, smiling through the tears, and looking off into the far distance, 'Oh yes, there is someone. I met him at school. He's the assistant caretaker. His name is Tyrone. I think I'm kind of head-over-heals about him.'

'We'd love to meet him,' said Dad.

'Yes, bring him round for tea,' said Mum.

I told Tyrone all that had taken place, over a couple of drinks at The Manhattan Bar. I also said they would love to meet him. He was as nervous as hell.

'What if they don't like me?' he said.

'They'll love you,' I said.

Mum had made a bit of an effort; she must have been baking all day.

Dad was great at putting people at their ease.

'What's it like being a school caretaker?' he said.

'Pretty boring actually,' said Tyrone, tucking into my mum's baking.

Gary had been told about me by my mum and dad. I was finding it difficult, for a change, to work out what he might be thinking. I could usually tell. We were very close. That early evening he seemed guarded. And then towards the end of the meal Gary turned to Tyrone and said,

'So do you both take it up the bum then?' Tyrone had reddened up and seemed on the verge of tears.

'Go to your room immediately. I'll talk to you later, young man,' said Dad. Both Mum and Dad were full of apologies.

'I suppose he must be finding it difficult to get his head round,' I said. Dad thought it was still no excuse for his behaviour.

'Let me try talking to him before we go,' I said.

I went up to his room. He was sitting cross-legged on his bed with his headphones on listening to music. I sat on the side of the bed.

'Can we talk,' I said.

'You're just a rotten, stinking faggot,' he said, throwing himself onto his pillow in floods of tears. All I could do was leave him. And yet I was feeling sore at heart.

'I can't reason with him. He's really upset,' I said coming down.

'He'll be even more upset by the time I'm ruddy finished with him,' said Dad.

'I think at the moment, you'll just make things worse, Dad,' I said.

Clarissa and Ned had had us both up for meals. Ned's four boys thought it was 'cool' and couldn't see what all the fuss was about.

'You've both got them well trained,' I said to Ned after they had gone to bed.

'I'm afraid you're wrong there, neither of us can take the credit for that. They're just really open-minded about most things in general, old boy,' he said.

I felt envious, because his second oldest boy was around Gary's age. But then I reasoned with myself, it was not like suddenly finding out that your own brother was gay. I intended to tell Matthew and David that Saturday at the pub. Tyrone asked me if I wanted him there for support. 'Thanks love, but

I think it might be better if I face them alone,' I had said. I knew he would be waiting for me when I got back home and that was enough. Gary had already told them. Matthew had bumped into him in town, and it all got blabbed out over a coke at a local cafe. I was met by a cold reception, although there was my usual pint of bitter and single malt waiting for me on the table.

'We know,' said David, 'your brother told us, he was heart-broken. He is worried that his friends will find out he's got a gay brother.'

'What really gets me,' said Matthew 'is how you've lied to us all this time. Or is it just some daft latest fad?' he said.

'No, it's not some latest fad. I've always been gay for as long as ever I can remember,' I said.

'So let me get it right, you and that, Tyrone,' he said, 'are a pair of screaming faggots?'

'We are lovers,' I said. 'I'd hoped you would both be big enough to understand, but it seems I was wrong.'

'You seriously expect us, to somehow get our heads round this, that everything will be all right and it we be all mates as usual? Said David.

I asked him why not, and after all wasn't I still the same person.

'No you're not the same person,' said Matthew, 'you are someone I don't know at all.'

'Look guys, you are being ridiculous,' I said. They finished their pints and left the pub.

'We're finished. Get that in you queer skull,' said David, as they were leaving. Selwyn, the landlord had overheard most of the conversation. I went up to the bar for another pint, to try to steady my nerves. He refused to serve me.

'Sorry,' he said, 'your type is not welcome round here. I've got a reputation and my license to think about,' he said. And so all I could do was leave. I went back home. Tyrone was listening to a Beethoven concerto. I didn't have to say anything. He could read it all on my face. He stood up and gave me a hug and then I burst into tears.

'Let's have ourselves a nice quiet night in, just listening to music. I'll nip to the off-license for some wine and nibbles and to hell with everyone else,' he said. I smiled and told him it was a good idea. 'They may come round,' he said, 'it's probably just the shock.'

I wanted to believe him, but in my heart I knew our friendship was at an end. I felt their betrayal, was the kind of pain that hurt me from a dark unthought-of place. Because it was least expected, it lingered on in my mind and my heart for weeks afterwards. Even when I thought about it months later, it remained a tender spot, the scared-tissue of the heart. It was an emotional wound that would not let me go. It was forever finding another hook, somewhere else to stab and lacerate me. It was torturing my mind, haunting my midnight hours, souring all my hope, cancelling out all my promise and laughing at all my happy moments, calling them but the sad delusions of an addled mind. Tyrone felt he couldn't reach me. Our love making was functional. I was somewhere else. I wondered if I would ever return. It was a desperate place of howling shadows.

And how my mind would play tricks on me. For all the happy memories of our friendship, would be suddenly and most vibrantly there before me. We would be boys again, playing knock-about in the backstreets, laughing and carefree on those summer afternoons that seemed to last forever. Then there were the school dances and first dates, trying our first drag on a cheap cigarette, or trying to hold down our very first pint of beer. What strange grief was this? Their faces were fully there before me. And they were always smiling, with kindness in their eyes and never a look of judgement. And then I would think I'd imagined it all. Surely, we were still the best of friends and the last few weeks, but a hideous dream.

Things were hardly any better at home. My brother refused to talk to me or have anything to do with me, despite my dad's entreaties. 'You do know you've broken your brother's heart?' my mum said. 'Things can never be the same. You've ruined all that. I hardly sleep a wink, thinking about it all.'

She had told Gran. I received one of her frosty receptions. She wanted to know what Matthew and David thought about it all, or whether I had been too ashamed to tell them.

'I've told them. I've nothing to be ashamed about,' I said.

'Oh, and I suppose they've welcomed the news with loud cheers and open-arms?' she said.

'Not exactly,' I said.

'What you mean is, you've told them and they've dropped you, like a ruddy hot potato. You had to go shouting it from the ruddy rooftops. No one in their right mind would ever admit to a thing like that,' she said.

'You've become a complete stranger to me. I don't know you anymore. I think I hate you,' she had said to me. And with that, I left the house.

The one person I needed most at this time was Tyrone. Yet he was the one person I was pushing away. He'd want to go out to The Manhattan Bar and I'd call off at the last moment. He'd get us tickets for some alternative theatre and I'd go, but sit through the performance, playing my own drama in my head.

'You've sat through the entire first half, and I don't think you've taken in a word of it,' he would say. I would ask him back.

'What's the point? You're not there,' he would say. And of course he was right. I didn't know how long he would be prepared to put up with my behaviour. I was losing everyone who was close to me. All of my worst fears were being fully realized. I went back up to school. I had pupils who had sat their GCE exams and their CSE exams. Most of them had passed and with good grades. Mr Jackstone was impressed and smacked me hard on the shoulder.

'Well as a reward, I'm going to let you loose on the first year sixth, at the beginning of the autumn term.'

I knew I should have been thrilled at this bit of news. I thanked him, but I was feeling nothing, nothing at all. The week before the start of term, I decided to go up to Edinburgh to see Natalie, my older sister and Chris, my brother-in-law. Mum had already phoned with the news. Natalie was eight years older than me. Despite that, we had always been close. And yet I was not holding out any hopes that she would be receptive, or supportive about Mum's news. And then she phoned me the day before I was due to travel.

'Hay, our kid,' she said, 'and what's this I hear about you batting for the other team?' She didn't sound either upset or surprised. 'I hear there's a boyfriend as well,' she said. 'You can bring him along if you like. Chris and I would love to meet him.'

Tyrone was working shorter shifts at school, due to the holidays, keeping the place ticking over and free of any vandalism. He had some holiday due, which he was able to take at short notice.

'I'm not sure though,' he said. 'They may hate me, and what about this, Chris, he said, 'your brother-in-law.'

'You'll be fine. He's is a great guy, you'll love him,' I said. Finally, at about eleven that evening, he had decided he'd take the risk and go up to Edinburgh with me.

Natalie and Chris were both jazz fanatics. They had met at a jazz festival in Clitheroe in the early seventies. In those days, they exuded the hippie ideal. They wore their hair long, smoked lots of dope, introduced me to all the exciting progressive rock bands, many of whom they took me to see live, at their campuses, when they were both undergraduates. And then, Natalie qualified as a Geography teacher and for some reason, Chris took an interest in insurance.

They married in Munford and got promotions up in Edinburgh. In the early days of their marriage, when money was rather tight, they'd rented a terrace house in a ramshackle area of town. It was very bohemian. During the summer, the kids played bare-foot in the street. Their parents cooked food in their front gardens, played lots of music at all hours, shared, laughed and lived, almost as one happy community. Natalie said it was the nearest thing to a commune outside of Woodstock. I'd been in my mid-teens at the time and loved the place. Since then, now thirty, Natalie was head of her department, at an independent girl's school. Chris had been an underwriter for motor insurance for some years, but was looking for something more exciting and challenging.

He was now a sort of project manager, come trouble-shooter, for a team of insurance sales people. They acted as some kind of bridge, between banking and insurance and did something terribly complicated with derivatives, which I didn't understand at all. Together, they'd rather a lot of money. They now lived in a luxury apartment of converted warehouses. From the kitchen window, you had a delightful view of The Fourth Bridge. What consisted of their living room area, well you could have fitted my house inside of it, at least twice over and still have room to spare. All the apartments were completely sound-proofed.

'You can make as much noise as ever you like, play heavy metal full-blast until four in the morning, and no one will hear you,' said Chris to me one day.

No one really knew anyone. They were all professional people, living separate lives. Although there new abode was certainly impressive, I much preferred their old haunt and the rag-tag folk who once peopled it. Chris wore a suite these days. He looked awkward in it. Natalie was quite the professional. The part actually suited her. She was rather bossy, but in a nice way. She got things done.

Ryan, their son, had come along, shortly after they'd moved up in the world. He was now five, had just started school and seemed to me in his free-child raga-muffin way, something of a wonderful throw-back, to the earlier days of their marriage, hanging out with the hippies.

'I don't know what it is about Edinburgh,' I said to Tyrone as we were sitting on the train, 'but it brings out the romantic in me.' He laughed at me.

There was lots of laughing, hugs and kisses as we entered their apartment.

'My dear,' said Natalie, 'and he's quite a catch. Pity he bats for the wrong side. And my God what a pert little bum he has.'

Chris laughed at her and said, 'aye up, you'll be frightening the lad away with all your talk.'

When Ryan saw me he practically jumped into my arms. 'Hello there, rag-bag,' I said, which was my pet name for him. He found it difficult to get Tyrone's name right. He kept calling him Teeroney, which everyone found highly amusing.

'Dad says you two are just like, Mum and Dad,' he said, 'with all of that slushy, yucky kissing stuff?' he said. Everyone howled at this.

Ryan had his tea much earlier than the rest of us. Natalie had something special planned, for later that evening. So we all sat down to the table, for a light snack as a put-you-on. Ryan was quite in his element, talking with his mouth full and enjoying being the centre of attention.

Whilst Natalie was putting the final touches to our evening meal, I went upstairs with Ryan to read him a bedtime story. These days he was madly into Enid Blyton and *The Famous Five*. I'd loved these stories, when I was a kid. He sat cuddled up beside me on his bed, in his *Star Wars* pyjamas, whilst I read to him. We were both transported back to another time, another age. I was a child once more, for but a brief half hour. I never could quite tell which of us was enjoying himself the most. We were both caught up in the enchantment of the moment.

Natalie had gone all out with supper. There was also plenty of wine and great single malt whisky for afters. Tyrone was visibly relaxing as the good food, the happy conversation and the excellent whisky, worked their magic. Their hi-fi was state-of-the-art. It cost thousands. It sounded great. Chris put on some Miles Davis on the turntable with its pickup, that I knew cost in the region of twelve hundred pounds. Even though the volume was low enough so we could talk, it felt like being inside the music. They wanted to know how we had met and got it together. And I ended up telling them all that had taken place, since I'd come out. I became tearful. Tyrone gently held my hand. Our love-making that night seemed particularly special.

They had a rather wonderful baby-sitter, so on the second night, the four of us went out to an intimate Italian restaurant, hidden away down one of the back streets in the town centre. It was their favourite. I insisted it was my treat. Tyrone and I loved the place, with its soft lighting. There was opera playing away in the background, and all of the simply prepared but gorgeous food, just happened to be some of the best I'd ever tasted. Chris asked for the drinks to be put on a separate bill, which he paid for. There were deep flavoursome and incredibly full-bodied red wines, some of which were forty pounds a bottle. We all laughed at Tyrone, who was enjoying them all, and getting a real taste for the high-life.

'So then, and how's God's gift to teaching?' said Natalie, sipping her wine.

'You know I love it,' I said.

'And I bet you've even got the so called no-hopers turned on to Shakespeare?' she said.

'Indeed, some of them. We act it all out in class,' I said, 'it's a right hoot.'

'I remember when he was no older than our, Ryan,' she said, 'he would be lecturing away to his teddy bears.'

Tyrone was giggling away, at that delicious stage between merry and pissed. I seemed to love him even more when he was like this. He'd start getting all of his words mixed up and talking a load of nonsense.

'More wine?' said Chris. He was unable to keep the smile off his face, as he filled up Tyrone's glass.

'Here, don't you think he's had enough?' I said jokingly.

'No I haven't,' said Tyrone, lifting up his glass.

In many ways, those few days in Edinburgh felt like I was in some kind of cocoon, safe from the world. Here, there were no cares and no people hating my guts because of who I chose to love.

On the third night, Tyrone and I took ourselves off to the city's small, but lovely gay scene. There were various bars we decided to sample. They were all full of a mid-week crowd of young and noisy revellers. We got chatting to a couple of young queens who had travelled from Dunfermline for the night. They were not in a relationship, simply best bitching partners. They were funny, loud and a little of them seemed to go, a very long way. We eventually ended up at the nightclub. It was down a back street and you went through a narrow side door, and up some even narrower stairs, to the club itself. There was big hefty bouncers to greet us at the entrance way. They both looked like they had just popped back from Cibber tossing, at the highland games.

'You both know what kind of club this is?' said one of them.

'Aye,' said a young lad behind us, 'it's for wee willie-woofters, just like us, so let's at them.' There were howls of laugher all down the staircase.

The music was infectious. Everyone seemed to be caught up in the beat of the hot summer's night. Lots of the young men threw off their T-shirts and danced wild and naked, down to their waists. Many of them were sniffing amyl nitrate and screaming out their joy, and we were screaming, laughing and dancing along with them. On the train journey back to Munford, I decided to come clean about all that I knew about my dad and his ex-gay lover. Tyrone listened carefully.

'That's why my mind was on other things,' I said, 'when you first came back from Ireland. I'm sorry.'

As we both stepped off the train at Munford station, I felt my heart sinking. It felt we had been surrounded by an ocean of tolerance and love and now it was back to all that hate. As we left the station, there was one of the bigger churches there before us, the other side of the road from the bus stop. And I thought there was the centre of all of that hate, the barbed-wire wrapped around the cant and the liturgy. It was raining heavily, as we waited for the bus home. My mind was suddenly caught up with the fever of the night, dancing wild and free and somehow one with all that it meant to be young. Whilst I was in Edinburgh, Natalie and I tried our best not to talk shop, but couldn't help ourselves doing just that. When she learned that I was in all probability, going to teach the six formers at the beginning of the new school academic year, she was surprised.

'My God, Robbie,' she said, 'how the hell did you go and manage that?' She then told me it had taken her five years, before they let her loose on the six formers.

'I had to earn my spurs darling,' she said.

A couple of days before the beginning of the new term, all the teachers went back to school for their pre-term briefing and to be given draft copies of their new syllabuses, for the coming year. I was delighted to see that for my first year six formers, I had been given *The General Prologue* from *The Canterbury Tales*, *The Wife of Bath*, the poetry of Dylan Thomas and *Mrs Dalloway*.

'God,' I thought, 'what a feast of delightful literature.'

Mr Jackstone took me aside, 'I know it's quite a challenge,

do you think you're up to it?' he said.

'I can't wait to get started,' I said.

'That's the spirit,' he said, gifting me with one of his rare smiles.

With Chaucer, I knew if I could get them to fall in love with all of that Middle-English language, they would be hooked. I got them to read small sections of *The Prologue* in class, and to translate two pages of their choice from it.

'It isn't going to be marked,' I said, 'I just want you to get a feel for the language and start to have fun with it.'

And then one Monday morning, I was walking down the corridor to their class, and I could hear them all through the open door to the classroom, speaking to each other in Middle-English dialogue. I was delighted. I came into the class and addressed them in Middle-English, and continued to talk to them in it for the next few minutes. We all then burst out laughing. I was enjoying myself at school so much and it always seemed to make me so very tender with Tyrone. We were always off to jazz or folk events in intimate venues and coming home to a night of the most wonderful loving. He was all soft, laying there naked beside me. I remember one night, rather drunk, just wanting to play endlessly with his hair, and kiss his wonderful ears.

'You utterly gorgeous creature,' I said to him one night, as he cuddled up in my arms in the half-light, sharing a cigarette. Our feet were all deliciously tangled together. He smiled up at me.

'I do believe we could grow old together,' he said.

'Dream on,' I told him, but at that moment I wished his fond fairy-tale could come true. There was no-one that I would have preferred to share the rest of my life with.

David called round on the Saturday morning. He was polite, cold and perfunctory. He had borrowed some rock records from me a few months before. He had come to return them.

'Fancy a coffee?' I said, 'I'm just about to make a brew,' I said. At first he seemed hesitant, almost as if he might stay. Then his face and his features became hard.

'No, I best be off. I've lots of things to attend to.' And then he left.

Tyrone came downstairs, bare-foot in an old T-shirt and a tatty old pair of jeans.

'What was all that about?' he said, wiping the sleep from his eyes. I told him. He came across to me and gave me a gentle cuddle. 'Never mind,' he said.

'God, I miss them so much,' I said, barely holding back the tears.

Tyrone tended to stay with his mum during the week and we spent Friday and Saturday together. Some Sundays, his mum would cook lunch and we would go for a few drinks at the club before-hand. Occasionally Sandra would be there. She never spoke to me. She would give me her best poisonous looks instead.

Maggie, Tyrone's mum, I had quickly grown to love. She had a great sense of humour and there was a kind and know-ing wisdom in the things she said. She was the sort of person I could confide in. We would both help out with the Sunday lunch. Tyrone would be putting the final touches to the roast, and me and Maggie would be preparing the veg.

'My God, you two just seem so Mr and Mrs Domesticated,' she said, laughing, and helping herself to a glass of white wine, on the sideboard. 'To be sure, a wee glass of wine, always helps me with the cooking,' she said. And we were both off laughing.

'Penny for them?' she said just before Sunday lunch, as I was gazing abstractedly out of the kitchen window.

'I was just thinking, it never feels this close with my own mum,' I said.

'Now I'm sure your good mother, loves you to bits,' she said, giving me a hug.

Things remained difficult at home. Mum was civil but little more. Gary was talking to me, in that he was keeping a civil tongue in his head, but I knew this was because of what my dad had said to him. It was all strained and false. I never went round with Tyrone, because I thought it would just make things worse, not that he would have come anyway. Gran had stopped talking to me altogether. Mum had said Gran wanted me to know that Gary and Ryan were now her only grandsons.

'To hell with her then,' I said, 'if that's how she wants to be.'

And yet, I remember that Saturday evening. Tyrone and I had gone to The Manhattan Bar and I'd broken down in fits of uncontrollable sobbing, over our second drink. We left the bar and came home early. We didn't really make love that night, Tyrone just held me close in his arms until I eventually fell off to sleep.

I'd wanted to use an overhead projector. I'd got some material on the use of rhyme and metre in the poetry of Dylan Thomas. I could have approached Tyrone to get it for me and set it all up before the lesson. Indeed, he was more than willing to do so.

'No, don't be daft; you've got enough to do. It's only down the corridor and I can set it up myself. I'm not completely useless in the technical department,' I said.

I'd left my six formers reading an informative piece of criticism on the continuing debate, *to what extent is Thomas one of the modern school of poets, and in what ways does he hark back to the earlier poetry of Gerald Manley Hopkins?* I had some interesting documents on Thomas's working methods of how he thought out his poems and the metres and tropes he chose to adopt. And so I went to collect the projector. It was as I was walking back to my classroom that I happened to overhear a raised voice. A teacher was shouting, or rather screaming at a pupil. He was shouting so loud, I could hear every word. I felt I needed to stand and listen to what was being said. The teacher that was shouting was Mr Jackstone. The pupil was fifteen- year- old William Henderson, now in his first year O' Level class.

'You dare to hand me in work like this!' said Mr Jackstone, 'this is *Great Expectations*, one of Dickens' best works. And what do you make of him, what?' I could hear William mumbling that he didn't know. 'No, you don't know, because you don't know anything, anything boy!' he continued. 'You are just stupid, dense, thick and completely brain-dead! You shouldn't be in this set at all. I don't think you could even manage the CSE set. Perhaps we should consider putting you in remedial with the paint and the ruddy glitter!'

I slowly walked back to my class. As far as I was concerned Mr Jackstone was way out of order. That boy had been emotionally abused by him. Mr Jackstone was a bully. The anger was burning in me, and I was finding it difficult to fully focus on the lesson in hand. Somehow I managed. And then I did something I should not have done. I chose to rationalize the incident. I told myself, it was just a one-off occurrence. In all likelihood, the homework he had handed in was really sub-standard. Why, the same pupil had sometimes handed in some very shoddy work for me, and as for his handwriting! And so I let the matter sleep in my mind. I was probably making a fuss over nothing.

I'd popped round to see Milly Armstrong. Her mum's condition had flared up and Milly had to do most of the cooking and the general housework. Her mum was feeling angry because of it. 'She should be out playing with her friends, not minding the house,' she said to me, as I made us both a cup of tea. 'Mind you, I'm rather glad in a way that you've called round,' she said. Milly was out of the house.

'Mr Jackstone is worried about her. Apparently her work is really slipping. I blame myself of course. Having to worry about me is no doubt affecting her studying,' she said.

'Mr Jackstone doesn't teach Milly,' I said, 'I do.'

'Well, he's been giving her loads of extra homework to try and get her work back up to scratch,' she said. 'He even gave her a whole pile of extra stuff to do over the summer holidays. He came round to visit. He explained it all to me and said it was all for her own good. So I gave him permission to give her any extra homework that he found necessary. How have you found her work?'

I told her that Milly's work was up to the same very high standard as it had always been.

'Well then, I'm relieved to hear it,' she said, 'it just goes to show that all of this extra work Mr Jackstone has been setting her, is really paying off.'

I wondered if Milly also found herself at the wrong end of

Mr Jackstone's tongue. I then was approached by Mr Jackstone himself, all very friendly.

'Remember I mentioned towards the end of last term about two pupils? I thought if I didn't do something they would both slip through the net.' I asked him if he meant Milly Armstrong and William Henderson.

'So you've had problems with them as well?' he said. 'I was wondering if you wouldn't mind helping out. I've got them both spending most of their lunch hour, doing extra work over in my classroom. The thing is I find Wednesday's a bit difficult. The music teacher likes me to help out with band practice,' he said.

'I didn't know you were musical?' I said.

'Oh yes,' he said, 'I used to play the French horn, in my youth of course. Well I know my way round a score, so I help out a bit with practice.'

At first I told him I'd too much on and would not be able to help him out. He said he perfectly understood and not to worry. I was worrying however and wondering why he was so obsessed with Milly and William's educational prospects. I went for an after work drink with Ned and voiced to him my concerns.

'He's a queer cove and no mistaking is that one,' he said.

'Oh, I didn't know he was gay,' I said.

Ned laughed. 'Are the strange vagaries of the English language? No what I mean is, there is something really odd about him. He's fiercely religious you know,' he said. I didn't know. He told me he was, 'head deacon, or some such nonsense at his local church. They're all rabid evangelicals. They seem to think the sun shines out of John Calvin's rear end, or so I've been led to believe. A funny lot, I can tell you. They'd gone and signed a petition about the teaching of Darwinism in our school and that children from their church should be able to opt out,' he said. 'Of course, Mr Jackstone,' he said, 'distanced himself from it all. He can be quite a willy old bird when he wants to be.'

He thought if I was to, 'blow the gaff as it were,' it might be a good idea to help out at his Wednesday lunchtime get together. 'Though I'd tread very carefully if I was you old man. He's got quite a lot of power. The board of governors regard him as their golden boy. Oh and the head also attends the same church,' he said.

I told Mr Jackstone that I'd managed to juggle things round, and could help him out on Wednesdays, at least for the time being. He didn't suspect anything odd in my sudden change of heart.

Milly and William were surprised to see me. I told them that Mr Jackstone was busy and he'd asked me if I would cover for him. He had put some old fashioned grammar exercises up on the blackboard. We didn't teach formal grammar. We got pupils to write it in essays and other written work. It was turgid stuff. When they weren't doing this, he had them doing endless English comprehension exercises. I loved English language, but all of this lot at any age, would have turned anyone off and sent them to sleep. I believed it to be punitive and in no way educational. I tried to think to myself, if he was emotionally abusing them, and just out on a campaign of systematic victimization and bullying, what could be his reasons for doing so? I could not come up with any immediate motives. Ned however could.

'When William was playing five-a-side he was not only

bloody good, he had a kind of natural grace about him. You could say, it was rather balletic, if you follow my meaning,' he said, over one of our many after work pints.

Some of the boys especially, stood out, in that they were rather sensitive, shy and in touch with their feminine side. Such boys tended to get picked on and called 'queer,' whether they were or not. Regardless of my being gay myself, I also knew that for some boys, this was all just a natural phase of their motor kinetic development. I knew that Milly wasn't gay. She had too many crushes on the current male pop idols' of the day. However, there was something very masculine and none feminine about her. Most of her friends happened to be boys. She didn't do all that girly stuff. And if one of her friends was being bullied, she would take on the bully and fell them with a single knock-out blow.

Milly and William did not stand out in such a way, as they were unable to fully integrate with their peers. But for all that, there was something that little bit different about them. And to some eyes, and especially seen through the eyes of bigotry and religious prejudice, they could be perceived as gay.

Mr Jackstone I reasoned, might be completely unaware of his prejudice, indeed he would tell himself that what he was doing was purely educational and all for their own good. But that was often how prejudice worked, largely unowned and unconscious. All I knew was, it had to be stopped, and it was probably only me that could stop it. I wanted to hide and hide and never come out from my shelter. And yet I knew I had no option except to act. The abuse had to cease.

8

Spring seemed to step suddenly out of winter's iron-fisted grasp that year. All the birds were singing from every tree and the cherry blossom was falling like scented snow. The children were formed into a crocodile and Mrs Ainsley, the teacher, led them out of the school gate. They were off to play on Horseman's common, beside Munford valley wood. I watched them as they were leaving, from the upstairs classroom window, a place that had become my prison. I would not be joining them. It was the late April of 1969 and I was eight. My sin was to have not got through all of my sums. Mr Gregsdale as usual, had chalked up a great pile of sums on the blackboard. At the top left hand corner of the board were the easier additions and then as you moved down the board, came the subtractions, the multiplications and the dreaded long division. I hated sums and everything about Mathematics more than anything.

'Now then, Robbie,' he said,' if you finish all of your sums and all of them are correct, then and only then, can you go out and play with the rest.'

He would then add just a bit more torture into the mix. 'My, what a wonderful spring day it is out there. If I was a boy, I'd love to be out there making dens and getting up to all kinds of mischief in those glorious woods,' he would say, standing up next to me. I would be much too slow to have gotten through all of those most hideous figures he had put up on the board.

The rest had finished and were greedily waiting for the next batch. And then he was chalking up a whole pile more.

'What, Dumbo, not even finished the first lot yet?' he would say. 'Well it looks like you will be here until kingdom come. You'll never get through your sums. This will be you, for the rest of your life, endlessly trying to do your sums and failing miserably. Oh look,' he would say, 'the beast, the dullard little toad is crying. He probably wants his mummy.' And then all the other kids would howl with laughter at the stupid kid at the front of the class.

This regime of tyranny had gone on since the February of that year. To me it felt like my entire life. I never thought it would end. I would be an old man on my death bed and I'd still be trying to finish my sums. And then I would die, my life would be over and God would send me to hell for not completing my sums. All was hopeless. I believed myself to be the most stupid child in the entire world. Somehow when God made me, he must have forgotten to give me a brain. I could hardly read either, and since I'd started my new school it seemed to be getting worse.

The other kids were allowed to use either a pencil or a ballpoint pen. Mr Gregsdale said that my handwriting was so bad, that I needed to use a fountain pen all the time to try and correct this. How I hated those pens. They must have come from the dark ages. They were made of wood, with a thick nib on the end. I was given an inkwell filled up with ink, to dip my pen in and 'woe-betide me,' if I got blotches all over my copy. If I did, this warranted a whollop with the slipper. He would make me leave my desk and walk up to the front of the class. I'd be told to bend over and then he would beat me once, sometimes twice, and as hard as he could with the slipper on my backside. The stinging pain and the public humiliation in front of all the other kids always reduced me to tears. And then he would always say, 'now then, that ought to liven up your ideas.'

I believed that if God wanted to create the worst kind of hell for all the sinners, he need not look any further than Musgrave House, the private primary school I was attending. And it seemed to me that the devil himself could not be more scary or intimidating than Mr Gregsdale, the self-styled headmaster of the school. The thing was, he was kind and seemed to have endless patience with all the other kids. I never heard him raise his voice so much as once with them. He reserved all his anger and his bile especially for me. I was his chosen child, the emotional punch-bag to support his warped ego. I'd been struggling at my old school and had fallen behind the rest. My parents were worried about my education. A customer of my dads' sent his boy to Musgrave House.

'It's a great school. The classes are really small, so your lad will get all the individual attention that he needs.' But then the customer happened to be a local GP on a good salary.

Although we were comfortably enough off, as they say, Dad wasn't exactly loaded. It was quite a financial sacrifice to send me to a private school. I didn't want to disappoint and said I would try my hardest. When the first report came through, posted by first class mail, it sat there on the breakfast table. It was a Saturday morning. It looked like a coiled snake ready to pounce! I was shocked and baffled, for it was glowing. When it came to Maths, I had been given a B minus and the comment, *still having a little difficulty here but, Robbie is making a real*

111

effort and progressing well. The report was all lies and I knew it was, but Mum and Dad were so very pleased with me, I felt I couldn't tell them the truth.

All the kids came from wealthy families. There were sons and daughters of solicitors, doctors, medical consultants, and the local justice of the peace, someone on the board of a bank, the daughter of a lord and lady from a large estate on the outskirts of town, and the son of the bishop of Munford. Beside them, my dad was in trade. And that was the difference. The kids themselves, when the adults weren't around, did not mind. They were made to see the difference and those children from trade were inferior in every kind of way.

It was many years later, that I was to find out that the head's father had been a master butcher, from Chelmsford. Although he was a master butcher, and had apparently won awards for his spicy sausages, at the end of the day, he was still in trade. Mr Gregsdale had risen through the ranks and no one must ever know his shady beginnings.

I was always led like a prisoner, down to the dining hall for my lunch and then back upstairs again, to my cell. I was singled out from the other kids, my purported crime, a dunce with his sums. My real and only crime happened to be the social class to which I belonged. And then, I remember one Friday at the beginning of June, with the sun shining in such an extraordinary way through the trees, outside our classroom window, it caused a poker-dot and dappled patterning all along the brickwork of the house opposite. The other children had left and I had settled myself down with the hideous figures. Mr Gregsdale came back into the classroom.

'Go on, it's much too nice a day to be stuck indoors. If you're quick,' he said, 'you can run and catch them up.'

I was more grateful than I could say, and I ran headlong from my prison, across the grim landing, down the wide staircase, across the large imposing hall and out of the front door. The children were nowhere to be seen. I could feel a great lump rising in my throat. I ran out of the school gates and down the road, lined with oak trees, their leaves gently swaying in the faint summer breeze. When I got to the end of the road, I could just make out the tail-end of the crocodile formation. And then I ran for all my worth to catch them up.

'Hello, Robbie,' said Julian, a fair haired boy I was friendly with, 'won't you get into trouble or something?' he said. I told him that for some unknown reason; today I had been let out of my prison to play. It seemed to me like the most wonderful lunch hour of my life. We made dens, we climbed trees, and we forged allegiances and laughed, shouted and screamed out our inherent irrepressible delight. It was perhaps the cruellest of his tactics, for it was to be the last time I was ever allowed out. I had tasted heaven, which made my personal hell seem all the more desperate.

Every school holiday I was given a pile of sums to do, and it seemed however hard I worked at them, every morning of every holiday, I never could get them done. I felt I should be working on them every day, but Mum would only allow me to do them in the morning. So I spent the rest of the day feeling guilty and fearful of the consequences, for not having finished all the work I'd been set. And so those sums blighted every school holiday for best part of three years.

The fees seemed to go up every year, so much so that by the time I was nine, Dad could no longer afford to send me there.

He was so very sorry that I was being dragged away from all my friends from such a wonderful place. I tried my best to pretend I was truly heart-broken, but I couldn't wait until I left.

On the very last day, Mr Gregsdale wished me well in my new school and offered me his hand. I refused to shake it.

'You always were an ungrateful, sullen wretch,' he said as I left.

Making sure I was well out of earshot, I mumbled under my breath, the worst expletive I could think of.

At my new school, the teachers suddenly found themselves with quite a task on their hands. I had almost been rendered stupid. And yet Mum believed that I had not been given anything to stir my soul.

'Learning to read is more of a spiritual matter, as opposed to an academic matter,' she had told them.

She got me a copy of *Tom Sawyer* from the local library and every night she would read a page and I would read a page. By the end of that summer, I had fallen in love with books and the English language. A flame had been lit in my heart, and it would never go out. I was never dull or stupid, only made so by a certain teacher's systematic emotional abuse.

It took me until my early forties, before I was ever able to talk about that period of my life. And then it was in therapy with a most gifted and empathic counsellor. I was finally able to cry out and rage through the pain of it. Abuse has a way of locking up its secrets through a sense of borrowed guilt, humiliation and shame. I knew I owed it to the little, frightened soul that had been me, to stand up for Milly Armstrong and William Henderson. I had to be their advocate. And so I asked for a meeting with Mr Jackstone.

I began by telling him how difficult I found it, and then

told him that I believed he was stepping outside his prescribed boundaries as a teacher, and that what he was doing with Milly and William, was abusive. I told him it had to stop.

'You dare to stand there and tell me I'm being abusive and to question my teaching strategies?

'I've been in this profession since 1954, thirty bloody years, and you who have been here for only a few brief months, think you have the right to pass judgement on me?' he said.

'I can tell you now that I have absolutely no intention of changing my methods,' he said. I told him that in that case I was forced to take it further.

'So you are going to put in a complaint about me?' he said.

'You leave me no option,' I said. He then put his face almost up to my own face.

'I'll break you for this! I'd make very sure you have full possession of all the facts, because not only will it be your position here that is on the line, but your whole damn career.'

He had been standing in for the remedial set of fourteen-year-olds for English language, until a replacement could be found. I suddenly found myself teaching them and removed from my sixth form class. I told him he couldn't do this. He informed me that as my head of department he could do precisely what ever he wanted.

The head told me that the whole idea was utterly preposterous.

'He is one of the best god-damn teachers in the whole school,' he said. He was red-faced and doing his best not to lose his temper with me.

'Perhaps you've been under a lot of strain recently. I know all about this queer business. I can't say I approve, but what you choose to do in your own time is up to you, as long as you don't bring the school into disrepute,' he said.

'It has nothing to do with that,' I said.

He wanted to stand-me-down, on full-pay, as opposed to suspending me, to reflect on my position. I went to the union and was told he couldn't do it. I had not done anything wrong and I was told that if I thought a student's welfare was being compromised, I had every right to report it. And so by the end of that week, I found I had made two enemies, instead of one. I had not been given any satisfaction from my head, and so it went to a formal complaint level with both the board of governors and Munford education authority. Although it was a Wednesday evening after school, I decided to phone Tyrone.

'I know it's mid-week but I need you,' I said. 'Give me half an hour and I'll be round. Get the amplifier warmed up and some nice Brahms spinning on the turntable and I'll supply the wine and nibbles,' he said. I thanked him, finding myself kissing the phone receiver as he hung up.

This had all been festering away for the last two weeks. He was a bit annoyed that I'd kept it all from him, but now that he knew everything, including the story of my own abuse from a teacher, he quickly forgave me. And so we played endless Brahms records. We found ourselves particularly connecting with some of the older mono fifties recordings. We smoked lots of cigarettes, drank loads of wine, hugged and cried together.

'This is what married life is all about, the bad times as well as the good,' he said.

'Do you know, one of these bloody days I'm going to lead you down that aisle,' I said. We both enjoyed the relief of brief laughter. As for the rest, there was precious little to laugh about.

The following evening there was a loud knock at the door.

116

It was Clarissa. She had a bottle of single malt in her hand.

'Two glasses on the kitchen table now, and I want to hear everything that's happened,' she said.

We both sat at the kitchen table facing each other, sipping our whisky and smoking our cigarettes. Like Tyrone, I told her everything, holding nothing back.

'Why didn't you come to me before?' she said.

'I didn't want you being compromised. That's why I didn't involve you.'

'I can take care of myself,' she said, 'I'm a big girl now. Anyway, because we are friends, as far as the powers that be are concerned, I'll be staying strictly neutral. That does not stop me from being able to support you through this bloody awful mess, and giving you lots of unsolicited advice,' she said, pouring me some more whisky. 'To begin with, Norman Jackstone,' she said, 'has got the governors completely in his pocket, so don't expect any help from that quarter. He is the school's main fund raiser. He's organised sponsored walks, tyre-drives, jumble sales and God knows what else, all to raise extra and much needed funds for the school. He has also been there even longer than me or the head. He's the school's longest serving member of staff. He's been there since the school opened in 1965.'

'I'm toast,' I said. 'Whatever was I thinking about?'

'You were thinking about the kids, kids you believe whose lives are being blighted and whose educational prospects are being stunted through a teacher who is abusing his position and his power. And hell, yes it is scary. You are taking on the big boys, and they will choose to wield every bit of artillery they happen to have in their armoury. And I do mean every bit of it,' she said, helping herself to another cigarette from the

117

open packet on the table.

'What do I do?' I said.

'Firstly, and I know this is difficult, you have to remember that you are not the one who is being disciplined. They will want to phase you out, so that you get to thinking that it is you who is the wrong end of a disciplinary hearing and not, Norman,' she said. I gulped down some of the whisky and found myself hacking on my cigarette. I tasted bitter ashes in my throat. Not for the first time, I wondered why I smoked the wretched things.

'I think, but I'm not at all sure, that he'll play the victim card. He'll be telling them how supportive he has been towards you, and even given you a sixth form class. He will say how he's bent over backwards, to help you progress successfully through your probation year. He will also imply that you have repaid him with nothing but base ingratitude. The education authority will want to arrange separate meetings with you both. They'll want to hear your side of the story. Keep it detailed but brief and get your story straight in your head.

'They will also want a written statement. That is what they will be referring to in the meeting. When you've written it, let me go over it with a fine tooth-comb,' she said.

'Do you believe me, or do you think I'm just making a fuss over nothing and should let the whole thing drop?' I said.

'If I thought that as a friend, believe me I would tell you so, because I'd want to spare you the pain of what lies ahead. No, I believe you completely and not just because you are a friend. What I'm about to tell you must go no further than you and, Tyrone,' she said. 'Actually, there have been rumours about, Norman,' she said, 'for a good many years. Other teachers, not in the English department, have said that they've heard him screaming at the kids and sometimes kids have come into their class looking distressed and even red-eyed with crying. When those teachers checked the school timetable, they quickly realised that there previous lesson was with, Norman,' she said.

'So why has it been allowed to go on for so long?' I said.

'Well one reason is that our be-knighted head, just happens to be best mates with Norman,' she said, 'and I'm very much afraid they are two of a kind. Norman was very fond of wielding the cane at every opportunity, before the school policy changed. Personally, I've always thought that any teacher, who must resort to corporal punishment, has already lost the argument. They are also both very religious. Norman,' she said, 'is a deacon and lay-reader for his church. They are rabid Bible-bashers of the worst stripe. Basically, they follow a Calvinist creed. They happen to believe they have been gifted with God's truth and that everyone else is sadly misguided and destined for eternal damnation. Not a particularly nice bunch of folk. They are also staunchly homophobic and they hate all Roman Catholics. And when they are roused up, to what they see as righteous indignation in the name of the Lord, there is no telling what they are capable of. Look at any movement of religious nutters, and there you have it,' she said.

9

That Saturday Ned called round. Tyrone was still in bed upstairs.

'I've got a lovely surprise for you both,' he said, sitting himself down at the kitchen table for some coffee. His uncle had invited us to his eightieth birthday celebrations. 'Hilary and I go down to Cheltenham every year. We wouldn't miss it for worlds. The boys go to stay with their grandparents in Surrey. There will be loads of best nosh and all the booze you could possibly drink. The place will be full of bohemians and artists of every stripe. He also likes to surround himself with young people, many of whom will just happen to be gay. I tell you, you'll both have a whale of a time.'

Part of me did not want to go. After all I still had a lengthy statement to write, and I had put aside the school half-term holiday so I could fully focus on it. Ned however, would not take no for an answer.

'I'll come over in the car with, Hilary,' he said, 'and drive you both down there, Saturday morning, eight o'clock prompt!' he said.

'OK, you win,' I said.

'That's the spirit, old man,' he said, breaking into a smile.

Henry Danbury, Ned's uncle, was not a duke, earl or grand lord of any kind. His father had invested a certain amount of money in railway stock, indeed all of his life savings. Just after the First World War, the dividends had been good, and he had made a considerable fortune. Lots of the old aristocratic holdings were going to seed. He had purchased Wenley Park, on the leafy outskirts of Cheltenham, at a knock-down price towards the end of the 1920s. Eventually his eldest son, Henry, had succeeded to the large estate. He had written to his nephew, in his grand copperplate hand, on finest water-marked paper with his ancient fountain pen in green ink, a couple of weeks before. Ned showed me the letter.

I've been somewhat daring. I've sent all the main servants away on a week's holiday. They deserve it, having to put up with this cranky old bugger three hundred and sixty five days a year. I've brought in some young folk from the local youth training scheme. They're all training to be caterers and waiters. It might all blow up in my face and go disastrously wrong, but Hay —hoe, you've got to give young folk a chance, and I'm hardly likely to growl at them if they happen to pass the bloody port the wrong way.

When we got there, driving through a mile long avenue of trees, resplendent in all of their rich autumn glory, other guests had already started arriving. There was a considerable amount of four-by-four vehicles, a couple of Rolls and an ancient Bentley or two in the drive, or should I say forecourt. Henry was standing at the door.

'Welcome, welcome all to my humble abode,' he was saying to all of the guests, his arms flung wide-open in his best theatrical fashion.

'Uncle,' said Ned, giving the old man an affectionate hug.

'Hilary my dear, you are looking as lovely as last time I saw you,' said Henry, smiling mischievously at her.

'Ah, Robbie,' he said, 'how nice to meet you again.'

'And who is this most marvellous young man at your side?' he said, shaking hands with Tyrone, who was blushing up to the roots of his gorgeous red curls and wanting to giggle with nerves.

'And I hope you are taking good care of my little car?' he said.

There were no actual sit-down meals, just a constant buffet at various tables and booths stretched out both in the grand house itself and located in various marques and pavilions, scattered throughout the grounds, where the food, wine, champagne, real ale, served natural gravity from great oaken casks, and the very best of everything flowed. At first we both stayed quite close to Ned and Hilary. But as we became more settled in, we found ourselves talking and mingling with the other guests, people of all ages and quite a few, deliciously, delightful old eccentrics.

'I've known that old rogue for over a ruddy lifetime,' said a retired brigadier, 'he buggered me in barracks during the heady spring of 1932. God, he was fit in those days.' Tyrone did not quite know where to put himself with embarrassment.

'So what you're trying to tell me,' I said, 'was that he was a great screw?'

'Indeed he was the best, the very best screw, in the whole ruddy Indian civil service,' he said. And then a few moments later, he brought an elegantly dressed middle-aged woman across to us.

'Let me introduce you to, Clorinda,' he said, 'my wife.' With this, Tyrone was all but choking on his champagne and canapés. There were lots of young people, and what could only be what appeared to be the entire young and queer peerage of old England. There were too many beautiful young creatures to name and Henry was good enough to introduce us to a few of them.

'When the disco starts in the far tent this evening, they'll be smoking dope, snorting coke and out there screwing like rabbits,' said Henry, 'and good luck to them. It's what being young is all about,' he said and then wandered off to talk to some of the other guests.

Later that evening, Tyrone and I found our way to the disco tent. In fact there were two, one for the straight young people, nearer the house and one for what Tyrone chose to call, 'the queer young peers.' The large marquee was heaving with lots of young lads, all of them I happened to notice were strangely bare-foot and many of them were dancing hot and wild with their tops off. The music was a mixture of eighties gay disco, but also some German import music, that was full of bass and rather hypnotic. I really liked it. They'd erected a wooden dance floor and the lighting system was one of the most impressive I'd seen, outside of London.

'I bet it took them days to set up all of this lot,' said Tyrone.

'Weeks I expect,' I said.

Despite all of the food and drink we had already imbibed that day, we were both very much in the mood for dancing. Tyrone was a real natural on the dance floor. Sometimes, I'd stop dancing for a few moments, just so I could watch all of that untutored grace and the fire of his unconscious move-ment, flickering and shimmering, between the lights, inside the beat and caught up somehow in the inner dance. A strange, wanton thing always spinning in an ecstatic perpetual motion, he surely was. He'd open his eyes, momentarily coming out of the crazed trance and notice that I'd been watching him.

He'd smile mischievously at me, knowing I was so turned on, so breathlessly in love with him. And then we would embrace and kiss long and hard, before moving back into the kissed-rhythm, the caressed lit glory of the dance, the wonder of the primeval, pagan stirring of young bodies in flight. It was our evensong and our communion, and the hallowed light from an autumn moon, large, liquid and almost terrible, shone through the gap in the canvass, the sentinel guardian, watching and smiling down on all our revels.

There was a recess down a dozen or so steps. Here some of the revellers sat crossed-legged on an assortment of bean-bags and scatter-cushions. They were passing spliffs around and seemed friendly enough.

'You guys could really do anything you wanted,' said Tyrone to one young lad with blond wavy hair.

'Yeh, I guess you're right. We could strip off, shag like crazy in front of everyone else, and no one would mind. We could even all decide to have an orgy in here. It's because we can that we don't, we don't need to,' he said. This got us both thinking. As we got talking, they found out what we did for a living and I realised for most of them, if they chose, they could do nothing. Daddy would still pay them their allowance. There was always money and they didn't have to work for it. However, most of them were either studying or working.

'God, I think I'd die of boredom if I didn't have something worth getting up for in the sodding morning,' said one young peer. And then one boy said that Henry had been best mates with his grandfather. During the fifties, his grandfather had ended up the wrong side of the law for importuning. He'd got six months in Pentonville. After that, he had worked with Henry, along with The Wolfenden Report and they had both helped to draft the 1967 act which partially legalised homosexuality.

The following evening there was a jazz quintet, a string quartet and down in the coppice beside the grove, all festooned with lanterns, a rather intimate and delightful performance of *A Midsummer Night's Dream*. Tyrone and I found ourselves enchanted and caught up within the moment. We both seemed to find lots of free time for wonderful, gorgeous and spectacular love-making.

'You beautiful, beautiful boy,' I kept saying to him.

'God, I sometimes think I'm living right inside a dream being with you,' said Tyrone, as we lay cuddled together afterwards, sharing a cigarette. He got up to get dressed, for we had decided to go back down and join in with the rest of what was going on. And then I saw the awesome, heart-stopping shape of his naked body, and I rushed across and pulled him back onto the bed for some even more hot and fevered afternoon loving. I was kissing his feet, and that wonderful arch of his soles. He always started to giggle. 'God, Robbie,' he said, 'your tongue really tickles.'

'I'll give you some tickling,' I said, 'if that's what you want.'

'No!' he screamed. But it was too late, for I had dived on top of him and I was tickling him and enjoying his wild screams and laughter.

And then it was back to school. The statements had been written and gathered in and both Norman and I were all but cross-examined by the local education authority. I was summoned to the head's office during lunchtime the following week.

'Well, no doubt you'll be pleased to know, Mr Jackstone,' he

125

said, ' has been found guilty of the so called complaints made against him by someone who has only been in the profession for less than five minutes. He has lost his headship of department, been transferred to another school in the area, has found himself on probation for six months and been given a final written warning. I hope you are pleased with yourself. May I ask what you have planned for an encore?' he said.

'I'm not to blame for any of this. I regret what has happened, but really, Mr Jackstone,' I said, 'brought all this on himself. I had to put the welfare of the pupils first.'

'Get out of my office!' he screamed at me.

And I thought that if a mere week before it had felt like living inside a dream, it now felt more like being inside a nightmare. And yet another part of me was relieved. It was all over, I told myself. Indeed Tyrone and I went off to a favourite restaurant on the outskirts of town to celebrate, a victory for justice.

The deputy of the English department, Fiona Rowling, was speedily promoted to head of the department. I was given back my first year sixth form class, though I had actually enjoyed working with the remedial kids too. Sipping our second glass of wine, round at Clarissa's place with Tyrone, she said, 'well this has been a sad chapter that mercifully we can put behind us.'

She could not have been more wrong. Mr Jackstone, still felt that he had only been acting in the interests of the pupils and he decided to make a formal complaint to the teacher's governing body, against what he saw as the grave in- justice done towards him. The true nightmare had just begun.

10

The governing body moved swiftly. The hearing was to be held the beginning of the third week in December, just after the school broke up for the Christmas holidays. They also sent letters to all the staff, as well as me, asking that if they had any useful information pertaining to this matter, that they should make a statement and that their confidentiality and full anonymity would be assured.

It was a Wednesday evening. I was getting ready, in a nice new shirt I'd bought, that I thought looked quite the part. I was meeting Tyrone at The Manhattan Bar. Before I was about to leave the house, the phone rang. The caller wanted to know if he was speaking to Robbie. I said that he was.

'You could call this a friendly call really. I'm phoning to tell you that you need to withdraw your statement. I'm really only thinking about your own well-being that is your continued well-being. Think about it,' he said and then hung up, from what sounded to be a public call box.

I told Tyrone what had happened.

'That's pure intimidation of a witness that is, you ought to report it to the police,' he said.

'Yes, but it's not a criminal investigation. I somehow don't think the police would be interested,' I said, smiling at him.

It was later in the evening, after we had drank quite a lot and were ready for home, when a complete stranger made his way to our table. He was thin, tall, grey haired and somehow seemed somewhat menacing. He didn't ask if he could join us, but sat down opposite us anyway, a heterosexual with a sense of assumed entitlement over anyone from the gay community. My hackles were immediately raised.

'I believe you are the little bastard who's trying to get Norman Jackstone the sack?' the stranger demanded.

'I'm not prepared to discuss my private business with a complete stranger,' I said.

'Listen you little faggot, I call the shots, and I'll leave when I'm good and ready.'

Just then, Arthur Devlin made his way across to us.

'Having trouble, lads?' he said.

'Yes, this man who we don't know from Adam, is being threatening and I'd like him to leave us alone,' said Tyrone.

'You heard what the gentleman said,' said Arthur, 'that means it's time to leave.'

The other man tried to out-face Arthur, but Arthur had the complete measure of the man.

'We could always finish off this conversation outside if you would prefer?' said Arthur. With this, the other man backed down and got up from the table and left. I thanked Arthur for stepping in and asked if he would like to join us for a drink. He stayed for a swift pint and then left. Tyrone looked be-mused, wanting to know who he was.

'That man, Tyrone,' I said, 'just happens to be my dad's ex-lover from the 1950s.'

'My God,' was Tyrone's shocked reply, which made me laugh for the first time that evening. 'And hell, he's fit for fifty!' he said.

'Yeh, my dad, bless him, certainly had good taste,' I said.

Tyrone had started to learn to drive a couple of years before he met me. He decided to take it up again. 'God, I'm as rusty as hell,' he said after his first lesson.

I got the insurance changed to two users for my car, and at weekends gave him a few pointers. Actually, he wasn't a bad driver at all, most of it was nerves. And then every time he took a lesson, he was that little bit better and every week he was gaining in confidence. And by the end of September, he took his test and passed first time.

His mum and I had scrabbled enough money together between us, to buy him his first car and to pay for his first year's insurance. It was to be our joint twenty-first birthday present to him. It was a five year old car, in good condition, with a rather distinctive light metallic blue paint job. On the day of his birthday, I came round to his house to pick him up. We were going to yet another delightful restaurant we had discovered. I'd parked his new car just round the corner to the house. He had absolutely no idea that Maggie and I had bought him a car.

'I'll probably be retired before I can afford a car of my own,' he kept telling us both.

'Yes probably,' we would both say to him, holding back our smiles.

And Maggie went even further by telling him, 'never mind, I dare say they'll do good pensioner discounts on your insurance.'

'Oh damn,' I said to his mum, 'I've forgotten my cigarettes. I'll have to just nip to the off-license down the street to buy a packet. I won't be a mow.' Maggie could not hold back her smiles.

'Are you two up to something?' he said.

'Whatever gave you that idea? Now sit down and have a slice

of your birthday cake,' she said.

I went and got the car. It drove like a dream. I parked it up outside the house and pipped the horn loudly! Tyrone and Maggie rushed out to see what all the commotion was. I jumped out of the car, said to him 'catch,' throwing him the keys, and then his mum and I were singing a very discordant rendition of 'Happy Birthday' at the tops of our voices. As expected, he was in floods of joyful tears.

'And all that guff you kept saying to me about getting good insurance rates when I was a pensioner.' He said. And then he was laughing and saying, 'I can't believe it, my own car, my very own car,' and then he was in floods of tears all over again.

The Italian pizzeria had been established as an Italian restaurant since the mid-sixties. It was located at the end of the town centre, overlooking the medieval priory ruins. It was rather hidden away, and you had to go down some narrow steps to what was a basement café. Its eight tables were all located in little intimate alcoves. The soft lighting was perfect. They played Neapolitan love songs as their piped music. And the food, the service and the wine, were all spectacularly good.

'The kids will be saying I reek of garlic tomorrow,' I said to him tucking into a rather succulent fillet steak.

'Ah well,' he said, throwing me one of his delightful mock philosophical looks, 'it will keep the vampires away.'

I told him not to be quite so sure about that because at that moment sitting there, looking so entirely gorgeous, I could quite happily gobble him all up on the spot. And then he giggled that delightful giggle that set my heart a dancing!

'God, I love this red wine or whatever they call it,' he said, speaking with his mouth full.

'And I love you getting nicely pissed on it,' I said.

Tyrone never really got totally pissed. He knew when he'd had enough. He would get merry and start talking, a lot of delightful nonsense. It's strange the things we love about people; especially those we happen to adore. That evening, under the subtle candlelight, I was aching and yearning for him, even although he was right there in front of me and smiling across the table at me with the eyes and the smiles of a lover. During the coffees and the afters, I reached into my jacket pocket and brought out a small blue box.

'And here's a little something else,' I said pushing it across the table towards him. It was a silver signet ring, moulded by a craftsman silversmith, a man who came out of retirement once a year to make a few dozen silver rings. He had been apprenticed to one of the old masters of the arts and crafts school. It was the kind of silver artefact that made gold seem like cheap tuppenny tat.

'It's beautiful,' he said becoming tearful once again.

We went on to The Manhattan Bar, but only stayed for a couple of drinks. We both wanted to get back to my place and up to the bedroom. Indeed, we were hardly through the front door, than we were ripping the clothes off each other's back and filling each other's mouths with our desperate and hungry kisses. I carried him upstairs, naked in my arms, and gently laid him on the bed. Our love that night was rough. We were tussling and fighting. Sometimes he was on top, and then I would be. 'God,' he said, 'sometimes I could kiss your ruddy face right off.' At last he let me into the deep warm and inviting space, and to possess all of him. He was honey-dipped in desire. The smell of him was coming up to me, full and strong, the pungent scent of all his young love. It was the best incense in the world. And next day at school, all my lessons seemed to be infused with an inner light. Everything I taught seemed to be understood. I was inspired.

'You seem particularly happy,' said one rather cheeky fourteen-year-old girl.

'I'm always happy,' I said.

'Why, Sir?' she said.

'I'm happy teaching you lot,' I said.

The whole class for some reason found this hilarious, even although I think they happened to believe me.

I decided to cook us both something special, that Saturday evening, and to have a cosy night in, listening to records. Tyrone had found a real find in a charity shop. It was some Brahms from the fifties. They were made up of interpretations; I don't believe have ever been bettered. They'd needed cleaning and new inner-sleeves, but other than that were practically in mint condition.

'God, this wine is good,' he said, sitting across the kitchen table from me.

'Yeh, I know, it's the same stuff we were drinking the other night at the restaurant. Drink it sparingly, it were just short of ten quid a bottle,' I said.

We decided to play all six records, his recent purchase. Tyrone fussed about with the candles, for the light had to be just so. When I listened to wonderful mono recordings, I would always wonder why they ever bothered to invent stereo. Tyrone was of the same opinion. We were happy to worship at the shrine of mono. We lay cuddled up in each other's arms on my old dishevelled settee, sipping wine, smoking and giving each other an occasional affectionate peck. We were half way through one of the heavenly slow movements, when we both were startled by the loud screeching of breaks and then a brick was thrown through the window.

The force of it pulled away one of the curtains and partially dislodged a curtain rail off the wall. There was shattered glass everywhere. We both screamed instinctively. I picked up the brick which had finally landed in the centre of the room, narrowly missing the turntable. There was a note attached to the brick. It said to back off. Tyrone was curled up on the settee, in fear.

'Come on love, it's all right, it's all right,' I kept saying to him.

I was trying to calm him down and to make him feel safe, whilst feeling scared out of my wits. I phoned the police and an officer came round about half an hour later to take our details and get a written statement from us. We were able to get a glazier to come round, out of hours. He cleaned up all the glass and boarded up the window for the night.

'I'll be round first thing to measure up and put you in some new glass,' he said. He was a middle-aged man, rather fatherly.

'It's all in hand. I'll leave you the invoice so you just pay me when you've got a mind,' he said. 'And both of you try and get a good night's sleep if you can.'

We'd both had a troubled sleep, waking up with small noises. At last, we fell off into a much deeper sleep, a little before sunrise. When we eventually woke, it was past nine in the morning. We were woken by a loud knock at the front door. I blearily took a peek out of the bedroom curtains. I saw the glazier's van parked in the road beside the house. We both popped into our dressing gowns.

'I'll get the door,' I said.

'I'll make us all some coffee,' said Tyrone.

I made my way downstairs and went to the front door.

'Hello there,' said the glazier. He was looking distinctly troubled.

'What is it?' I said.

'I'd brace myself for quite a shock if I was you,' he said.

I stepped outside. What met my gaze froze my heart.

'Oh my God!' I said. And then Tyrone had run through from the kitchen. He joined me out on the street and was practically hysterical. Someone had splattered red paint all over the front door and across the brick-work, in great capital letters six feet high, the word faggots. The glazier came in, and he took immediate charge of things.

'The pair of you just sit down. I'll make the coffee,' he said. 'Actually, to hell with the coffee, what's needed is sweet tea. And you wouldn't happen to keep a bit of brandy?' he said. A few minutes later, he brought us through some steaming mugs of tea, and he had put a generous drop of brandy in them both. He had also turned on the gas fire.

'Come on the pair of you, get yourself nearer the fire,' he said.

After he had got us settled, though we were just holding onto each other still in shock, he phoned the police. It was at this stage I told a senior officer that I was being nobbled as the chief witness in a disciplinary hearing.

'We'll put a tap on the phone, even although most of the threatening phone calls are usually done from a public phone box. They often do them out of town, so that there's even less chance of tracing them. Let's just hope they decide to get a bit cocky. That's when they're most likely to get careless,' said the officer.

By lunchtime, the new window was all fitted, and I'd nipped up to a cash point to pay him and to also give him a little bit extra for all his troubles. He was almost reluctant to take any payment at all; indeed I had to shove the money into his hand. It turned out; he had known my father and uncle, for many years.

'There's been many a brick thrown by a drunken yob through their shop,' he said. 'I'm proud to help anyone connected with, your dad, and your uncle,' he said as he left. We had restored the curtain rail and the curtains were all back in place. By early afternoon, about to go round to Maggie's for Sunday lunch, there was now no evidence of the previous evening's horrific incident. The outside of the house however, was quite a different matter.

11

Despite all of the terrible things that were happening to us, not all was desperate. Tyrone found himself with a rather nice pay rise. It was completely unexpected and therefore all the sweeter. And then Fiona, my new head of department gave me my final report. I had passed my probation period with flying colours and my post was made permanent. And so it was back to that Italian restaurant for more celebrations and lashings of red wine and special afters. Clara, the moggie, was due her M.O.T. I decided to give Billy my business. He was now chief mechanic at a garage just off the town centre. Tyrone, more out of nosey curiosity than any other reason, wanted to drive down to the garage with me.

'I want to get a good look at this old flame of yours,' he said.

'Well don't be getting all jealous on me, cos he's a complete dish,' I said.

I was feeling just a little bit nervous. This was the first time we had met since our tearful parting. I wondered would I still have all those same feelings for him. He came out to greet us. I'd phoned him before hand, so as not to shock him. He and Tyrone shook hands warmly.

'Well,' said Billy, 'I'm glad we've got that out of the way.' And then the three of us laughed.

It was strange, but although he was still as gorgeous as ever, I did not feel the urge to climb into bed with him. The passion

I had felt for him was gone. He was now just a fond memory. I also knew he had a little boy, taking up most of his time these days.

'She'll get my full personal attention,' said Billy patting the bonnet of the car.

Dad came round with the dog, to look at all the damage. He brought Gary round, somewhat in-toe, giving him an impromptu lecture about the evils of bigotry and homophobia. Gary was sullen as usual, and said very little. I didn't expect much else from him.

It was a few days later that there was a loud knock on my front door. It was Gary. He ran into my arms, burst into tears and told me he was sorry. Later that evening, we also had some more company. It was Matthew and David.

'We've been a couple of right prats,' said Matthew.

'I don't know what got into the pair of us,' said David.

They both looked shame-faced.

'And hay, as our way of making amends, me Matthew and your kidder there,' he said, ' will clean up the front of your house and re-paint the front door.'

'Thanks lads,' I said.

I told them that after they had left that night, I'd been barred from the pub. 'You leave Selwyn to us,' said David.

I brought them up to date with all that had been happening at work and they listened sympathetically.

'Well it's times like this that you need your friends,' said Matthew. 'We are both here for you.'

I told Tyrone about the sea-change the following day, round at his mothers'. He was still not entirely convinced. Nevertheless, he joined me that Saturday evening, back at our local. I'd certainly missed all of that great tasting beer. Gran was now talking to me again, saying how silly she had been and she was all hugs and kisses. Strangely, where as I totally believed everyone else's change of heart, knowing it to be genuine, I thought Gran was simply choosing to save face in front of the rest of the family.

I received another phone call. It was the same voice. 'Still not learned your lesson yet,' he said, 'I can see more persuasive measures seem to be called for.' And then he put the phone down.

That Saturday afternoon Gary had popped round with the dog. Tyrone came round before tea-time. I asked if Gary wanted to stay for tea.

'No,' he said, 'I'll leave you too to have a smooch,' he said, smiling mischievously before he left.

The evening meal was cooking away nicely, when I suddenly remembered I'd forgotten to get any wine. 'Don't get all in a dither,' said Tyrone, 'I'll nip down to the off-license and get us a couple of bottles of something vaguely drinkable.'

I told him as it was Saturday; they didn't open for another hour. He decided to nip into town. He had taken the bus, leaving his own car at home. I threw him the keys to mine. I hadn't driven the car for the last couple of days. It was one of those Octobers, filled with misty mornings and all the trees were a riot of deep golds and reds, I just wanted to be a part of. I had caught the bus to work, getting off a couple of stops early, so I could enjoy the rest of the walk up to the school.

There was a small supermarket as you entered the town centre. It was about a five minute drive away. It was also open until late in the evening. Tyrone left the house at five minutes past five. I expected him back long before six. By a quarter to seven, I was starting to worry where the hell he had got to? I kept going to the front door and looking down the hill for any sign of him and then coming back into the house and pacing about the place. And at half past seven, a taxi pulled up outside the house. Maggie got out.

'Turn everything off, lock up and get in,' she said, pale-faced from the taxi.

'Why?' I said.

'There's been an accident, our Tyrone, has been injured,' she said.

When we got to Munford General Infirmary, Tyrone had been rushed into theatres. All we knew at this stage was that he had crashed the car into a lamp post at speed. He was having his condition stabilized, so it was some time before we were able to see him. He had broken his right arm, his right leg in three places, his collar bone and three ribs. He had also lost quite a lot of blood. We both stayed with him throughout the night. Maggie was on one side of the bed holding his hand and I was on the other. We were both finding it difficult to see through the tears. I remember the slow ticking away of the hours, and there he was with wires and tubes everywhere, looking so small and vulnerable as he lay there. He was concussed and unconscious for three days. The doctors were beginning to shake their heads, wondering whether or not he would pull through. I'd gone off to one of the rest rooms on the fourth morning, just to grab a brief respite. Maggie came rushing through.

'He's regained consciousness, he's going to be all right,' she said. I burst into tears and she hugged me unable to hold back her own tears. When we went back into his room, he was groggy but able to talk.

'It was the breaks, they just suddenly gave out, and then the car went careering down the hill, and I lost control. I could see this kid walking as slow as last week, with a pram about to cross the road. I'm there pipping my horn at her and shouting out of the window for her to get out of the way, but for some reason she didn't hear me. And so I swerved the car, out of her way. The next thing I see, right there almost in front of me is this great lamp-post. And then it all went black.'

By the next day the doctors were now convinced that he would make a complete recovery. They told us that he would probably be in hospital for the next six weeks, and he would need quite a bit of physio on his leg after it had mended.

'Fortunately, Mrs Kelly,' he said, 'he's young and young bones heal.'

The consultant always spoke directly to Maggie, and practically ignored me. Maggie, being Maggie, was having none of this, not now that she knew Tyrone was out of danger.

'This is, Robbie,' she said, 'my son's partner.' He looked at me as if I was a piece of dirt that had drifted in from the street and then walked away.

They quickly moved him to the orthopaedic ward, which was filled with boys and young men who had either fallen off their bikes or come to grief due to sporting injuries. Tyrone had one arm and one leg in traction. Also his face was still misshapen and covered with yellow and purple bruises. When I arrived back on the ward, he was sitting up in bed, propped up with lots of pillows and drinking a cup of tea. He seemed quite chirpy which gladdened my heart.

'I must look like a complete fright?' he said.

'Oh you do my dear,' I said, 'but I still love you.' And then we both laughed. I realised that it was the first time we had both been able to laugh since the accident. The ward sister came across to us.

'There is a police officer waiting in my office. Do you feel up to speaking with him?' she said.

We both nodded our ascent. He was a plain-clothes officer from CID. His name was Larry Hickston. He wore a suit that looked rather crumpled. Indeed everything about him had a sort of crumbled appearance. However, he was friendly enough.

'We've had our boys in forensic go over your car with a fine tooth-comb. I very much regret to inform you both that your car was tampered with. It's been sabotaged,' he said. It took us a minute or two to take in what he had just told us.

'But how, officer?' I said.

'The brake wires were cut, but not completely. It was quite a professional job. Whoever was driving that car, would have got one or two short journeys in it, no more, before the brakes failed.'

I told the officer the car was mine, but that we had joint usage insurance.

'I'll need to see all the paperwork for the vehicle when you have time,' he said.

'Of course, officer,' I said.

'I don't want to be alarmist, but I reckon the person who tampered with your brakes, intended you to be behind the wheel of that car and they didn't intend for you to walk away from that crash. Someone wanted you dead. That's why I'm involved. We are treating this as attempted murder,' he said.

It was two days before the disciplinary hearing and they sent up a convener to interview me. Her name was Susan Thwaites. She was a lawyer in corporate law. As well as going through all the details of my statement, I also told her about all the events that had recently happened.

'We don't know for certain, whether or not the attacks are simply motivated by someone who is homophobic, or they are connected with the hearing and someone wants me out of the way,' I said.

'This puts a whole new complexion on everything. I'm going to see if I can get an extension on this, what with everything that has just happened to you, and your partner in hospital. I'll get back to you before lunchtime tomorrow,' she said.

She did get back to me the following day, and I was much relieved to hear that everything had been put back to the first week in March of the following year. And then Clarissa came round. She wanted to know all about Tyrone's continuing progress, although she had been a regular visitor, along with Maddie, Ned and Hilary, Matthew, David and Gary. Indeed, Gary was seen as the token visitor from our family. This really hurt. Dad always asked how he was getting along. Mum kept wittering on about how young bones were quick to mend, despite my dad continually reminding her that he had been nearly killed. Gran remained silent on the matter and never once asked about his progress.

'Our dear and most beloved, headmaster,' she Clarissa, very much in the mood for biting irony, 'has decided to do the proverbial runner. He has suddenly gone and taken early retirement on supposed ill-health grounds. Apparently, the governors knew all about it, around the time you first lodged your complaint. And that's not all,' she said, 'four other teachers have suddenly decided to come out of the woodwork and testify. Three of them are gay, and when they tried to make a complaint, the head was able to shut them up by threatening to expose them. The other male teacher had a bad sickness record, and he was able to use that over him. His abuse has been going on for years.'

'My God,' I said, 'I've been surrounded by enemies.'

She gave my hand an affectionate stroke and said, 'and fortunately by friends too.'

12

The detective inspector, Larry Hickston, was a daily visitor on the ward. By the end of the first week, we were on first name terms. Tyrone was making an excellent and altogether speedy recovery. All our fingers were crossed that he would be home for Christmas, with lots of physio out-patients support. As he began to recover, he started to remember other things. It was one bright December morning, a few days before Christmas. Tyrone was sitting up in a chair, his leg supported on a stool, his crutches near-by.

'I don't know why, but do you remember, Robbie,' he said 'the day of the head teacher's conference?' I said that I did.

'Well, if you remember, your car had just come back from the garage. I was staying over, even though it was mid-week, cos we were going to see a favourite drag-act at The Manhattan Bar. I was working an odd shift that day, ten until six because of that ruddy conference. Well you left me with the car. I drove up to school, but I couldn't get parked because the car park was full to busting with cars from the conference. So I had to park the car in Seaton Drive, two streets away from the school. It was a very secluded back-street, really out of the way. Anyway, this woman came out of her house. "You can't park that old rust bucket there," she said. I was frantic, cos I was already late for work. I decided to turn on all my charm and she let me park there. "You can park it there till six," she said, "but not a minute longer mind you." I thanked her with a theatrical emphasis and blew her a kiss as I walked off down the road. When I got back, just a little before six, I knocked on her door and presented her with a box of chocolates. I found out her name and everything. She even invited me in for a cup of tea. Her name is, Elsie Braithwaite,' he said. '"And I hope the car is all fixed?" she said as I was leaving. I must have given her a puzzled look, but then you had your M.O.T badge stuck to your windscreen along with your license. So I didn't think anything more about it.'

'Gentlemen,' said Larry, 'I do believe we may have the person who tried to murder you.'

'What, Elsie Braithwaite,' said Tyrone, 'and she seemed such a kindly old soul.'

'No not, Elsie,' said Larry, 'I reckon she saw someone tampering with old Clara. I need to get back to the office right away and I'll keep you posted,' he said. 'Oh, by the way, who was the drag-act you went to see?'

'Well she was a kind of, Carmen Maranda, with a potty mouth,' said Tyrone. Larry burst out laughing.

'It wouldn't be, Maisie Mow,' he said, 'by any chance would it?'

'Aye, that was her,' I said.

'I didn't know she was still on the go,' said Larry. 'When I was a young Sgt, she used to perform at all our Christmas staff parties. It's a small ruddy world,' he said as he left.

He came back later that afternoon. He had managed to talk to Elsie. She had plied him with biscuits and cups of tea. She had also told him that at around two in the afternoon, a man turned up in overalls and a tool bag, and started to get under the car. The man told her he was from AA although he was not able to give her any formal identification. She also was able to supply a full description of the man. The description fitted the one of the man who had tried to menace us in The Manhattan Bar, a few weeks previously.

For a very brief period, even Billy had been under suspicion. This had been quickly dismissed by forensics as Billy happened to be left-handed. The sabotage had been carried out by someone who was right-handed. It had probably been done at speed and from a tight restricted angle. Billy and the rest of the mechanics at the garage always worked from a pit, giving them lots of room and leverage. I told Larry that I didn't think it was the same man as was making the threatening phone calls. He sounded different.

'Both of you tend to speak, not exactly with the Queen's good English,' said Larry 'but not in broad Munford.'

'What are you getting at? 'Tyrone said.

He then asked us if we could actually speak in broad dialect. We both proceeded to give him a very amusing and colourful example. When he had stopped laughing he said, 'was the man in the phone box simply talking in a more received pronunciation kind-of-way, whereas the man you met in the pub, was talking in broad Munford dialect?' As I recalled how he spoke, I could feel a sudden chill shooting up my spine.

'Gentlemen,' he said, 'I believe we are dealing with one and the same man.'

The insurance finally paid out and I was really lucky in managing to pick up another second-hand moggie, with one careful owner. She wasn't quite Clara, although she got called Clara Two. She had been manufactured in 1965, the year they recorded *Rubber Soul*. She was maroon and I'm afraid it was a love affair from the first moment I saw her. Tyrone loved her too.

We had to wait until late afternoon on Christmas Eve, before Tyrone's consultant said he could be discharged home. David came up with the van, because it had much more leg room. I watched as it pulled into the hospital car park, with the ward sister giving a guarded, but nevertheless amused look, as she read the slogan on the side of the van, *Toilets Are Our Business*.

Tyrone, being Tyrone had to make a very theatrical farewell to all of the staff. Maggie had turned up earlier with chocolates and flowers, and then he had to hug and kiss everyone, even the male doctors and nurses. The younger ones didn't mind, in fact they seemed to rather like it. His consultant wished him all the best but would only give him a somewhat rather formal hand-shake. And so we reached his house, with *Welcome Home Tyrone* bunting all outside the house, and Maggie running out to meet us. He was able to climb out of the van himself, with minimum help and hobble up to the front door with his crutches.

'Eeh, I'm going to spoil you something rotten,' said Maggie.

Everyone was laughing at this, including the neighbours, who had all turned out and would be helping Maggie to put on quite a spread for all and sundry for the following day. Even Larry said he would probably pop by for a mince pie and a glass of sherry. He popped round somewhat sooner than expected, around seven that evening.

'Well you can all relax. I decided to put a bit of pressure on Norman Jackstone,' he said. 'By the end of our little interview, I didn't even have to take him down to the station; he was blubbing out a full confession.'

'You mean you had him singing like a canary?' said Tyrone.

'You've been reading too much Raymond Chandler,' he said, making us all burst out laughing.

'Apparently, he had got in touch with one of his old cronies, someone he used to know, before he had found the Lord. All he had intended was to scare you off, hoping you wouldn't testify because if you did, then he knew his career was finished. When he heard what had happened and how young, Tyrone, here nearly lost his life, he was all for giving himself up there and then. His contact, however, a Mr Warren Singleton,' he said, 'started to get rather intimidating with him. He told him, if he blew the gaff now, then there was no telling what would happen to his wife and family. As of now, both men are safely in custody. Their case will be coming up sometime in the New Year. Oh and, Mr Singleton,' he said, 'has previous about a mile long.' He then helped himself to his fourth mince pie. 'Could I have another glass of sherry?' he said. And then Maggie walked across to him, 'here, have the whole ruddy bottle love,' she said and then we all found the relief of laughter.

Clarissa would be acting head from the beginning of the new term. She called round with Maddie as did Ned, Hilary and the four boys. And Maggie, completely in her element, kept opening the door to all the callers.

'Come in, come in, the more the merrier,' she kept saying. And the food and the drink were flowing as well as the laughter and the kind of tears that have both joy and poignancy all kind of mingled together. But Larry had one more surprise for us all. He came back round that Christmas evening, with Maisie Mow, who performed her act, for free, in Maggie's front room, to the delight of everyone. I thought she was as blue as blue could possibly be.

'I thought I better tone it down a bit, you know with children being present,' she had whispered to Maggie afterwards. And Maggie wondered if that was the censored version of her act, what the real thing must be like!

When all the guests had finally left at around midnight, Tyrone had a make-shift bed, for the time being, in the front room downstairs. Apart from holding hands, we had been deprived of the touch of each other for weeks.

'Come on,' he said, 'I won't break you know,' he said to me.

We held each other for what seemed an eternity, and then we were kissing like the very act of kissing, was an entirely new thing that had just been discovered and like we would never quite get over, the novelty of it.

'Welcome home, Tyrone,' I said, somewhere between our kisses, as he drew me in closer and hugged me tightly.

At the beginning of January just before the school went back, I had my twenty-third birthday. I spent it quietly with Tyrone and Maggie. Tyrone was now able to walk about the ground floor of the house, with his crutches. He seemed to be getting stronger every day. His physio was delighted with his progress.

'Some people you really have to push like hell' said Adam, his physio, 'but with you, you really drive yourself. And that arm is now as good as new.'

By the March of that new year of 1984, he was able to go back to work, though to begin with he was on light duties. He was pleased to be back. The disciplinary hearing was cancelled. The court case was to be held at Manchester Crown Court at the beginning of April. It lasted three days, and we both attended. They went through a fairly graphic description of the injuries Tyrone had sustained, complete with the pictures that were taken shortly after the incident. I could see Tyrone getting quite upset by the images. I gave his hand a gentle squeeze. He threw me a somewhat tearful smile.

'I'm Ok, it just brings it all back, seeing it all like that,' he said, during the short adjournment, whilst we grabbed ourselves a hasty cup of coffee. Norman's accomplice showed no remorse and did his best to lie to the prosecuting barrister. He tried to lay the blame all on Norman. Being a liar, he kept tripping himself up badly and if the matter had not been so serious, it was almost laughable.

'I was nowhere in the area. I was in Manchester at the time of the attack,' he said.

Elsie Braithwaite was brought in as one of the witnesses.

'Good old, Elsie,' said Tyrone to me in one of his best stage-whispers. We both crossed our fingers.

Norman was quite another matter entirely. He was full of contrition and backed up everything he had told Larry in his original confession. He even said at the end of his cross-examination that he was prepared to take whatever punishment was handed out to him. He said he had done a terrible thing and blighted the life of an innocent young man, who happened to be in the wrong place, at the wrong time. And for the first time, I actually found myself feeling more than a little compassion for Norman.

On the third day, the madam judge did the summing up and then the jury retired, to decide their verdict. Both were found unanimously guilty, though they had accepted Norman's plea that he had not been in any way the instigator of the sabotage of my car. We broke for lunch, to come back for the final sentencing. Tyrone and I went to a rather nice real ale pub I knew, down a cosy back street. They also did great bar lunches. Larry joined us.

'I wish I wasn't still on duty,' he said, eying up our beer with an envious eye. He too felt quite sorry for Norman and hoped the judge would hand him out a more lenient sentence, but did not hold out much hope of this.

'After all, we are talking about attempted murder,' he said.

Norman was up first. There were lots of things the judge decided in his favour, not least of which were his obvious contrition and the fact that his actions had brought about the end of his career as a highly respected teacher. He was given a twelve year sentence. Both Tyrone and I smiled at each other. The sentence seemed fare.

His accomplice was not so fortunate. The sabotage of my car was seen as pre-meditated, completely calculated and planned. There were various other charges that were added to his sentence, like the phone harassment. He had also tried to resist arrest, assaulted an officer whilst doing so, before being overpowered. The most serious charge was attempted murder. He was given eighteen years. Tyrone was also awarded costs for damages, through a criminal injuries scheme. We thanked the barrister.

'Never has my job been easier,' he said. 'Talk about someone being ripe for the plucking.' He wished us both well and hoped we would now be able to get on with our lives. Larry joined us both back at that pub, where we all fully imbibed of the fabulous ale.

'I don't know how to even begin to thank you enough for all you've done,' said Tyrone. He went and phoned Maggie to tell her the news. He came back laughing, telling us that she and the neighbours were going to have a bit of a shin-dig that evening to celebrate.

'And what are you two going to do?' said Larry.

'Well it's Friday afternoon. I reckon we'll both go down to Canal Street for a few hours and book into a hotel for the night,' said Tyrone.

'That sounds like a great idea to me,' I said.

'You know sometimes, I'm just a tad envious of the queer life. It's all so wonderfully uncomplicated,' said Larry. He then got up to leave and we both hugged him warmly.

Spring was peeping through the buildings all along Canal Street and by five that afternoon; it was full of young revellers. Music was ringing out from the bars, infectious, happy, strident and brazenly celebratory. I knew we would be dancing our young rocks off later that evening. We were both absolutely ravenous.

'If I don't eat something I think I'm going to die of starvation,' said Tyrone.

I laughed at him, for I felt exactly the same.

'It must be all that adrenalin,' I said, believing that we were both probably having a mild hypoglycaemic attack or something.

'Only a pile of the worst kind of junk food will do,' said Tyrone.

'You're on,' I said. We both walked off arm in arm, to find somewhere on the high street.

Tyrone's wounds, unfortunately, went much deeper than flesh, sinew and bone. We delude ourselves with our tough personas and talk of emotional resilience. And yet we are but frail, tender and fragile things, gossamer blown on the breeze, egg-shell folded around the startled ghost of an insubstantial utterance, the stuff of our borrowed days. At first he would turn away from me after making love, instead of snuggling into me. He would snap at me over nothing and storm off home for no reason at all. He had once loved it when I bought tickets for a Hallé concert in Manchester. Now he would complain about the programme and refuse to go. One Saturday evening at our local he had argued with Matthew and David.

'All of your making up, it's all false. It happened too fast. You only did it to save face. Once a homophobic bigot always a homophobic bigot,' he said, storming out of the pub on the rest of us.

'My God, Robbie,' said Matthew, 'what did we say to cause that outburst?'

'I think that was meant for me,' I told them. 'All of that stuff from the car crash, it is working itself out like a great bruise,' I said.

He was just as fractious with his mother. Nothing she did for him was right. And then by the June of that year, he had moved out. He rented a bed-sit, shabby, unkempt, with an exorbitant rent in a good part of town, where his landlord knew he could charge, whatever he wanted. He refused to take either my advice or Maggie's. We both said it was a bad move. I had wanted him to move in with me.

'Will you both just back- off, you're crowding me out,' he said.

Sunday lunchtime, a couple of weeks later, he had argued with Maggie and me. It had ended up with him storming out of the house, getting in his car and driving off at speed. Maggie was in tears, and whilst I was trying to offer her some comfort, I found myself in tears too.

'It's like there's this great wall round him and he won't let me near him,' I said. And then we finished off a bottle of single malt together.

The following week we had gone out to The Manhattan Bar as usual. We must have been there for about an hour. Tyrone had gone to the gents. He had been in there for quite a while. When he came back to our table, he looked like he had been crying.

'Whatever's the matter?' I said.

'I don't love you anymore,' he said.

'Tyrone, I said, 'you don't know what you're saying.'

'I do know what I'm saying. Since the car crash, nothing's been the same. Everything is spoilt and ruined. There can be no going back. Things can't ever be as they once were,' he said, although he had tears streaming down his face as he said it.

'Please, Tyrone,' I said, 'don't do this. I love you.' I was trying to hold back the tears.

'You've become too needy. I need my independence. You just need to back right off, it's over, we're history,' he said and then he got up and left, walking out of the bar and out of my life.

I somehow managed to drag myself to school the next day, but every lesson felt like going through the motions. Between classes and throughout the day, I noticed him from time to time moving about the school, now out on the periphery of my life. I couldn't bare it. Clarissa caught me between classes. She could see from my face that something was very much up.

'He's dumped me,' I said.

'You're coming back home with me tonight and no arguments,' she said, hurrying off to one of her classes.

'I can't even begin to imagine my life without him,' I said to her, back at her flat. Maddie was making tea. My body ached for him and yet I had not cried since he had walked out on me. We were through our third glass of single malt when the tears finally came.

My relationship with Matthew and David could never really be the same. There had been too much water under the bridge. We all knew it and therefore refused to acknowledge it. And then one Saturday afternoon in town, I happened to notice my father getting into a car with Arthur. Both men were smiling and probably off to a secret rendezvous. I realized that my parents' marriage was nothing more than a sham and it always had been. It would not have surprised me, if my mother also had taken a lover at some time or other. Life was leaving nothing but the bitter taste of ashes in my mouth. I needed a change. I needed to start again.

I still went to The Manhattan Bar, but not quite so often. Tyrone was there. He acknowledged me with a polite nod of his head, nothing else. He was flirting, laughing, kissing all the young boys who came into the bar. I knew most of this was merely for show. He was getting really drunk, something he never did with me. And one night I found him barely conscious inside the gents. I ordered a taxi and got him safely back to his flat and then left him. I could do no more. It was like he was destroying himself from the inside out, and I could do nothing to stop him.

At the beginning of the summer holidays, I attended an interview at a school in Leeds. It was tough and I was up for one post with twelve applicants. They seemed impressed, but said they would let me know. A week later, they wrote to inform me I had been successful. I gave the new head master a term's notice. Clarissa and Ned both tried to get me to reconsider. Another mid-week of Tyrone's drunken flirtations with other men, finally decided me. My house was on the market by the end of the week.

I had found and purchased a terrace house in the east area of Leeds. All my things had been despatched there the week before Christmas. On the 2nd of January 1985, with the snow falling outside my parent's house, I climbed into my trusty old moggie and drove off to Leeds and the beginning of my new life. After the first day of the new school term, I came back home to my empty and cold house. I knew no one and I had never felt more lonely or isolated.

'My God,' I said to myself, 'what have I done?'

It was then that the thought suddenly came to me, to advertise for some gay lodgers to share the house with me. I'd fill this lonely warren of a place with laughter. I was only just turned twenty-four, and yet I was behaving as if my life was already over.

'This will not do at all,' I told myself. I had all of my young life ahead of me. The best was still to come.

Part Two: The City

13

Despite having to survive on a student nurse's pay, Callum was very particular about the cigarettes he smoked. It was all a matter of style. They were always French. They were expensive and they tasted wonderful. He bought them at a tobacconist that had been there since the Edwardian era. I often slipped him a ten pound note to buy some. I was a dreadful cigarette cadger in those days. But then, smoking them, we both felt quite the part, luxuriating in a borrowed sophistication, well beyond our present means, which somehow made it all the more delicious!

Unlike Callum however, if I was in the mood for a delightfully rough one-night-stand, I wanted to smoke cheap cigarettes, awful beer and fire-water branded whisky. It helped me to fully get into the experience. I'd also dress down and not bother to shave for a couple of days. I also believed that our borrowed sophistication sometimes frightened them off.

Callum McAlister was one of my lodgers, along with Rory O'Riley. They were both nurses. Rory, the same age as me, was doing his post registration sick children's qualification; Callum was a first year student nurse He was a cheeky, brazen red-headed eighteen-year-old. We were the best of friends.

The Leeds gay scene, back then, in the mid-eighties, was very different from the corporate and carefully managed thing it is today. I particularly liked one of the bars. Rory and

159

Callum thought the place was a hell hole. I usually went there by myself, when they were both on late shifts. It was small, almost claustrophobically so. The windows were all boarded up, except for some near the ceiling. It was nearly always crowded, by about eight in the evening. People of all ages frequented the place. Everyone seemed to smoke. My eyes would stream with the fumes. And then there was the noise! People would be screaming and laughing. The jukebox would be belting out disco music, whilst a drag act would be singing, 'I Am What I Am,' to anyone who cared to listen, up on the stage. There would be hairy bears and their cubs, clones in their cheque shirts and long moustaches. The lesbians, very friendly with other gay men, were furtive, aggressive and paranoid with each other and the bright young things in their sequins, put on the same performance every night for the punters. Middle-aged men in suits, drank and laughed with working class rent boys, transvestites and men who sometimes just loved to 'frock-up' would be standing chatting away to thick-set men from the building trade. And the drink flowed, in amongst all the smoke and the noise, which all became a sort of delightful narcotic, numbing the senses to a dulled-out but happy drowse.

The smells were pungent and numerous. Lots of the young men, wore the latest scents, the women often wore musky perfumes. There was always the smell of amyl nitrate in the air, and many of the rougher young men, who never bothered to wash at all, added their rich and dank odour to the proceedings. The urinal was always full of butt-ends, and boys were nearly always screwing in the lock-up. The stench of stale boy and piss, was often overpowering, and yet I thought rather wonderful, all at the same time, even as I sometimes had to stop myself from gagging! I rarely picked up. Nevertheless, a young man or two would often come over for a chat and a quick snog, and if I was lucky, a grope. Indeed sometimes, I would have two young things, either side of me, gagging for a fag or a sniff of 'poppers', which usually got you a hot, young tongue darting down your throat!

Brian was around my own age. I met him one Saturday night at the club. I was standing on the balcony which overlooked the dancefloor. It was nearly two in the morning. He was hesitant and awkward in his introductions. We didn't kiss. He held my hand as we sat in the taxi. He was a curly-headed blond; with an infectious smile. He lived with his landlady in digs, up by the university. His landlady was still up, watching the last of some late night telly show. An old brown dog, with arthritic legs, hobbled his way over to me to greet me. He retired back to his bean-bag which served as his bed; in the corner of the living room.

His landlady finally took herself off to bed. Brian moved up closer on the sofa. We kissed at last. It had been worth the wait. Like me, he was hungry for some hot loving. All his awkward hesitation was quickly dispensed with along with his clothes; as soon as we got into his bedroom. I remembered a strange birthmark, a little way up from his navel. He had rather fantastic ears.

The following morning, crisp and cold; he walked into town with me. He waved to me as I got on the bus, taking me back to my terrace house in the east side of Leeds. I didn't expect we would meet again. He was just one of many one-night-stands; so very wonderful in their own way.

My new school was quite a lot smaller and somehow more

intimate than my old school. There was fewer staff. I was soon welcomed in as one of the family. Trevor Routledge, the head master, was in his late forties. He was dynamic; made sure he always had room in his busy timetable to still teach his beloved History. He was friendly and approachable, and I could tell that the staff adored him. So did the kids. Often I would come into school and there he would be in the forecourt, chatting away and laughing with a small group of them. He even knew what their favourite hobbies and interest were. And I thought how very different he was from my last head teacher.

My head of department, Phyllis Wright was middle-aged and adored the novels of D.H .Lawrence. 'My dear, I read *Sons and Lovers* once a year. It's become a sort of ritual. I can't get enough of him; I really can't,' she said.

Callum and I were quite content to be house slobs, able to live in a midden. Rory was not! One morning during the school half term, when the other two had a couple of days off work, Callum and I sauntered ourselves down for breakfast. Rory was standing, hands on hips, glowering at us both.

'Have you seen the state of this place?' he said.

'Yeh, its fine,' said a still sleepy Callum.

'Callum Arthur McAlister,' said Rory, 'your mother would be ashamed of you, and as for you, Robert Samuel Stebson,' he said, 'a graduate and a teacher. Well what can I say?' he said.

'Why are all the windows misted over?' said Callum.

'That happens to be polish for the windows. It's surprising how we have been able to see out of them. They're a disgrace!' he said.

'And as for the state of this cooker!' he said, going back into the kitchen area.

'Oh you don't need to worry about that,' I said, trying to be helpful. 'When I bought it, they told me it was a self-cleaning oven,' I said.

'That's because it has a drip tray you idiot!' he said. Callum was off laughing.

'And you've got nothing to laugh about young man. The state of your bedroom! I've cleared out your dirty clothes. And as for your socks, they nearly walked down the stairs all by themselves and begged me to put them in the washing machine,' he said.

'Right, I'm going to set to, give this place a cleaning within an inch of its life, and I want you two out of my hair for the morning. Go and amuse yourselves in town or something. I'll meet you both for lunch at our local. You can stand me lunch, Robbie,' he said, 'and the pair of you can buy my beers.' And then he was setting to, with a great deal of noise and kerfuffle and the smell of pine disinfectant everywhere. We stood at the bus stop, a minute's walk from the house, waiting for a bus to take us into town. We looked rather sheepishly at each other and then began to giggle.

'I suppose we are complete domestic slatterns?' said Callum. The three of us were always buying each other presents. They were not expensive ones, just little tokens to show that we cared. We went into one of the large and exclusive department stores on the main street and bought Rory a piny and some oven gloves. And then Callum was nosing about the men's toiletries department, always after the latest aroma to wear on the dancefloor at the nightclub.

'There is nothing better than the smell of stale boy,' I told him. He gave me one of his best mock-disdainful looks and said, 'yes darling, but that is because you're a hopeless case.'

I was eager to browse round the records, at a shop that sold only classical records. There were two separate recordings of Elgar I had wanted. They had both been recently released and they had good write-ups in the art's sections of the Sunday newspapers, we tended to read. I decided in the end to buy one of the recordings as opposed to the other, for I would be left short for our Saturday evening revels later that day. Callum told me he had some boring things his mother wanted him to get her, whilst he happened to be in town. So I could get the first round in and he would see me at our local. When he arrived, Callum was carrying a bag which obviously had a record inside.

'Here,' he said, 'I know you wanted it.'

It was the other recording of the Elgar.

'Oh, Callum,' I said, 'you really shouldn't have,' I said.

'Call it an early birthday present if you like,' he said.

'But my birthday is at the beginning of January next year and this is March,' I said.

'So,' he said, 'who the hell is counting?'

Rory joined us a short time later. He had obviously calmed down. And once he had his first glorious pint of bitter inside him, he was back in a very good mood. He laughed at us but thanked us for his presents.

'We really will try and do more around the house,' said Callum.

'Oh look, there's a herd of pink elephants flying across the sky,' said Rory. And then we were all off laughing.

They were doing some building work at the bottom of the road. They must have knocked off for the day, as it was now pouring down with rain. There was a young builder; I guessed he couldn't be more than twenty, if that. He was rather small, full of the grime, dust and dirt of the building site, with a rather cute and cheeky face. He was also a blond skin-head. He seemed to be looking over at me and then furtively looking away.

'See that lad over there, drinking his lager? I said, 'well I think he fancies me.' The other two looked over briefly.

'I think you must be imagining things darling,' said Rory.

'I think he's ruddy gorgeous,' I said.

'I'm afraid, I'd have to stick him in the bath tub first,' said Callum.

'Oh, I love him just how he is,' I said, smiling.

'Slut!' the other two said in unison.

There was a fruit machine in the passageway, between the back bar and the main bar. The young man seemed to be content to play away on it, with his pint of lager, perched precariously on top of it. I had got into an interesting conversation with the other two, about how so many interpretations of Elgar were really rubbish. We had caught a performance at Leeds town hall the previous week. It had been rather dull and uninspired. When I looked over to the fruit machine, the young man seemed to have left. I needed to piss, so I took myself off to the gents. He was standing at the urinal taking a piss. I could not believe my good fortune. But then I told myself, he was probably straight. But then I stole a quick and furtive glance, and he was sporting a full-blown and completely delightful erection! He was also smiling at me.

'Fancy a screw?' he said.

'I ruddy do,' I said. We decided to go back to his high-rise flat across the road from the hospital. 'Give us half a mow,' I said, 'I'll just tell my friends I'm otherwise occupied. I'll see you outside.' I went back to the others. I was feeling that delightful sense of giddy anticipation and all of my young hormones were doing a dance through my head and singing joyfully through my veins.

'Guess what, I've clicked. I'm on a promise,' I said.

'Lucky sod,' said Rory.

'Make him squeal like a pig,' said Callum. 'We'll take care of your records for you,' he said.

When I got back outside, I thought he had gone. I heard him whistling over to me. He was huddled up in the side doorway to the pub, doing his best to avoid the wind and the rain and to light a cigarette. We then went back to his flat. The lift was out-of-order. It always was. He was on the tenth floor. The stairways stank of piss. I wondered when I got to the top, whether or not I'd still have any energy left. He asked if I wanted a coffee.

'Sure,' I said.

The mug it came in looked none too clean and neither was the flat or himself, regardless of his occupation. This was all turning me on even more.

'Screw the coffee,' he said at last and he was kissing me, sticking a young and hungry tongue deep into my mouth. I moved my hand, rather cold from the weather outside, under his grubby jumper. He gave a little yelp with the cold. When I moved it away, I put my fingers up to my nose, to smell his young, unwashed, builder's essence. He just smiled at me, knowing I enjoyed his smell. We had each other undressed, fairly quickly. His naked feet, grubby and smelling of the day, with their dirty soles, I caressed and kissed. He laughed at the close attention I was giving them.

'I could always nip and have a shower, if you like?' he said, with a mischievous grin.

'No, please don't, I love you just as you are, all wild and natural,' I said.

'You dirty bugger,' he said. We were both off laughing again. I entered his warm, inviting space and he smiled. 'God, that feels so good, I mean really good,' he said.

It all happened there in the living room on his dishevelled settee. The TV was on somewhere in the background. He was gorgeous, just gorgeous! I think he happened to know it. I loved the smell, touch and taste of him, and we were fairly busy for the next couple of hours.

'Eeh, you screw like a real professional, you do,' he said. Eventually, he looked up at the clock on the wall. It was ten past five.

'I suppose we better stop,' he said. I asked him why.

'Me lass finishes work at five, and she gets the bus straight home,' he said. I smiled at him and got dressed. Before I left, however, he gave me yet another of his hungry kisses at the door. I hurried off down the ten flights of stairs and back out into the street. It was still raining, but not quite so heavy and the wind was blowing the sign of the pub. The street lights all along the road had come on and the hospital looked more like a lit-up village. I walked back up to the house, and as I reached the corner of our street, I could hear the majestic strains of the music of Elgar, blasting away from the hi-fi, probably annoying all the neighbours. And I thought to myself, these are the wonderful days of my youth! Enjoy them whilst they last, I said to myself, cos days like these will never come again. And then I smiled and turned towards the house.

Phyllis, my head of department and her husband Bob, were regular visitors. Sometimes Rory and Callum joined us, other times they were working late shifts. Like me, Bob was into classical music, especially Beethoven, Brahms and Elgar, recorded between the years 1952-1964. He described these years as the golden age of classical recordings. I happened to agree with him. And then one evening my entire vintage hi-fi packed up.

Something had shorted-out the whole system, blown the motor in the turntable, taken out three valves and the capacitor from the amplifier, and wasted the tweeters in the speakers. I was effectively without music. And then all the lights went out.

'You could always read,' said Phyllis, trying to be helpful, I suppose, after we had got the junction box in the cellar back working.

My spare amp I'd given to Tyrone.

'You know,' Bob said, 'you don't have to buy new. In fact most great hi-fi was made from around 1965 to 1974. Lots of really silly people, with more money than sense, got rid of their old systems and upgraded.' He told me about a second-hand shop on the outskirts of Leeds that sold reconditioned hi-fi. 'I bet you anything, he could fit you up with something, and you'd still have change from a hundred pounds,' he said.

Every year the school put on a performance of a Shakespeare play, with actors made up from sixth formers and staff. Phyllis asked if I wanted to have a shot at directing it.

'Are you kidding?' I said.

'No, I'm perfectly serious,' she said. And so I found myself agreeing. They were doing *Hamlet* that year. I was as nervous as hell. They'd given the leading role to Thomas Lewthwaite, the head boy, with a right old attitude to match. I sensed there was going to be problems with him, but I was unable to say why. The rest of his teachers thought the sun shone out of his proverbial; so I kept my reservations to myself.

One Saturday afternoon, just before the Easter holidays, Rory and Callum got into the car with me and pootled off into the outskirts to a radio shop. The proprietor was a be-spectacled man, nearing retirement. He believed he had just the thing, especially if I listened to my music through headphones. He sold me a belt-drive turntable, a sixties solid-state amplifier and a pair of inexpensive headphones. I had change from £70 when I left the shop. My finances did not stretch to a pair of speakers as well.

'Look guys, it will only be a very temporary arrangement until I can afford to get the other system fixed,' I said.

We would have to listen to our music, as a solo experience via headphones. I was not really holding out any hope of it actually sounding any good. The neighbours however, I'm sure must have been grateful that there was no more loud music, blaring out from our little house. We devised a timetable for who got to listen to his music and when. Finally fitting it all up when we got back home, Callum chose the first record to try out on it. He picked out some fifties jazz. He got first go, and as he listened away, he was giving me the thumbs up sign. And so I went next. It sounded glorious. Strange really, that something that was meant to be only a temporary solution is still the system I often find myself using today, for late evening sessions; thirty two years later!

The school production was veering very much off course, with the leading role being a right old pre -Madonna. He was clever, and had all his lines learned, laughing at the slowness of the others, who were still struggling with their lines. I told him,

'It's Shakespeare we are doing, not a ruddy West End musical.'

However, every soliloquy was a chance for him to really ham it up. It was dreadful. And then he ended by having a screaming match with make-up, who happened to be Phyllis! She had a shorter fuse than me and she ordered him off the set, never to come back. And so I ended up, with a week to go to opening night, needing to step in as the Danish Prince and having to learn all of those ruddy lines! Surely he must have been the most verbose of all of Shakespeare's protagonists! Rory and Callum insisted on coming to the opening night.

'So you want to see me die on stage?' I said.

'Only when you're supposed to, at the end of Act Five,' said Callum, giving me one of his best innocent smiles.

A couple of days before opening night, during the crucial dress-rehearsals, Thomas's father came striding in, as if he owned the place. He was head of an engineering works, just off the town centre. He was smoking a large cigar.

'What's all this I hear about my son being ditched from the leading role?' he said, coming right up to me and blowing his cigar smoke into my face. I was about to answer him, when Phyllis popped her head from behind the curtain, her mouth full of pins.

'It was I who ordered your son off set,' she said. 'I'm head of the English and Drama department at this school. School productions happen to be about team-work, not simply there to bolster your son's ego!'

'This is an outrage!' he exclaimed. 'The governors will hear about this, you mark my words! 'And then it was first night, and

170

somehow I managed not to make a complete fool of myself. I even remembered all my lines. We got three curtain calls and I realised, it had been a success. The head took to the stage, where he thanked all the pupils and the staff for their immense efforts, and then I found myself with a special mention for the debut direction and having to stand-in at the last moment, to take on the leading role. Horatio was a twenty-eight year old Geography teacher. I screwed him on the last night of our little production. One more notch on the bedstead.

'I don't even know if I'm really gay,' he said, getting himself dressed again.

'So, which do you prefer?' I asked him, 'an afternoon going to watch Leeds United playing at home, or going to see the opera?'

'Well, the opera of course,' he said.

'I reckon you're gay. And if that really was your first time, I'd say you are quite a natural.'

He smiled at me. 'Did anyone ever tell you are rather gorgeous?' he said before he left. Tyrone had often told me so. I found myself unable to answer him. Damn it, I thought, why did he still manage to get to me in this way?

14

I was standing in one of the attic bedrooms, watching the rain falling across the rooftops, a gully of slate with endless row upon row of terrace houses. I knew there would be little chance of a let-up that afternoon. It was a Saturday, Rory and Callum were at work. They would be working all weekend and so I'd decided so spend a quiet evening in, listening to my records. Why did so many people talk about being bored and at a loose end? I did not understand the meaning of either the word or the phrase. There was always something to do. Although I loved going out, availing myself of concerts, the theatre, the opera, our favourite Italian restaurant and the heady delights of Leeds gay scene, nevertheless, I could be just as contented at home, indeed blissfully so.

I'd spent a couple of hours, messing about in the kitchen, putting myself a nice meal together. I'd even bought a tolerably drinkable bottle of red wine to go with it. I'd promised myself an evening of Brahms. Sitting at the table with the last of the yellow light, left by the rain pouring through the window, my meal tasted rather good and so did the wine.

Eventually, I sauntered myself into the front room and the delights of Brahms. I always turned out all the lights and would light some scented candles instead. At such times, I was often gifted with an insight that somehow the entire universe was made out of joy, beauty and a kind compassion, that not only connected with all things, but was all things, and that all strife and ugliness, was but a delusion. The naked shape of a lover, and the arch of his back, sunlight dancing across Borrowdale, were all the same, and the reasons, though having rejected religion, I could never stop believing in God and all that was other, unknowable and ineffable. It was the breath behind my breath, the shadow-light, the part of me that would always walk in eternity, whilst carving out my hum-drum days in the world of everyday. This realization connected me up and made me feel whole.

When the others had come back home from their late-shifts, wet-through from their walk back from the hospital, they would look at me, they would know I had been touched by God. I had been listening to Brahms. At such times, they would leave me to myself, until I was ready to gradually come down and re-connect with the world of things.

All of this took me back to my childhood. Dad had an old valve wireless, in the back of the shop. It was tuned in to the Light Programme. Just occasionally, they would play some opera. Dad would stop whatever he was doing and a strange other-worldly look would come into his eyes. And he would stand there and listen. Sometimes a stray tear would run from his eye and down his cheek. And then the aria would finish. He would sigh and then return to his work, but not so much resigned, as somehow able to go on because of it.

I would come through and join them both at the kitchen table. Callum would offer me one of his French cigarettes; Rory would be making the coco. The talk then was kind of hushed, though we smiled and our laughter was like the hazy smoke of our cigarettes, rising slowly up to the ceiling and dissipating on the dappled evening air. The other two would sometimes stay up for a while. I would usually take myself to bed quite early. At such times I liked to read, usually poetry. Dylan Thomas was a particular favourite at this time. The verse had burned through him, God's irresistible fused-light through the tallow, the blaze of sudden sunlight, the ocean-swell and the wind of desire, howling through the Welsh valleys, which made up the stuff of his mortal flesh.

Rory was working a late shift. I'd finished my marking early and Callum popped his head round the kitchen door. 'Fancy a couple of pints at the pub?' he said.

'That sounds like a good idea,' I said.

'You do know he's completely besotted and infatuated with you?' he said to me, during my second pint.

I asked him who he was talking about, thinking he was referring to some young guy or other; we had both met on the scene.

'Rory,' he said. I was shocked.

'But we're mates,' I said.

'And what ruddy difference do you think that makes?' he said.

I took a rather large gulp of beer and then an even larger gulp of air, straight afterwards.

'Oh God,' I said. 'I didn't know. This complicates things.'

'You know for a teacher, you can be really dumb at times,' he said. 'Have you not seen the way he fusses over you like a mother hen?'

'He does that with us both,' I said.

'That's true, but he does it more with you. He treats you like Dresden China,' said Callum.

'The thing is, I really like him as a friend but I just don't fancy him. It's not that there's anything wrong with him, he's just not my type,' I said.

'I think he knows that and that's what makes it hard for him. I mean, you're a damned attractive bloke you know,' he said.

'Oh don't tell me you fancy me as well?' I said, 'let's have a ruddy three-some and be done with it.' He told me sarcasm didn't suite me. 'And for the record, I do think you're kind of cute, but you're not exactly my type. You're not ordinary enough,' he said.

'Has he told you all this?' I said.

'Naturally,' he said.

'Well should you be giving away his confidence like this?' I said.

'He wanted me to say something. He thought it might clear the air. He even said that if it made you really uncomfortable, he'd move out.'

I was unable to answer him. I wanted Rory as a friend. Already, they were both beginning to feel like, the best friends I'd ever had. Why did sex have to get in the way and spoil everything?

The following day at work I got a summons to Trevor's office between lessons.

'God, have I done something wrong?' I said.

'Good God, Robbie,' he said, 'no.' He then jumped out of his seat behind his desk and came across and gave me one of his crushing bear hugs.

'No, it's just that I was clearing the attic at the weekend, when I realised I still had an old pair of speakers. You were saying that your new amplifier isn't powerful enough to drive your existing set of speakers. I thought they might serve. I don't want anything for them. I'd just like them to go to a good home,' he said.

Trevor drove an old sixties Hillman, that had definitely seen better days. It chugged up the road, and I was always surprised when it actually made it up our hill. He arrived one Saturday morning, just before lunch. Being Trevor, he was all bluster and mad activity, getting the speakers out of the back seat of the car. Five minutes later, he had them connected to my amplifier and ready to go.

'Do I get to choose a record then?' he said.

I told him to be my guest. He chose an Ella Fitzgerald album, she sounded like she was in the room.

The other two were glad they could play their music through speakers again. I'd fallen in love with listening through headphones, so I didn't have to turn the music down. Nevertheless, it was nice to come down on a weekend morning to the sound of a musical or some Bach, wafting its sweet incense up the stairs.

There was something so very make-do-and mend about my system, and that's what I loved about it. It felt rather like our lives. We were three young gay men, who had been thrown together by chance, full of hormones, attitudes, opinions on every subject under the sun and dreams of all wanting to do something really special with our lives, without knowing what.

We had been living together now for six months and with the exception of my time with Tyrone, I was as happy as I'd ever been. Wednesday evening we sometimes popped down to the scene, especially during the school holidays when I didn't have to be up early for work. The nightclub was rather quiet on Wednesdays, and they usually only opened the top room. The music was played a lot quieter up here and the lighting was

176

more subtle. They were playing mostly old Mowtown numbers.

Callum, as usual was dancing away on the small dance-floor with its corridor of mirrors, flirting with every young boy in sight, enjoying his youth and his queerness, with a celebratory swagger and delightful arrogance. It made me smile. Rory had left early because he had an early shift the following day. Callum came back over to where we were both sitting, breathless with all of his exertions. But then a favourite track came on, and he dragged me onto the dance floor, where we danced hot and wild, for the next ten minutes. It was then that I suddenly was aware, how altogether cute and pert was Callum's young butt. It was a delightful thing indeed! I told myself he was my housemate and that I shouldn't be having such thoughts. It felt almost incestuous. We sat back down and continued with our drinks. He pushed his face forward and gave me a kiss full on the lips.

'What was that for?' I said.

'Does there have to be a reason?' he said. We kissed again, more slowly and with a hungry passion. I knew I wanted him, and I could see an equal look of desire in his eyes. We quickly left the club and got a taxi home. We said goodnight to each other, all very formally on the top landing. And then I turned into my room and went to bed. It must have been about half an hour later, when I felt someone getting into bed beside me. It was Callum and he was naked.

'Budge up then,' he said. We kissed, darting our young tongues, deep into each other's hot, moist mouths. I realized he had the most wonderful nipples, and although I knew he wanted to be taken, I was going to have to wrestle for the joy of him.

'You're a wanton little slut,' I whispered to him, screwing him like my life depended on it.

'I know,' he said, causing us both to giggle, but being aware not to make too much noise, and wake Rory.

We had fallen to sleep in each other's arms. Neither of us wanted Rory to find us like this. It would hurt him too much. Callum got up to return to his own room and gave me a gentle and somewhat chased kiss on the forehead. It made me smile, especially when I thought about our impassioned love-making, only a few brief hours before!

I decided to invite Trevor and his wife Pat round for a meal. I wanted to thank him for the speakers.

'I'd love to come, but I'm afraid it will just be me.'

He then told me that he never knew what Pat, his wife, was really up to these days. I was puzzled and I could see he was enjoying his enigmatic moment. He laughed and patted me on the shoulder saying, 'all will be revealed.' Both Rory and Callum wanted to be part of the party. Rory said he would cook. They were both curious to meet a line manager, who they thought was vaguely human.

'I don't know what it is,' said Rory over the breakfast table one morning, 'but as soon as anyone becomes a ward sister, they transmogrify into Hitler in drag.'

Trevor was forty-six, with wild wavy hair, rapidly going grey. He also wore thick spectacles. His expressive features, had that lived in look about them. I sometimes used to think that if he had chosen to work on the world stage in diplomacy, instead of teaching, there would have been universal peace years ago. He was simply affability itself! The Saturday morning of our little party, Callum and I were given a long shopping list, together with our orders.

'No going for a sly drink, cos I want you both back here. I've loads of things for you to do.' He was being delightfully bossy, with a wry twinkle in his eye.

Rory had cooked a leg of lamb, with all the trimmings. The wine was going down well, and the four of us were chatting and laughing round the table. Trevor had brought with him a rather delightful bottle of best highland malt. Rory and Trevor found they both had a passion for The Tudors and Stewarts period of history.

'The textbooks get it all wrong of course,' said Rory, now well-oiled and being quite the high Queen of the evening proceedings.

'There was a great deal more behind-the-scenes political manoeuvrings and Machiavellian machinations. And as for the under-hand pacts and the poisonings from an unknown hand, it certainly made for a very interesting period of English History,' he said, re-filling everyone's glass with some more whisky. When Trevor finally got up to leave, with his taxi waiting for him outside, he thanked us all for a most enjoyable evening.

'May I be so bold as to ask you out for dinner, it will be my treat? You can tell me some more about your interesting ideas on English History,' he said to Rory. 'Oh, I forgot to mention gentlemen, I'm also as queer as queer can possibly be!' And then he left, laughing at our puzzled faces, as he got into the taxi.

Rory had been living on the promise for the next few days, singing and whistling happily to himself around the house. Callum and I could not help smiling. Rory, with the exception of me, was into older men. He simply found them more interesting.

'They've seen life and they have a lot more to talk about,' he would say.

'I don't want them to ruddy talk,' I said, 'all I want them to do is to grunt in all the right places whilst I'm screwing them stupid.'

Rory gave me one of his looks and said, 'you are a completely hopeless case.' I believed he may be right.

15

Leeds had become my playground for afternoon assignations, with street-sluts, wanton- boys who should know better, but who I was glad didn't. I'd had young plumbers, joiners, a lithographer with bitten nails and dirty ways, a young lad who had come to read the metre, and the apprentice boy, Ronnie, who cleaned our windows for his dad. He was twenty with greasy brown hair, cheeky-faced, sly-eyed and was supposed to be going steady, with his lass from the local council estate! I was having the time of my life! He'd even bring his ladders and bucket into the house.

'They'll nick ought round here,' he said with his cheeky grin. I loved the young, stale smell of him, especially after he had been out on his rounds for most of the morning. And he was a hungry, almost desperate lover, kissing, biting and clawing, and so delightfully muscular underneath his grubby tee-shirt.

'Does your girlfriend even suspect?' I said to him, one bright Saturday morning with the May sunshine drifting in shafts through the window, and his little muscular legs, up over my shoulders.

'Nah,' he said, 'she doesn't have the imagination. Now will you shut up and screw me, cos I've got the next street's windows still to clean.'

Callum commented, one evening that he happened to notice that I'd had, young Ronnie, yet again. I asked him how he knew. 'Because, he's left his shammy-leather in your attic bedroom again,' he said.

It was the evening of Rory's glory. He was all dressed up in a suit and tie. We both thought he looked great and we told him so.

'Make sure he seduces you between the second course and the sweet menu,' said Callum.

'And when he takes you back to his place, get him to screw you silly, and don't take no for an answer,' I said. And then Callum and I were off giggling like a couple of school-kids. It was not until two days later, with the three of us sitting in the snug of our local, that Rory was able to fill us in on his evening.

'Well, darlings, he is still married to, Pat,' he said 'but they've been separated for over the last five years.'

He told us he had two teenage kids, Ryan, aged seventeen and, Trish, who was fourteen. 'He sees them all the time.' He told us he was still best mates with his wife and he thought her long-term partner Clive, was a great guy. They all went on holiday together and everything. It was all terribly cosy.

'Yes, never mind about all that. Did he screw you?' asked Callum.

'I'm getting to that bit in a minute,' said Rory.

'This restaurant he took us both to. It was way out in the country. I believe it used to be an old coaching inn or some-thing or the other. It was part pub, all intimate, with the most subtle of lighting, and part restaurant. There were all kinds of Victoriana dotted around the place too. The food was all French and cooked to perfection. We only had the house wine, but it tasted delicious. And yes he did take me back to, his place and yes we did make love, but not the sordid variety you two keep going on about,' he said.

'Oh, for God's sake, a screw is a screw, at the end of the day,' I said.

'Let me just say, that everything went extremely well in that department,' said Rory. He was smiling with the memory.

'Was he well-endowed then?' said Callum.

'Darlings, his wife had nothing to complain about, during their eighteen years of marriage.' Callum and I found ourselves sniggering.

Trevor and Rory would not go on to have a full-time relationship. Instead they would remain good and close friends, who would sometimes go to bed together. It suited them both perfectly. And not for the first time, I thought about the infinite variety and flexibility of gay love. It certainly came in all shapes and sizes.

Martin Baines, the Horatio of our little school production, was hankering after a relationship with me. I kept bumping into him on the scene. I liked him a lot, and for a twenty-eight-year-old Geography teacher, he had boyishly good looks and was actually interesting. He was also only a ten minute walk from my own front door. He loved Impressionism, was rather bohemian, he was fiercely vegetarian, and was actively involved in canvasing during local and general elections, promoting The Labour Party but a committed and fully paid up member of The Fabian Society. His little terrace house was something of a shrine to William Morris. He loved the music of Delius and Vaughan Williams, and bought us both tickets for a concert given by The Leeds Symphonia; an evening dedicated to the music of Vaughan Williams. It was haunting, infectious and completely delightful. Afterwards, we both went back to his little house and made love. He didn't like being screwed. It was all stroking, licking and sucking, with scented candles; all very sensuous. And from there, somehow we seemed to be an item.

Callum had met Alastair Southwell. He was a civil servant. He was nice enough, but terribly ordinary-looking. He would never stand out in a crowd. He dressed one step down from smart and two steps up from casual. Even when not at work he often wore a white shirt and a dark blue tie. If you blinked you really could have missed him. He did like the music of Beethoven and had rather good taste, as to the interpretations of his work. There had recently been some re-releases of classic sixties Beethoven recordings, digitally remastered for vinyl. I'd bought a couple. I thought they sounded dreadful! He brought me round his own original copies of these recordings, which were sublime!

Alastair was also in a relationship; indeed he had been so for the last eight years with Barry Hepworth, who worked front-of-house in hospitality. Barry knew about Callum and he believed he pepped up their relationship. He was also quite agreeable to the occasional threesome. It was all very French and Callum adored playing the mistress! And so in our own ways, we were all happily sexually preoccupied at this time, in our various involvements. There would be seven of us all sat round two tables at our favourite Italian restaurant: Martin and I, Callum with Alastair and Barry and Rory with Trevor. The conversation was erudite, witty, and artful, with lots of laughter and copious amounts of good wine, to help the proceedings along.

Rory had got to know Trevor's teenage children and Rory and Trevor's wife Pat, would sit by the hour, discussing interior design. Rory had gone to listen to a string quartet in Harrogate with Clive, Pat's partner. It was all so very cosy and we all told ourselves how happy we were. And then for some reason or other, Callum would fall out with Alastair about something and nothing, and I would have a row with Martin. We would end up avoiding each other in the staff room. It was all pretty childish really, when I look back. At these periods, Callum and I would start to feel all lustful towards each other.

'If you don't take me right up those stairs this minute,' he would say to me, usually right in front of Rory, 'and make wild and passionate love to me, then I'll just have to kill myself because of unrequited love.' And all of that lust would burn strong between us. Wine, cigarettes and amyl nitrate, helping to fuel the flow of our love, which was not really love at all.

We not only adored poetry, we saw ourselves as poets between the sheets. No one had ever had a romantic relationship like ours, it was all *Wuthering Heights* meets D.H. Lawrence, and couldn't everyone else see that what we had was the real thing and every other kind of love, a mere imitation, not worthy of comment! The foreplay was always short. 'Let's skip the entrée,' Callum would say, 'and let's just get down to the main course.' And then, I'd turn him over on his soft belly and he would lift up his delightful buttocks, and I would screw him with crazy desire! And how, just entering him, aroused me so much, I had to think of something really gross to stop me from ejaculating. At these times, I would think of women and their painted toe-nails. This was usually sufficient to stop the flow of my love. And then he would always turn himself around, placing his legs up around my shoulders, for what he chose to call, 'the grand finale.' With the heart-stopping sight of the soles of his delicious feet, this usually came quickly enough!

We would always come down from our sexual high, wondering what it had all been about. Martin would ring me, Alastair would call round with flowers and tickets for the opera, and then Callum and I could hardly bear to look at each other and we would avoid each other for days. Rory found us tiresome, for we would speak to him and not each other, blaming each other for it ever having happened in the first place.

'If you think I'm taking sides, the pair of you can think again. I'm getting tired of all this. Either be one thing or the ruddy other,' Rory would say with some heat.

I would look at Callum when things were going well with me and Martin, and wonder what I could possibly have seen in him. Perhaps it was a distant whisper of Tyrone, nothing else. My relationship with Martin ran its inevitable course. We rarely argued, although I would grow heated and irritated, with some innocuous comment he had made. And then I would storm off.

We went to art exhibitions and sculpture parks and had 'interesting' conversations about intentionalism in art since the late 1950s. We drank herbal tea; chose curtain patterns and how it infuriated me when we went out, that he never got drunk and never ever really let himself go. Our love-making was sedate, gentle, almost stitched together out of hessian. It was like I was standing back from myself in the very act, and it seemed defused into an art-deco sepia-tone. I was bored in my heart and bored in my body. Part of me wanted to end our relationship, with the heady fireworks of a grand falling-out. He refused to grant me even this. He told me he had applied for another teaching post in Coventry.

'I don't think you'll be joining me, although you are always welcome to visit,' he said in his quiet way.

It felt like the diminuendo at the end of a romantic symphony, the setting of the sun and the hazy twilight of spent love.

16

Whilst I had been living in Leeds, I often liked to trawl the gay bars and clubs alone. Rory and Callum called these periods my 'bouts.' As far as they were concerned, I was just out on the pull. Sometimes they were right, and I'd lost count of the casual one-night stands I'd had. But to me, it was much more than this. I would hang out at the rougher, down-at-heel bars, with their claustrophobia and their smoke, drinking in the sounds, sights and smells of the place. The bottled beer was just about drinkable. The Irish whisky was good! And I would smoke cheap cigarettes. They always caught the back of my throat. And then there were places, not actually on the scene itself, but connected to it. These were the back-street out-of-hours drinking dives, peopled by the lost, lonely and the interesting. I bumped into twenty-four- year- old Luther Davis, in one of these bars. He was black, fairly clean, with big brown, you could say, almost sorrowful eyes. He was gay. I knew he fancied me, and yet it was sometime before he invited me back to his council flat in the west end of Leeds.

'I want to be a record producer,' he told me the first time I met him. 'I've even put this portfolio together, with all the stuff I've done. I want my name up there in big, flashing lights, like Trevor Horn and Quincy Jones,' he said. And then he would get all sad, because he was stuck working in a factory. The place was destroying his soul. He'd left home as soon as he could.

'I hate to say it, but my mum, she's a slapper. You know seven kids, all on benefit, and a different father for each kid. Christ knows who my dad is!' he told me. 'My step-dad, he's just a thug. When I was fifteen, I was in baby-sitting my younger brothers and sisters, whilst him and me mum were out getting wasted at the working men's club down the road. All the kids were in bed, and I was watching *Calamity Jane* on telly. I love Doris Day; I mean if you're gay, who doesn't? He said. 'Anyway, me step-dad comes in, and sees what I'm watching. He turns it off and tells me I'm watching stuff that only queers watch. And then he kicks seven bells of crap out of me. I reported him to social services and everything, but they ended up taking his side. He gave them a load of bull about how I was joy-riding, getting in with a bad crowd and taking drugs. I left as soon as I'd turned eighteen,' he said.

'I'd love to screw you,' I said to him on one of these late evenings.

'Yeh, I know you would. And I'd really like that. But not tonight,' he said.

'You mean you want me to back off?' I said.

'No, I'd like you to come back. But I just want a bit of tenderness tonight,' he said. And so we waited out by the taxi-rank, in the driving wind and the rain, with me thinking, 'it's one in the morning, and I've got school tomorrow.'

We ended up in his tenth-storey flat. He kept it nice. I could see he had decorated the place himself. It had cool minimal lines, and all the effects were paired back. He had an innate sense of artistic taste. He had two decks, his pride and joy, in his living room. He put on some blues music at a low volume. We drank our coffee from clean mugs, and kissed at last. I'd wanted to kiss him for weeks. For some time, even when we were both naked, there on his threadbare couch, he just wanted me to hold him. 'Now you can screw me,' he said at last, smiling up at me.

'Are you sure you really want me to?' I said.

'Yeh, and screw me hard, for I guess that too, is another kind of tenderness.'

Afterwards, he cuddled in. We went into his bedroom, and quickly fell asleep on a carefully made bed. He had to be up for work by six. I left and got an early bus home. I was teaching on rote that morning, but was almost back to my normal self by lunchtime.

Julian Argyle had some terribly important position or other, for the Sheffield health authority. What it was exactly; I've completely forgotten. But they paid him a whole bundle of money for doing it. He was thirty six, with rather a lot of style, heaps of disposable income, his own set of interesting friends, a ground floor apartment in a good area of Leeds, which stank of class and for someone who was, in my eyes, approaching irreversible senility, being now the grand old age of thirty six; not bad looking. I felt seduced by him, through good manners, interesting conversation and that kind of affability of which Rory was basking in with Trevor. And he loved to spoil me. I was his pet. We were always going to the theatre, sitting in all the most expensive seats. He took me to exclusive restaurants, mostly French, up for weekend trips to London to see the ballet, concerts at The Barbican and all the grand opera, we could stuff inside our ears! And once again, I told myself I was happy. Both Callum and Rory was just a teeny bit envious of me at this time, and I rather enjoyed the fact that they were. I also sometimes felt, like his bit of working class rough on the side. This thrilled my soul! My personal hygiene had always been good, but it was never quite up to Julian's fastidious standards.

'Darling,' he would say to me, 'go and have a bath or a shower or something, you are starting to hum.' And then I would giggle, like some errant urchin and go and have a bath in his sumptuous bathroom, filled up with every conceivable kind of grooming product, garnered from expensive shops from London. I don't think he ever spent less than twenty pounds on a bottle of shampoo!

He was terribly passive in the bedroom department. And although I usually was the one with all my lovers who ended up, as it were, dominating the sexual proceedings, I rather liked a bit of a tussle and a fight for it. I was amused by the fact that thousands of pounds of money, went through his hands at work every week, and he was responsible for hundreds of workers, yet I had him underneath me, purring like a pussycat and suppliant to my will. The wonderful irony of it would set me off giggling.

'Whatever are you laughing at?' he would say. And how could I ever tell him, how absurd he looked; this hospital big-wig, with his legs in the air, anticipatory of my uncouth favours.

And then the family came across to Leeds for a few days. They stayed in a guest house close by. They were gracious with Rory and Callum, less so with me. To them I was still their little, rather errant child. I'd out-grown them and broke out of the straight-jacket. Mum and Dad were still holding the pretence of a marriage together, the supposed miracle of Canaan where the wine remained as water and the outward show, stood for the whole thing. Gran was her usual acid self, carefully dropping her one-liners into the conversation, with her comments.

'Well, you've made you bed so I suppose you'll just have to lie on it. And there is nothing that I or your mother can do to change that.' Dad would turn to her and tell her to give it a rest.

The only person, who seemed natural, was Gary. He felt real and authentic. He was pleased to see me. He was now a tall, lanky fourteen-year-old, in the middle of his first tentative and somewhat scary relationship with a girlfriend. A sly snog behind the bike sheds at school had blossomed into a teenage romance. Julian came round to see them, in his BMW with its daft smoked-glass sun-roof. He even took a couple of days off work, insisting on taking them out for a drive up through the north Yorkshire moors.

'Well my dear,' said Mum when he had gone, 'you could do a lot worse for yourself.'

And then Gran butted in with, 'yes he's certainly an improvement on the last one.' I knew she was referring to Tyrone. I felt hurt and angry.

Julian was happy to drive them all back down to the station, and I was so very glad when their train finally pulled away from the platform. There had been the usual kisses and hugs before they got on the train. It all felt so incongruous to me. I hated the act. And then I had to endure the impromptu lecture from Julian, about how I should be more giving and understanding with my gran and parents.

I told him where to get off. He had wanted to spend the rest of the day with me. I told him I just needed time by myself.

'Well my dear,' said Rory ironing his uniform for work, 'you managed to get through it.'

'Just,' I told him.' It felt like the only honest conversation I'd had for days. I was grateful for it and I found myself laughing. Callum was working a late shift, so there was just the two of us.

'I need to finish off this bit of ironing, but then what do you say to us both going down to the pub, for a good old bitch and getting ourselves, well and truly rat-arsed for the afternoon?' I told him that it sounded to me like the best idea in the world.

Julian's friends were all gay and very well-heeled. I felt like his latest mascot. I detested feeling like this. They found me charming and amusing and could not help but be superior and condescending.

'You're probably wasted in such a barren back-water,' said David, a solicitor from Doncaster.

'No, I love my job, the staff I work with and the kids that I teach.'

They didn't say anything, but I could tell by the looks on all the faces around that dinner table, that they thought I was deluding myself.

'There are some great public and independent schools out there you know. They'd love you,' said Ryan, an accountant who didn't know these days how much he was worth or how much he earned in a year. I was coming back from the bathroom. I could hear their babble of chatter from the half open door. They were talking about me.

'Yes darling, he's quite delightful. You never can tell what you can pick up from the provinces these days.'

With this comment, I knew I was expected to play *Eliza Doolittle* to his *Professor Higgins*. But then, when I wanted to be, I could be a sarcastic and cutting little cat! My claws were primed and I was ready for the fray. If they talked about some sublime classical recording, on some expensive record label or other, then I would start talking about the same piece on one of the budget labels. And when they talked about literature, I could tell, most of their ideas had come from *The Times Literary Supplement* and *The Listener*. And so I would ask them for their own subjective opinion of the novel or collection of poetry, they happened to be talking about.

'Why did you have to behave like that?' said a very put-out Julian as we drove back to his place, later that evening.

'Your friends are snobs. I can't help it if they don't have a single original idea in their heads,' I said.

And even in the half-light of the car, I could tell he was secretly seething! And I thought one more pretentious evening like that and we would be history. I was also hungry for some honest, working class love!

I received a letter one morning towards the end of June that year, from my old friend and colleague Ned Farrows. He told me the sad news of his Uncle's demise.

Apparently, he was still on the job with some rent boy or other from the village when it happened. His heart just gave out. What a way to go! I got the news from Sullivan, his butler. Naturally, I had to sift through his words to get to the truth of the matter. The funeral is to be held next Saturday, if you want to pay your last respects. Hilary and the boys will also be there. Bring a friend or your most recent fuck-buddy, Henry would have loved that, you know, keeping up the faith! Also, I'd love to see you, if you can make it.

A local bishop, the very Reverend George Tilby, would be taking the funeral. They were old friends. Like Henry, he was a confirmed old bachelor, had a penchant for antique furniture, good Claret and bred and reared race horses as a hobby. He was just the right side of sixty. Two of his horses had won The Cheltenham Cup four seasons running. The proceeds had been split between The Church of England and various favourite charities and good causes, one of which was for, *The Lost Boys of Soho*. I lie to you not! They turned out to be a young struggling boy band from East Soho who were trying to make it onto the local indie-scene that he had somewhat unusually taken a fancy for, well at least its lead guitarist, who just happened to be gay and very beautiful.

Julian naturally thought we would both be going to the funeral. He'd gone and had his car, specially valeted in exited anticipation. I told him I was going by myself. There were lots of old and painful memories, I still hadn't processed from my earlier life, I told him, and I needed to be by myself. When I met him for a mid-week drink at a gay bar in town, he was rather huffy about it, but nevertheless respected my decision.

'Pity you won't be getting to see the real thing,' I could not help myself from saying, the next morning, before leaving for work. God, I could be such a bitch!

Callum was in the middle of a dreary round of night shifts. I asked Rory if he was free and whether or not he would like to come with me.

'Oh, Robbie,' he said, 'thanks for the kind offer, but you know how nervous I am with strangers. I'll simply clam up and I'll probably cramp your style.'

'Nonsense,' I told him, 'you're coming.'

He gave me one of his best smiles before saying, 'you can be so masterful at times.' I told him to sod-off!

We travelled down in Clara Two, taking the scenic route and avoiding the traffic and therefore clocking-up nearly five hours, instead of three. We arrived up at the house just before lunch. The funeral was scheduled for two in the afternoon. Ned and Hilary were standing at the imposing entrance to Henry's old place, greeting all the guests. There would be more people at the church.

'My God, old man,' said Ned, giving me one of his great bear hugs, 'but it's great to see you!' I returned the compliment. I introduced Rory as my best friend. Ned was Henry's only surviving relative and he had bequeathed the entire estate, along with his fortune to him.

'Believe it or not, I actually wanted to remain as a teacher. I don't really do all this grand lord of the manor stuff.'

He told me that Hilary had said to him one morning that he ought to build a gymnasium in the grounds, if he missed teaching so very much!

'Well done you,' I said turning to Hilary and giving her a fond hug.

'I dare say he'll get completely used to lording it up in say a month,' I said.

'I'd give it a fortnight,' said his eldest boy.

Whilst we were getting ready, Rory had gone all quiet.

'I don't know what I'm doing here. I don't know anyone. Do you think they'd mind if I just stayed back in my bedroom, until it's all over. You could always tell them I've had an attack of recurrent malaria, from my time in the tropics,' he said.

'You'll be fine.'

I told him not to worry and that it was Henry's day, he was the belle of the ball!

The large church, about the size of a small cathedral, was packed with standing room only for the late-comers. It was all high Anglican, indeed it was so high, it made the Pope appear as if he were a member of some Low Church institution! The bishop was very impressive, all in his full regalia. You would have thought they were burying royalty! There was a boys' choir singing in four part harmony, some rather wonderful passages from a rather impressive requiem. It was sublime! I could tell Rory was impressed. He himself was a Roman Catholic.

'My God,' he whispered to me, 'this lot puts our lot to shame.'

'Yes, and if you play your cards right you might even get to be screwed stupid by the bishop for afters. He's as queer as a fifties musical, or so I hear,' I said.

The biggest surprise came with all the people who wanted to get up and say something or read a favourite passage. Naturally, he had been a patron to the local art scene. It was the ordinary people however, who he had helped. There was a woman; she had been a single mum, stuck on benefits. He had helped her out and paid for her to go to college. He'd done it all in secret. He didn't want a fuss or anyone knowing about it. It really had been a question of not letting the right hand knowing what the left hand was up to. He had in fact been the only kind of Christian; I really had any time for. And to hell with all the bells and the smells and the silly pomp!

Back at the house, and after the first couple of glasses of vintage champagne, I could see that Rory was starting to relax and begin to enjoy himself. A man in rather simple morning attire, nothing in the least bit ostentatious about him, came across to talk to us. His face looked vaguely familiar. It was the bishop. He insisted that we call him George.

'I've known that old bugger for decades,' he began, 'he was like a best friend to everyone he met. It didn't matter what background they came from. My God, did you see all of those weeping servants, all sitting there in seats of honour right at the front of the church? Those were real tears, despite their jobs being completely safe. They adored him,' he said.

I was aware the place was also full of very cute looking young gentlemen, of both an aristocratic and queer persuasion. My hormones were calling out to me, as was a certain rather cheeky smile from a blond, blue-eyed young peer.

'Don't forget you're married,' said Rory who saw where I was looking.

'What, you mean, Julian?' I said, 'oh, I've completely forgotten about him. And might you dabble, George,' I said, 'seemed quite taken with you, I could tell? He even went and got you another glass of champers, and then got all embarrassed, when he realized he'd forgotten to get me one.' Rory began to blush and I started to laugh.

I managed to get a word or two with Ned, as the warm late June afternoon was passing into a balmy evening, of delicate twilight and dappled shadows, out along the coppices and out-houses. We walked for some time in silence, coming up to the extensive rows of greenhouses. I'd left Rory to get better acquainted with George.

'So then, how is everyone back in sleepy old Munford?' I said.

I already knew that Clarissa had retired. She had written to me only recently, promising to come up with Maddie during the summer. She had also said she thought the school was now in very safe hands with the new headmaster.

'I know what you really want to know, though you are strangely reluctant to say it, old man. You want to know how, Tyrone,' is doing don't you?'

'I can hardly bring myself to utter his name, without my wanting to burst into tears,' I said.

'He no longer works up at the school,' said Ned, 'he hasn't done so for quite some time now.'

I asked him if he knew what he was doing and where he had gone to work. There was another difficult silence between us.

'I'd heard rumours, but only rumours, that they had to let him go from his caretaking job.' I asked him why.

'Well, apparently he kept turning up drunk to work. And one day the pupils saw him puking up behind the bike sheds, and they reported him,' he said. 'I'm so sorry,' he said, 'he was such a nice young man. And you two just seemed so right for each other.'

I was trying to hold back the tears. He saw my struggle and gave me a hug. And after that we both walked slowly back to the house.

The cute young man I had seen earlier with the blond hair and blue eyes, blue eyes encased in a very distinctive pair of large glasses with white frames, came across to talk to me. He was rather nervous and self-conscious at first.

'God, I hope I'm not barging in or anything,' he said.

'No, not at all I'm glad of the company,' I said.

'You're not with anyone are you, like that chap I saw you with earlier on' he said.

'He's just a very good friend. I think he's trying to chat up the bishop at this moment, he prefers older men,' I said.

With this, we both laughed and started to relax in each

other's company.

'My name is, Richard Addlebrooks,' he said.

'Robbie Stebson,' I said.

We found ourselves shaking hands and smiling.

The servants kept coming round with wine. We asked for some beer, and five minutes later we were sinking our lips into a glorious pint of the local brew.

'I much prefer beer,' he said.

'Me too, 'I said.

He wanted to know all about me and what I happened to do for a living. And then I found myself talking to him for the next quarter of an hour, about my passion for English literature and my particular philosophy, as regards to teaching. He seemed really interested and kept stopping me to ask questions and needing further clarification. He told me he was twenty and a second year student at Cambridge, studying Law. He didn't like Cambridge.

'It's too much like Eton and I'm afraid once you've seen one Eton cock you've really seen them all,' he said. This made me laugh out loud.

'And then there is the Eton attitude, all entitlement and bloody arrogance. God I hate it! We get waited on hand and ruddy foot in halls of residence. They treat the staff like they were dirt. And do you know, at all the formal dinners, they have food fights and expect the catering staff to clean it all up afterwards. God, I hate them,' he said with some heat. He was rather delightful, when he became all flushed and animated. He told me that when he graduated, he eventually wanted to specialise in legal aid work representing women survivors of domestic violence. 'I think it's a crying shame what some women have to put up with, from abusive men. I want to help them in my own small way,' he said. I was impressed. Like me, he was a crazy visionary.

Rory came back over with George. We all sat together, in one of the smoking rooms, with its leaded lighted windows, chatting for a while. There was to be a string quartet in the library at nine in the evening. Rory asked us if we cared to join himself and George. We both declined. And then they walked off to their quartet.

'Would you like to go to bed with me?' he said.

'I'd absolutely love to,' I said, 'but not just yet. Let's have another drink or two. I'm really enjoying getting to know you.'

He told me I was sounding like, 'what's her name,' from *The King and I* and then for the next half hour we were both sharing with each other our complete and total delight in Hollywood musicals. Eventually, he put out his hand to me in a beckoning way and we left the proceedings and went up the long flight of stairs, with all its many oiled portraits festooned all over the walls, and on up to his bedroom.

In the half light of the little bedroom, we removed each other's ties and our cuff-links. And then we gently kissed. He removed his glasses and put them gently, on his bedside table. He really was lovely. We kissed again, sitting down on the bed. My hand was tentatively moving under his shirt, to feel the sudden delight of his naked belly. Worship and reverence were woven together, in the mellifluous embrace. I kissed his forehead, a strange thing to do, and then he rubbed his head against my chest. 'Oh God,' he said, 'I love this.'

'Me too,' I said. We both laughed. He seemed to fall into the shape of my hands. At last we kissed, long, hard and hot.

He produced a condom, from God knows where, and smiled at me. His meaning was obvious.

There was something so fluid and so natural to it all. I wanted him to keep the lamp on his bedside table on, so that every-so-often I could just look at him. I thought he was so very beautiful. And then in the honey afterglow of our love, he lay nestled in my arms whilst we shared a cigarette, chatting, laughing and pecking each other with our insistent kisses. We woke up in the early light of morning and made love again, before falling off into a much deeper sleep. It was nearly ten o'clock, when we finally stirred. And then just before lunch, everyone was leaving. I hugged Ned and Hilary before saying goodbye. I caught Richard at the entrance to the long driveway. He was being driven back up to London by his parents, who were also guests. We shook hands and smiled, knowing our paths would probably never cross again, but having enjoyed the all too brief interlude. Rory too had had his moment with George. For some time we were silent as we drove back up to Leeds; as if common speech would somehow disturb the memory.

17

It was the beginning of the school summer holidays. Our little house was reduced to a hushed silence. Callum was still in the middle of his stint of night shifts, so we moved quietly around the house until he got up, usually at four in the afternoon. I would often go and gently wake him at around this time with a mug of tea. Rory was mugging up for his hospital finals, keeping to his room, when he wasn't working. And so it felt like all my playmates were otherwise engaged. I would have liked to have got out of the house, but during the first few days of my holiday, it did nothing but rain. I occupied myself with lots of reading and listening to my records through my headphones.

I kept Rory going with snacks and mugs of coffee. He had a desk and a study lamp in his room. The place was filled with textbooks, screwed up bits of paper, a waste bin filled with discarded notes, ball pens and marker pens, all with their caps well chewed, endless ink bottles, diagrams of anatomy, graph paper filled with feeding times for children and a chart for some kind of complicated formula, for the giving of dialysis to sick children, under the age of ten. Most of the time, I left the muggers and the snorers to their own devices. And then one very wet morning, the phone rang. It was Ned.

'Hello there, old chap,' he began, 'with everything that was going on, I forgot to mention, the old fellow left you a little something in his Will.' That something was a collection of around three hundred records of classical music. They were mostly mono recordings from the fifties, and they were all on a quality budget label of the times.

'You might not want them,' said Ned. I told him, that as his uncle tended to have rather excellent taste, I probably would. He had also bequeathed me the hand-made pine cabinet they came in, together with a collection of musical criticism, which included the complete works of Sir Donald Tovey.

'I could dash up to Leeds with them if you like?' he said. And so a couple of days later, he pulled up outside the front door, in his uncle's 1934 Bentley, complete with the stash of records, cluttering up the back seat and all the neighbours twitching their net curtains, at the sight of such an unusual mode of transport! Rory came down to say hello, and a sleepy Callum, bare foot and in his pyjamas and on his way to bed, was eager to meet Ned. I had been friends with Ned long enough to know when he had something on his mind.

'There is a delightful little watering hole, just down the street, we can have lunch there and have a few jars of their best ale and I can even put you up for the night, unless you're needed back to attend to your royal duties,' I said.

'I was rather hoping you would suggest something of the kind, old man,' he said.

'My God, you can read me like a book.'

Sitting over our second pint of glorious ale in our local, he told me that Hilary had had a stonker of an idea.

'We've decided to turn the whole of the east wing of the house into a school for pupils with special needs. When I say special needs, I don't mean severe, but young folk who struggle with the traditional education set-up, the kind who end up getting excluded and that sort of thing. We'll have to set up bursaries and grants and all that kind of thing and it will all have to be properly vetted and costed. I want there to be lots of art, music, drama, sport and outdoor activities on the curriculum. We also thought that during the summer holidays, we could run residential weekends for other teachers, providing them with tools on how to teach and work with pupils with challenging behaviour,' he said.

'Have you any idea how you are going to realise all of this?' I said.

'Not a bloody clue,' he said.

'Well that's as good a place to start as any,' I said.

'I was wondering if from time to time I could use you in a sort of consultative role, I mean you have never been what they might call the run-of-the-mill, where teaching is concerned,' he said. I told him I would be happy to help out in any way I could.

I was feeling happy for him. Those records were more often than not from a cast of nobodies, but absolutely wonderful! There were lots of recordings from the fifties, mostly in mono. They happened to be utterly sublime and just the kind of recordings that Julian and his dinner-party set, would no doubt turn up their noses at. I thought about young Richard and him wanting to work with women who had suffered domestic abuse, Ned and his school for pupils with challenging behaviour and my wonderful collection of vintage records. I could not but help myself from comparing all of that, against the value system and judgements from Julian and his friends. And I was finding him and them, utterly wanting.

Callum's stint of night shifts came to an end. He was having a sticky patch with his boyfriend. They had fallen out again and weren't speaking. Meanwhile, my relationship with Julian, was hanging on a thread. He was playing host. He rarely cooked. The caterers had been in all afternoon, together with a florist, his cleaner, who he had paid extra to make his flat, even more immaculate than usual, and he'd even gone as far as to have a menu for his four guests, printed out in French. He was nervously pacing about the place.

'My God,' he said, 'those menus should have been back from the printers by now. I placed my order with them on Tuesday!' I reminded him that he had asked for them to be delivered on Saturday afternoon. It was now barely two o'clock.

'And give yourself an extra scrub when you're in the bathroom,' he said, 'you are looking particularly grubby today young man.' I was veritably drowning in vanilla! I wondered if his friends bothered to cook either. They all said they did, and handed round recipes of their supposed feats of gastronomy. I believe they got in the caterers, probably the same caterers, who laughed behind their backs while pocketing their money.

Julian had shelled out over two hundred pounds, for a three course meal, all carefully wrapped in tinfoil that only needed re-heating when the guests arrived, and over three hundred pounds between the various bottles of wine and whiskies. If we were all feeling a bit down, Rory, Callum and I would splash out on a posh meal in, complete with wine and whisky. I reckon we still had change between us from fifty pounds. To us, that was decadent behaviour. And so the guests arrived, the usual crowd of middle-class bores. They talked of politics and how Arthur Scargill, should be hung, drawn and quartered. They were all Tories; so much so, they made Margaret Thatcher seem like a Socialist. I decided to put the proverbial cat up in the pigeon loft, by asking the solicitor if he ever did any legal aid work.

'Oh, only when I have to,' he said in his blustery manner, 'but I try to avoid it as much as I can. I and my fellow partners, we're running a business, not some ruddy charity.' I asked him what his thoughts were about women stuck in relationships with men who were violent and abusive.

'Oh, I think they know exactly what they're getting into when they marry these brutes. They always come blubbing and wanting free legal advice, when they've caused the whole thing in the first place. Well they needn't bother coming to me for help,' he said.

'This lamb is particularly delicious this evening,' he then said turning to Julian who was preening himself with the complement.

'Yes,' I answered for him, 'I always think the caterers do such a fine job, especially with the lamb. They're real experts.' There was silence round the table.

'You must excuse me gentlemen, I'll leave you to your Tory nosh.'

I then got up and left the table, walked out of his flat and right out of his life. It was still quite early in the evening, so I took a bus into the city centre and was in time for last orders at one of our favourite gay bars in town. Rory and Callum were sitting over in the corner and I went across and joined them.

'I thought you were wining and dining tonight?' said Rory.

'Let me ask you both something. What has, Julian,' I said, 'his odious bunch of Tory friends and the Stewards and Tudors, all got in common?'

They both looked at me with blank faces.

'They're all history,' I said.

I was in the mood for dancing. So was Callum. Rory declined because he had work the next day, and still lots of revision after that.

'No rest for the wicked, girls,' he said, leaving us to our carouse.

It was a hot summer's night and the nightclub was full of cute young revellers. Callum and I were caught up in the moment, dancing like crazy and enjoying the site of all the young men, dancing bare to the waist and the heady smell of poppers and summer sweat, the most gorgeous odour in the whole damn world! I'd just been paid, so the pair us had been drinking far more than was good for us. We went upstairs to the upper room. The fever was on us both again, and soon we were hungrily kissing, and wanting each other.

'Oh God,' I said, coming up for air, 'not all this again!'

'Tell me to stop then and I will,' he said. I didn't want him to stop. At that moment, he seemed to me the most desirable young man, in the entire world. I wanted him like an ache and a strange primeval yearning that would not let me be.

18

Callum and I tried to be on our best behaviour, especially when Rory was around. There we would be at the breakfast table, almost as if butter wouldn't melt, but would find ourselves sniggering at something innocuous.

'God, you two are insufferable,' Rory would say and get up from the table in disgust.

And then Trevor insisted on inviting the three of us out for a meal at a rather nice French Restaurant on the outskirts of town. Rory thought Trevor had an agenda, Callum and I thought he was just being his usual kind and affable self. Rory knew him so much better than we did.

'I've been approached several times by the board of governors for a headship of an inner-city school in Liverpool. They're really struggling and are now threatened with closure, if they don't somehow get their act together, over the next academic year,' he said, taking a sip of his wine. 'They believe I'm the only person who can turn the place around. Their faith in me might well be miss-placed, but if that school fails then seven hundred kids from struggling family backgrounds, will all be displaced to other schools throughout Merseyside. I don't know if I can have that on my conscience. I received a phone call from one of the governors, a couple of days ago, and I finally accepted. So I will be leaving at the end of the next school term.'

We were saddened by the news and I wondered what

kind of headmaster might take his place. He said Phyllis had been acting deputy for the last eighteen months, since Hilda Musgrave had gone off on long term sick. He thought she was bound to get the post, and that the school was therefore in safe hands. I looked across at Rory, who was sitting in the half-light of the restaurant. His face said everything. I could tell he was devastated by the news. Trevor caught his look too.

'Come on, Rory,' he said, 'Liverpool is hardly a million miles away. We'll still be able to see each other,' he said. 'Yes of course,' said Rory, 'don't mind me, I'm just being silly.'

Two days later, Rory sat his hospital finals and a week after that he got the results. He had failed and would have to re-sit in the January. Callum and I tried showering him with hugs and presents, all to no avail. He would often keep to his room. We were unable to get him to come out with us on Saturday nights, onto the scene. He wouldn't even come out for a couple of pints to our local.

'I've got ten days holiday coming up,' he said to us one morning over breakfast, 'so I've decided to pop back down to Essex to see Mum. You two will have the place all to yourselves, without me getting in your way or cramping up your style. You can have each other as much as you like,' he said and then burst into tears. We were both unable to console him.

I would like to report that Callum and I were shamed into mending our ways, and that we were able to take some responsibility for there being so much on his mind, a contributory factor to his failing his finals. I was still on my summer school holidays, and Callum had a long weekend off work, before a ten day stretch. It was a sunny Friday in mid-August and we agreed to meet in the snug at our local, a little after nine that evening, when his shift finished. He came into the pub, having changed into a pair of jeans and a red T-shirt, which clung to him in all the right places. I wanted him, and I knew he wanted me.

'You know, all of this stuff between us, it's entirely ridiculous,' he said, sipping his gin and tonic.

'I completely agree,' I said. 'It must stop,' I said.

'But not tonight,' he said, 'let's go to bed together just one last time and then we'll call it quits.' And I felt helpless to resist. We stayed out until closing time, getting outrageously pissed, thus further fuelling the needy furnace of our desire.

We barely got through the front door, before we were hungrily kissing, biting and clawing and then chasing each other upstairs and into his bedroom. Our love making was intense, almost frightening and something that felt like it would never be abated. I was taking him, with my arms wrapped around his lithe torso. I felt his nipples, they were erect and hard. I knew he was utterly aroused, and his state of arousal, raised the heat of my own desire. He kept turning his head, and raising it from the pillow, for a desperate kiss.

We had intended going into town. We were both up and dressed. Callum cooked us breakfast. He also wanted to wash up. I was scanning the headlines and sipping the last of my coffee. The August morning sunshine was blazing through the small kitchen window. A sudden shaft of sunlight glanced across his features, catching the gold and red highlights in his hair. I put down my cup, got up and walked slowly towards him. He saw the lustful look in my eye. 'Not here, there's no curtain on the window, the whole neighbourhood will see us,' he said. I knew I was past caring. I came right up beside him, and he was squeezed up tight against the sink, his hands in the hot soapy water. I was nuzzling his neck. 'Will you get off, you bastard!' he said. He was angry with me. I started to undo the button on his jeans. He was struggling, but they fell quickly around his ankles. Seconds later, my own trousers were down. There was no lubricant needed by either of us. Nature supplied all that was necessary. But then, my cool reason and common-sense suddenly took over.

'Look, do you want me to stop?' I said.

'Just screw me, you crazy bastard,' he said.

It felt so very different from all the times I'd fucked him before. His prostate was a hard wall. His own pleasure was coming back to me, like bolts of lightning. It hurt, and yet I wanted it to. He was screaming, and so was I. After that, I did not know where either of us had gone or where we were. We certainly were not in a kitchen in Leeds. I wondered if we were even on this earth. Was this what death felt like! Sometime later, I was aware that we were both re-arranging ourselves. 'Let's leave all of this, and catch the bus into town,' he said, awakening me from a dream.

The following morning we tried to have breakfast, but ended up going back upstairs for more loving. Later in the day, we tried going for a walk, but could not wait to get back home and back upstairs. And so the whole weekend went on. We were hopeless addicts, junkies to love. Finally, exhausted and aching in every limb, we cuddled up together on the sofa in the front room, listening to Beethoven records and trying to raise our conversation above the carnal. And then we both realised, we must have missed several meals and that we were desperately hungry. Half an hour later, we were both tucking in to the largest set-meal Chinese takeaway on planet Earth!

A tearful Phyllis and Bob popped round on the Monday, to tell me that she had not got the job. It had gone to a complete outsider. And then whilst they were still there, Trevor came round, for he had just been given the devastating news. He said he was almost tempted to withdraw his resignation. Phyllis however, would not hear of it. I was going to phone Rory to tell him the sad developments. Callum said, 'leave him to enjoy his break with his mum. Bad news will always keep.'

It seemed strange, but since Phyllis had come round, our ardour had been completely cooled. We had stopped being hungry, desperate lovers. We were friends again, and friends that were part of a threesome of the very closest of friends. We all needed each other. Rory came back a few days later, full of apologies for his behaviour.

'I just get so jealous,' he said, 'I can't help it.' And we in our turn apologized to him. The three of us then decided we needed to treat ourselves with a meal at our favourite Italian restaurant and the opera. We were all the best of friends again. Things between the three of us remained good, through all of September and well into an October of vibrant autumn colours and hazy mornings, of dappled sunshine.

'Us three against the world,' we would say and we believed it. And then I had to go and spoil things, and nearly put our entire friendship in jeopardy by taking up with twenty-two-year-old Jason Sanders, the ferret in the woodpile.

19

Jason was twenty-two and was doing his student placement at our school. He taught English and was supervised by Phyllis. I didn't think much about him at first. It was as if he was on the edge of my awareness. He was quite good looking, but not strikingly so. I thought he might be gay and yet he possessed that almost arrogant self-assurance and sense of entitlement that made me wonder about both his sexual-orientation and his educational background. I decided he hadn't gone to a public school, but his cultured voice suggested either a grammar or a good independent. He had in fact gone to a church school in Harrogate, from where he hailed and still lived with his parents.

From time to time we had staff nights out. Twenty or so of us would gather at a favourite curry house and then go on somewhere for drinks afterwards. Trevor, who really hated these events, for they always felt so staged, nevertheless felt it was his duty to attend and help things along. Usually Trevor, Phyllis and I would end up chatting away to each other and leaving the rest to their own devices.

On one particular evening, just prior to the autumn half term, young Jason hung on assiduously, especially round me and I was unable to shake him off. We had ended up in a large pub, just behind Leeds Town Hall, where Rory, Callum and I often ended up after our classical concerts. It was a rather good turn-out that night, indeed we had taken over one large section of the pub. I had nipped to the gents, whilst Trevor was getting in the next round. Jason had followed me into the gents, and then he said, 'fancy a snog then?' and as he said it, he was beckoning across to the lock up. We went inside and locked the door behind us. He was a hungry little slut and he had suddenly aroused an equal passion in me, I didn't know was there. A week later, we were in a relationship, though nothing was to compare or indeed come anywhere near, that first feverish encounter. He was to be my last infatuation.

He was eager to move in. He had to take two buses up to the school every day from Harrogate and he found it such a bore! Rory and Callum were a bit suspicious of him at first. He turned on all of his considerable charm, which had very little effect on either of them. They loved me too much and saw that I was unhappy when he wasn't around. They agreed to let him become the other lodger. We were all innocent sheep that had unwittingly let a fox into the fold.

And then the first Saturday morning of the half term holidays, Callum wandered into the kitchen, munching on a bowl of cornflakes.

'I think we've got company,' he said.

I went into the front room where, I could see a very familiar looking car, pulling up outside the house. Moments later, two young men got out. They were both hooded up, for it was raining heavily and there was a strong autumn wind. They came up my little path and rang the doorbell. I went to answer it. One of the young men removed his hood and I was looking straight into the face and the lovely eyes of Tyrone.

'You look like you've just seen a ghost,' he said. We laughed and hugged.

'What a lovely surprise,' I said welcoming them both inside.

A few minutes later, we were all sat round the kitchen table drinking steaming mugs of coffee. I gathered quickly that the other young man, called Mark Kendal, was his boyfriend. I felt a touch of jealousy, but was also pleased that not only had he moved on, but that he now seemed to have turned his life around for the better. There was a look, so very fleeting, from Jason across the table to Tyrone; it was one of pure poison. I could tell that he hated his rival for my affections. Rory and Callum were curious and gracious.

Tyrone, who had never been able to keep any secrets about himself in the old days, was very forth-coming about his life since we had last seen each other, and was eager to fill me in on all that had happened to him, since the last time we had met.

'I'll not lie to you; my life was going to the dogs. I was turning up pissed to work every day and they had to let me go in the end. Things went from bad to worse, and then my doctor recommended that I see this guy in Manchester, who specialised in something called post-traumatic stress counselling. So off I toddled, to see, Edmund Bedford,' he said, 'this therapist in Manchester, in these creepy old rooms down a backstreet. At first I felt really awkward, but over the weeks I gradually relaxed and learned to trust him. I owe that man my ruddy life. Naturally, as you might expect, things got worse, a lot worse, before they started to get better. I took an overdose and then tried to slash my wrists. I spent six weeks on a psyche ward, four of them under a section of the mental health act. When they discharged me, I went back to see, Edmund,' he said, 'and one afternoon I completely broke down, cried like a baby, and I broke through.'

'God, you always were such a drama queen,' I said.

The flippancy of the remark was very different from the feeling behind it; I was trying not to show. It wasn't lost on Tyrone, who gave me a tearful smile. Everyone else round the table, felt uncomfortable. Then Tyrone and I started talking about something really trivial, relieving the tension. He had got himself a new job as a postman. He liked it but did not love it, or the early morning starts and being out in all weathers. He had met Mark, a fellow postman, who worked in the rural offices on the outskirts of Munford, at a staff night out.

'So what brings you both to these neck-of-the-woods?' I said.

'We've come to see this progressive rock band. They're really fab. They've played up and down Lancashire and we just had to see them again.

'They're gigging at a pub in town. They host lots of up and coming live bands, or so I'm told,' said Mark.

I thought he was lovely. He was rather fussy and a bit camp, but in a really endearing way. He was just a nice lad. They were putting up in a guesthouse nearby. The concert was for that evening. I had always loved progressive rock and I was curious as to any emerging new talent.

'I bet they'll be selling tickets at the door,' said Mark.

'Hay guys, I don't want to cramp your style,' I said.

They both assured me, that I was welcome to tag along. Rory, Callum and Jason would have preferred their teeth being pulled, than to attend a progressive rock concert, famous, emerging or otherwise. I decided to go.

The pub was situated down a back street, in Leeds town centre. The beer was all keg, and rather dreadful. The place was full of students. There were one or two young men, who certainly took my eye. As was usual, there were two other backing bands on before them. They were all noise, attitude and without talent. The decibels were blasting. They sounded kind of punk. I was glad when they finally left the make-do stage. The group we had come to see managed to play their set, with the volume level turned well down. The lead singer had a rather lovely and very distinctive voice. They were somewhat folkie, with lots of twelve-string guitars and recorders. I found them delightful.

The following day Rory, Callum, Tyrone, Mark and me, all sauntered into town, to a lovely pub and eatery we had discovered, some months before. It was one of the oldest pubs in West Yorkshire. They did a fabulous traditional Sunday lunch. Tyrone wasn't drinking as he would be driving. Jason always went to see his parents on Sundays. The Sunday dinner was a ritual in his family, he found difficult to get out of. I was glad he was not one of our gang.

There was not even so much, as the slightest of unpleasant atmospheres, between the four of us. We chatted, we laughed, we tried to out-camp each other, calling and referring to each other as 'she,' and 'what's she like?'

I was coming back out of the gents, and walking down the small corridor and back to the main section of the pub. Tyrone was coming in the other direction. He stopped and looked at me.

'Are you happy?' he said.

'Yeh, of course I'm happy,' I said.

He took hold of my hand and gently squeezed it. He told me that he still missed me and that there was scarcely a day, when he wasn't thinking about me.

We drove back up to the house and they both finally left, a little after four that overcast afternoon. And so we hugged and laughed and jollied them into the car, waving them off as the car chugged off up the street.

'I'll make us all some tea,' said Rory, as we came into the back room. I then felt overwhelmed with emotion. I sat myself down at the kitchen table and cried my heart out. Rory and Callum were cuddling me and trying to give me what comfort they could. And at that moment, how glad I was of their friendship!

'You've got to get him back. You two were meant to be together,' Callum said to me, when my tears had finally subsided. Rory agreed with him.

'How can I do that?' I said. I told them he was with Mark now.

'I couldn't do that to him, he's a really nice guy,' I said. Neither of them had any answers and we sipped our tea, as the evening shadows crept across the room. None of us were thinking or concerned about what it would do to Jason, if ever Tyrone and I got back together.

Jason always came back, around seven in the evening. I couldn't put on an act and the others told him, I just needed some time by myself. Again, I was grateful that they were able to distract him by suggesting that they all nipped down the road to our local, for a couple of hours. I said I would join them later, and this was able to appease him slightly. When they had gone, I put on some Elgar, and cried some more. By the time I joined them in our local, all my tears were spent and I was able to hide, to mask and to go on with the stupid performance, I happened to call my life.

Sex with Jason was a rather curious affair. At first I found

219

him so attractive and my hormones ruled over both my head and my heart. As we got further into the relationship I began to notice that it all felt like sex by numbers.

It was almost as if he was standing back, watching himself making love. He seemed to know every technique in the book and more besides. I craved for spontaneity.

I could set my watch by the ritualistic nature of our 'love making'. At half-past eleven, most evenings, he removed his pyjamas. By eleven thirty-two, he had removed mine. And then until a quarter to twelve, he would orally 'pleasure me.' He would say, usually at eleven forty, 'is that good?' I would lie to him that it was. At quarter to midnight, he would lay himself face down on the pillow expecting to be screwed. And I would perform, what felt like marital duties, my mind usually on other things, like whether or not it might be a good idea to introduce the notion of archetypes and symbolic emblems in the novels of Thomas Hardy, with my six form group. At the stroke of midnight, I rolled off him, and he would always get up to use the bathroom. By five past, we had turned away from each other, and went off to sleep.

We differed on most things. I loved Dylan Thomas and D.H. Lawrence; he loved T.S. Eliot and thought that James Joyce was not only the greatest novelist, but the greatest writer of all time. He thought Virginia Woolf's contribution to English letters was negligible, whereas I believed she was the most underestimated of writers, and the greatest of the school of Modernists.

I loved The Romantics, he adored The Realists. He loved all things atonal in the classical music department and for him Beethoven and Brahms, was for the birds! There was an all-Beethoven evening at Leeds Town Hall, by an ensemble playing original instruments. It sounded stripped-back and academic to me, Beethoven consigned to a museum. He was very much taken by it. Rory and Callum were of the same opinion as me.

One of my favourite novels was *Anna Karenina*. My copy of it, bought second-hand, many years previously, and translated about seventy years ago into English, before that, was a very tatty affair. I had read in one of the arts sections, from some Sunday newspaper or other, that there was a new translation. All the critics, as well as the academics, loved it. I went out and bought it. Jason was the first to read it. He thought it was a great improvement on the various older translations he had read. Callum and I then read it. We hated it!

'Whatever do you find to dislike about it?' said Jason.

'I find it is much too literal. They've somehow managed to kill off all of the book's lyricism and innate charm,' I said.

'I can see, you're all for paraphrase over the real thing,' he said.

'I don't rightly know,' I said, 'it just reads all wrong to me, that's all.'

Rory decided to read it, for he wanted to know what all the fuss was about. He hated it too.

'It reads like the telephone directory,' he said.

Callum and I laughed at this timely critical analysis of it. Jason hated losing the argument. He would fume away to himself for days.

'You all gang up on me,' he would say to me.

'Don't talk such nonsense,' I would say.

I often differed in my opinion with my older students. All of this made for a healthy debate in the classroom. Jason thought that students, of all ages, were simply there to be taught. His opinion was therefore the only opinion that mattered.

'They will get plenty of opportunity to vent their ideas, when they go into further education,' he said, one evening when the four of us were sitting in our local, over a drink.

'God, Jason,' said Callum, 'you're so narrow-minded.'

That in the beginning was the low level of things. We all remained friends, although sometimes the banter, got a little out of hand. Jason was clever in a calculating kind of way. He had worked out the sexual dynamics of our little household. He knew Rory was sweet on me, and he had worked out for himself, that although me and Callum were hardly lovers, we never-the-less enjoyed the occasional dabble. To Jason, they were a threat. He wanted them out and me all to himself.

There was one evening when Rory and Callum were working late shifts. Jason and I took ourselves onto the scene, and one of our favourite gay bars.

'You know those two have got it really cosy,' he said as we were sipping our beer.

'What do you mean?' I said.

He then seemed eager to change the subject.

'Oh, nothing,' he said.

He was smiling at me, and I was still more than a little infatuated with him. We ended up at the club, dancing away until two in the morning. And I was thinking life was rather wonderful. It was a bubble I wanted to live inside forever, even although the more sober thinking part of me, simply knew it couldn't last. And so we danced, wild, reckless, forgetful, sniffing our poppers and blowing our tin whistles and hooting and hollering with the rest of the revellers, quite the daring young things, with no thought for tomorrow.

We would all come together, for delightful mid-week meals

in, with wine and whisky, or the four of us would go out to our favourite Italian restaurant, maxing out our credit cards. We never bothered how much we spent. Jason did bother. He certainly was not prepared to pay for the excesses of the rest of us. He kept tabs.

'That's three bottles of red wine we've had already,' he would say to me. 'Do you really need, yet another bottle of wine?' he would say to Rory.

'I don't care if it is, and if I want to drink ten bottles of wine, I shall certainly do so, Jason,' Rory would say, thus shutting him up.

'You are so very trusting,' said Jason to me, one evening, when we were on our own. 'You think they respect you. They don't.

'That night, the other week, when you didn't get back until really late, because of the parents' evening, they forgot I was even in the house. There they both were, sharing a bottle of wine in, Rory's bedroom,' he said, 'the biggest bedroom in the house, I might add, and they were gossiping away and bitching about you. They take you for a mug and keep saying, what a cushy number it is, living under your roof.'

'Whatever you've heard, you've simply got the wrong end of the stick.'

I told him that Rory and Callum were my best friends. I said I thought they happened to be the best friends, I've ever had. They were like soul mates.

'Ok, have it your way. You just continue to bury your head in the sand, whilst they take you to the cleaners.'

'And just how, are they taking me to the cleaners? They pay their way,' I said.

'You should see all the times they both use the phone, when you're not around.'

He said that Rory was always on to the phone to his mum in Tilbury; sometimes he said he was on the phone for over an hour. He said that Callum was worse. He was always phoning Alastair, or phoning his mum in Saltaire'

'You phone your folks in Harrogate,' I said. 'Yes, but hardly ever,' he said. I tried to dismiss, all that Jason was saying. His poison was working in an insidious way, the slow drip, drip on my mind. I started finding myself standing back as an observer, with the other two. I was now looking for any sign, or the merest hint from anything they may be saying, or anything they may have done. And I was storing it all up, for future reference.

What Jason did not know, was how I had experienced treachery before, with my other friends, Matthew and David, and how bitter, was that realization. And maybe I told myself, I was giving them too much of the benefit of the doubt, because I didn't want to face the truth. Had they ever been friends at all, or just looking for a chance to get one over on me? I believe Jason was standing back and looking at the effect, all of his poison was having on me. I started to back-bite about them.

'God, I came down this morning for breakfast, and I couldn't find a single clean cup or bowl,' I said to Jason. He chose to remind me, that Callum had been entertaining Alastair, the previous evening.

'And you mean to tell me, they didn't even have the common curtesy to wash up after themselves?' he said.

'Yeh, I suppose so,' I said.

'And you had given him full run of the house, your house, whilst we had to slum it at the local,' he said.

224

'Do you know, you're right,' I said, finding myself getting angry with Callum, for the first time in my life.

'You really need to have it out with him. You need to nip it in the bud, put your foot down and, let him know who is boss,' said Jason. And then for the rest of the evening, he was buying me my favourite shorts and was the most affectionate and accommodating lover, in the bedroom afterwards.

And so I had words with Callum. We were all sitting round the tea table.

'Callum,' I said, 'I don't think it's really fare, when I allowed you and, Alastair,' I said, 'to have the place all to yourselves, for you not to wash up after yourselves.'

'*Allowed*,' he said.

He looked incredulous at what he had just heard and repeated, '*allowed.*'

'After all it is, Robbie's house,' said Jason, 'and in that sense, you are just a lodger here, indeed we all are. He could chuck us out at any moment, if he so chose.'

'Now wait a minute,' I said, 'I never meant to imply, any such thing. My God, you two are not lodgers, you're my best friends.'

'Well it seems to me,' said Rory, 'that you have a funny way of showing it. Callum, fancy a drink at the local? We'll leave these two to contrive their plots. We both know when we're not wanted.'

'Please, let's all just calm down. I apologize for anything I've said. Let's just forget it,' I said.

'There you are, giving into them as usual,' said Jason, 'stop being so ruddy spineless.'

And then it was Jason who got up and left the table, and a

few minutes later, we could all hear him leaving the house. I thought that things had blown over and everyone seemed to be civil, at least with each other. Then Jason spoke to me one evening, when they were both on late shifts.

'I can't take it anymore,' he said, 'I can't take all the lies, the deceit and the way they are just using you. And you just don't see it. Either they go or I go,' he said.

'Let's just sleep on it.' I said.

The following morning, the phone bill arrived. It was normally at most, forty pounds. It was for £273,40p.

'How the hell am I going to pay that?' I said. Everything Jason had said seemed to make a hideous kind of sense. They had been taking me for a ride. They must have been phoning away to their mothers, without any thought for the consequences. I felt the hot iron of treachery! That evening I confronted them both with the bill. They seemed as surprised as I was.

'Do you really think, we would run up a bill like that?' said Rory.

'Well, I didn't think you could do such a thing, and I thought you were my best mates,' I said.

I then found myself becoming tearful. Jason was by my side.

'You see what you've both reduced him to?' he said.

The following day was a Saturday. Callum and Rory had gone out by themselves, the night before. They told me they were both moving out. Rory had got a room, back in the nurse's home and Callum was moving back in with his mother. I didn't want them to leave.

'Look, we'll go through the figures again,' I said, 'there must be some explanation. I don't want to part like this.'

'You and, Jason,' said Rory, 'have made your position,

perfectly clear. We will not cramp your style any further.'

For the rest of the weekend, Rory and Callum kept to Rory's bedroom, coming down to the kitchen to make themselves snacks and cups of tea. It was usually Rory who came down, giving us both poisonous looks.

'Don't let them intimidate you,' said Jason, 'they know they've been found out and now they are trying to make it, as unpleasant as they can, before they leave.

20

Jason had finished his student placement and had passed it comfortably. He also had some annual leave, before returning to college up in Ripon. He was going through for a few days, to see his parents in Harrogate. His father would help him to move in the rest of his stuff. He gave me a passionate kiss, before he left. That was on the Monday morning, first thing. And then I went to school, my mind distracted with all that had gone on over the last forty-eight hours. When I finally came home, the house was empty; they'd gone. I sat myself down at the kitchen table, and wondered what I had done. I then burst into tears. I could not ever remember, feeling more completely wretched.

A mild October gave way to a blustery November, blowing the leaves off the trees, which now pointed angular branches up to a barren sky. Ravens and crows had taken over it seemed from the sparrows, finches and the friendly morning song of the blackbird. Nature was showing her bleakest face. The kids huddled in doorways and mooched about in the cloakrooms, during break and lunchtime, unable to venture outside because of the endless rain. Leaves blew up against the classroom windows and everything seemed, hard-edged and unyielding. I had lost my two best friends in the entire world, and I felt trapped, in a now loveless and hateful relationship with Jason. My own life felt as bitter and as ungiving, as the pitiless weather out of doors.

The sex between us became brutal. We were both servicing a biological need, nothing more. Any tenderness had gone. We argued and shouted at each other. Sometimes, I wondered if it would actually come to blows. And then one morning before he left for college, we had yet another blazing row. He got up from the table and punched me full in the face, busting my lip. He was all apologies.

'Just leave me alone,' I said, 'I'll see you tonight.'

After what he had done, he could not look at me across the table, over our evening meal. He went out to the pub. I was glad he was out of the house. I found myself marking my books for school, and feeling more irritated than usual at careless spelling mistakes and bad grammar. And I was writing in red pen, scathing and cutting remarks. Other teachers did this, not me. I felt a sense of shame, for taking it out on the kids like this. My God, I told myself, Shakespeare couldn't spell and Mark Twain always left it up to his publishers, to punctuate according to their taste.

The phone bill remained unpaid. I had received a reminder letter and now they were threatening to cut off the phone, unless the bill was paid in full, over the next seven days. On that Saturday morning, Jason went to use the phone. The line was completely dead.

'There must be a fault on the line or something,' he said to me as I looked up from my copy of the Saturday *Guardian*, a paper he called, *The Trotsky Gazette*. He read *The Times* which I called *The Sun* with posh words. I told him we had been cut off.

'But how on earth will I contact my folks?' he said.

'You'll have to use a public phone box my dear,' I said to him.

I decided later that day, to venture down to the nurses home

229

to see Rory and whether or not I could get him to see his way to paying something, towards the phone bill. My main reason for seeing him was that I missed him like crazy and I wanted to find some way of renewing our friendship, and starting to build bridges. I had to ask at the reception, which room he was in. He was down in the basement, with the water pipes overhead in the corridors. It smelt like an old laundry. The dank heat was almost unbearable. I knocked tentatively at his door.

'Oh, it's you,' he said, 'you better come in I suppose.'

His bed was strewn with textbooks. 'Make a space for yourself,' he said. He remained stony-faced.

'So what brings you from your love-nest,' he said. He was in the mood for biting irony.

'It's hardly that,' I said. 'We fight most of the time.'

'So why have you come?' he said.

He was drinking some coffee from his filter coffee machine. He didn't offer me any. I told him about the unpaid telephone bill and that; we had now been cut off. He laughed when I told him about the recent exchange over it with Jason, but it was a cold humour, a humour that enjoyed the meeting out of poetic justice.

'I suggest you ask for an itemised bill. No doubt you will be attending our little get-together at a certain favourite Italian restaurant, for Trevor?' he said.

'Yeh, I suppose so,' I said. He said when we went there, it was Trevor's night.

'So I want no argy-barging between the main course and the sweet course,' he said.

'You mean we will behave like the British and German soldiers on Christmas day, during World War One?' I said.

'That's right, strictly football. Now you really must excuse me, I still have loads of revision to do. If I don't pass my hospital finals this time, then I'm out of a job. So I would be grateful, if you must communicate with me, that you do so by letter. Not that I can guarantee that I will bother to answer your correspondence. Now, good day to you,' he said, getting up and opening the door. I felt I had no option but to leave.

I phoned up my telephone providers, who said they would send me out an itemized bill but to allow up to ten days, as I was no longer one of their customers. I was feeling sore and sad over my all too brief meeting with Rory. And I wondered how Callum was still feeling about it all. I wrote to him at his mother's house. He didn't grace my letter with a reply. Twelve days later, the itemized bill landed on the door mat. Jason was spending the weekend in Harrogate at his parents. Really, it was just as well.

He had run up a bill of £230 phoning Harrogate. Only £43 had been run up by Rory, Callum and me, for the entire quarter. There was the evidence. I had been duped and I had paid a much greater price than the actual phone bill. I had lost my closest friends. I phoned my providers back and was told that there would be a fifty pounds re-connection charge, added on to the bill, and a further thirty pounds that had been incurred, since the original bill had been sent out. That left a debit balance, just short of £354. When I returned from school that Monday evening, Jason was there. After our meal, I confronted him with the bill.

'I don't expect you to pay it, but you can get the hell out of my house and out of my life,' I said.

It was then all tears and apologies from him. He agreed to

231

pay the bill in full. He would borrow the money off his dad. When I came back from work on the Wednesday evening, Jason had cooked tea, something he never did. There was also a bulging brown envelope in the centre of the table, propped up by the teapot. I knew it was the money.

'My dad came all the way from Harrogate, post-haste with the dosh,' he said. He was looking expectant. I really believed that he actually thought we could somehow salvage things. I slowly finished my meal. I then opened the envelope and carefully counted the money inside. It was all there. I got up from the table, and put the money in my pocket.

'Thanks,' I said, 'now you can get out.' At first he stayed where he was, sitting at the table. He laughed and thought it was a fine joke. My face was hard.

'My God, you're serious?' he said.

'Never have I been more serious, about anything in my entire life,' I said. He then asked if he could stay until the end of the week.

'No, you can leave now and come back and pick the rest of your stuff up, at the end of the week. Quite frankly, I can no longer stand the sight of you.' I said. I reached into my pocket and handed him a five pound note.

'Here, get yourself the train back to Harrogate. They run until nine in the evening. Now, as I said, get out.'

He went upstairs and packed a few things into a hold-all and then left the house. When he was gone, I sat down at my writing desk in the front room and composed two letters, one to Rory and one to Callum, explaining all that had now taken place and asking for their forgiveness, for ever doubting them. I then took myself for a walk, just to clear my head. The autumn wind was blowing hard, nearly knocking me off my feet. It was not only bracing, but strangely soothing my frayed nerves.

As we approached December, the whole school was in a kind of mourning over Trevor's imminent departure. And then it was the last day of the school term. All the kids had got together to buy him a leaving present. He got up to thank everyone and had to sit right back down, because he had burst into tears. We all stood up to sing the school hymn, 'To Be a Pilgrim' I don't think anyone in that assembly hall, had a dry eye. The leaving do for the staff, had taken place a few days before. And then it was our final leave taking, at our favourite Italian restaurant in town.

The winds and the rain had gone, to be replaced by a frosty glow everywhere and bright blue morning skies, to somewhat cheer the heart. I could not get into any kind of festive spirit. I thought I would try to enjoy myself that evening as best I could, for the rest of Christmas did not hold out much hope. We met for Trevor's leaving do, our treat for him, a couple of days or so before Christmas, but a safe margin after all the office parties in town.

I thought I was well turned out, in my new suit, finally groomed and wearing some expensive after-shave. I caught the bus into town, at the end of the street. The cold air was bracing as I stepped off the bus and the festive heavens, were filled with stars. Being gay meant that when it was called for, you could always put on a good act, after all before you came out; all of life was just an act. I knew Rory and Callum would be doing the same.

We all wanted Trevor's last night with us, to be truly special. I arrived a little after seven. The other three were sipping their aperitifs, from tall elegant glasses. They welcomed me to the table. Trevor got up to give me one of his usual bear-hugs. The other two smiled their acknowledgments. They had found us a nice table, tucked into the corner, but still overlooking the main part of the restaurant. The subtle lighting, bathed us with its sepia rays. Callum's French cigarettes were on the table in a soft pack, his trade mark. His 1950s paraffin lighter, was by the side of the packet. Those cigarettes had been an all too familiar feature on the kitchen table, especially when the three of us would gather there for our evening coco before bed. The sight of them was a poignant reminder, of all that I had lost.

We showered Trevor with our gifts, between the starter and the main course. He was tearfully moved.

'It's OK,' I said, 'you can leave the speech till after coffee.'

'Well you know what I was like the last day of school, I doubt that I'll fare much better,' he said.

We all decided to have steak for the main course and we had ordered some rather good strong red wine. What we didn't know was that Trevor had had a quiet word with the staff, behind the bar. After we finished our first bottle of red, the waiter came back to the table with fresh glasses and no less than four bottles, already opened, of some special reserve. I took my first sip. It was like hundreds of tastes and sensations, were somehow taking place inside my mouth. It was the best wine I had as yet tasted. I'm now nearly sixty years of age, and have drank some very fine wine in my time, but few have compared with the wine I was drinking that night. We loved to talk about classical music. The pupils had clubbed together to buy him a box set of Beethoven.

'My God, they're absolutely bloody amazing,' he said. 'I bet they took Phyllis into their confidence, as to what to buy me for a leaving present. A silver mug with my name engraved on it would have done.'

'It certainly would have done, just for any common or garden headmaster, but not for you,' said Rory. The three of us agreed and raised the first of many toasts for him, throughout that night.

As the good wine began to really flow, we all relaxed and the banter between us all seemed just like it had always been. We were laughing at the anecdotes, being catty and supremely cutting, with camp undertones, without anyone taking the least offence. Again, just as it had been in the good old days.

'What's this I hear about you three falling out?' said Trevor, during the sweet course. He told us that Rory had mentioned something, a few weeks back.

'Oh, it was a tiff about nothing and something,' said Callum dismissively.

'Yes, everything is fine on the old homestead,' chimed in Rory. I simply smiled my agreement. God, I thought, we were not only acting, the three of us were giving him an Oscar winning performance!

After the meal, Trevor was getting a taxi and going home by himself. He and Rory would be spending, Boxing Day together. Trevor had family commitments the following day. Before leaving the restaurant, we hugged and kissed and waved him on his way, in the taxi. The three of us stood in the street, looking and feeling awkward. I knew the other two would be off to a cosy jazz club we had discovered some months ago. It was down a back street off the town centre. They served drinks until late. I knew if I chose to join them, they would not have stopped me.

I also knew that they didn't want me there. And so I quickly made my excuses.

'You must forgive me,' I said, 'I'd like to join you, but I'm absolutely wacked.'

As they were walking off together down the street, I wished them both a merry Christmas. They turned round to look at me, smiled but did not return the felicitation. That really hurt. I knew I could have gone back to Munford to spend Christmas with the family, but that had its own problems. Instead, I got lots of food in from one of the better supermarkets and a pile of booze, to drown my sorrows.

Christmas Eve was a day of crisp fine weather. I decided that afternoon to take myself for a bracing walk up to the park. It was a good hour's walk to get there. During the summer months, it was filled with people. Today, it was deserted. I walked myself down to the water, watching white birds skimming off the middle of the lake, before taking flight. This wintery scene somehow added to my overall sense of desolation. Even the café by the lakeside, was closed, its shutters all boarded up and batted down, everything moth-balled and under-wraps, until the beginning of spring.

I could have gone out into town that night and onto the scene. I didn't fancy all the crowds and needing to wait for hours, for a taxi back home and having to pay double fare. Instead, I decided to wander myself down to the local.

I usually went into the back bar, especially with Rory and Callum. I found myself a corner seat up by the window in the main bar. It was early evening and the place gradually began to fill up. Strangely, although it was our local, the three of us had kept ourselves to ourselves. So we had never really mixed with the locals. Sitting there in the main bar, they all seemed like strangers. I knew one or two of them by sight, but not enough to strike up a conversation with.

A young lad was in with his mum, several of her women friends, rather loud, and he was enjoying his first legal pint of lager. It was his eighteenth birthday. There was a group of his other friends, mostly boys of his own age, rather boisterous. They kept going off to play darts. He took my fancy for he was gorgeously rough-looking, with the eyes and the manner of a local slut.

I believed he was no innocent, despite the coy looks he kept giving to his mum and her friends. He turned around and caught my casual glance. He smiled at me mischievously, and I thought to myself that maybe it wasn't going to be, such a lonely Christmas after all. There was a council estate a little way up the road from where I lived. I often walked through the estate and noticed many a young lad, rough and friendly. They came down to use the shops, on the main shopping precinct. The people from our end, were on speaking terms with them, but many of the terrace houses where I lived, were owner occupied or private rental, whereas all the houses on the estate, were council properties. It was a case of tuppence –half-penny looking down on tuppence.

I went to the gents, and I happened to notice that the back room had been used for the actual birthday do. There was bunting all over the place, celebrating his birthday. I also heard one of his friends calling him Wayne. He had bits of party-poppers in his hair, and someone had swathed him in Christmas tinsel, which he wore like a priceless mink shawl. He was very animated. The more he drank the more outrageous and camp he became.

I gathered that his mum and everyone else knew he was gay. No-one it seemed gave a damn. And then his friends, who all looked straight, kept hugging him and ruffling his hair, whilst he laughed and was almost, falling about giggling with evident happiness. For a moment, it seemed like everything was reduced into slow motion, and I was watching those friends, laughing with him and hugging him. It made me think about my own friends and how close, we had once been. I was feeling tearful. I quickly got up and left the pub.

'Yes, don't worry I'll get a taxi there and back,' I had heard Rory saying to Callum, when we were in the restaurant. And Callum saying,

'Mum always has the meal on the table by twelve o'clock,' Callum had replied to him. I gathered from this, that Rory would be spending Christmas day, with Callum and his mum. I was feeling like the kid in the playground, without any friends.

And so Christmas morning arrived, overcast and dull. The whole street seemed deserted. I knew my neighbours from either side were away for Christmas, visiting relatives. It meant I could play my music as loud as ever I wanted. I was feeling like a bruised and battered cub, and all I could think about was that I needed to nurse my wounds. Plenty of self-care was required. I couldn't be bothered watching television. I played rock, classical and jazz records, belting it out through the speakers. I knew I could spend the day getting wasted with booze, but I also knew that this would simply make me feel really depressed. I decided to limit my drinking to a bottle of red wine, with my Christmas day dinner. I picked out *David Copperfield* to read. It was a very dog-eared paperback edition. And then with some Brahms on the turntable, I settled myself down for the rest of the day.

When I finally went to bed that night, a little before twelve, I was still feeling sad, but sane. I could manage this. I could get through it. It was not going to destroy me. And yet I thought my life would never be as happy again. The last year, sharing a house with Rory and Callum had been like the pauper boy who had been allowed to be king for but a day.

21

In the early January of 1986, a fortnight later and having marked up my twenty-fifth birthday, I returned to school and to a new headmaster, called Eric Byfield. He hailed from Sydney, Australia. He was around fifty-years-old, of diminutive stature and spoke with a rather high-pitched voice. Most of his working life he had worked in an Australian bank. He had gravitated into teaching, towards the latter end of his thirties and had built up a reputation for getting schools to work, well inside their allotted budgets. Our school was always considerably above its budget.

They also appointed a new deputy. He was a thirty-year-old graduate from St Andrews. His name was Malcolm Stables. He was obsequious and sycophantic in the extreme, hurrying around the place with quite a lot of steam and bluster, following Mr Bayfield's orders and his cursory whims, with something of a scorched backside! He was a figure of fun from the first. Both staff and pupils were rather intimidated by Mr Byfield.

The school had always been about broadening the pupils' education. This included lots of school trips out to industry, historical sites of interest, the theatre, art galleries and exhibitions. There was a film society and a photographic club, all ran as extra-curricular activities. The staff gave their out-of-hours services for free, but these societies were heavily subsidised. They were amongst the first luxuries to be targeted.

'We are not a public school,' he said at a staff meeting, with his high-pitched voice, 'we really cannot afford these things.'

Although we were not to lose music and drama, these subjects were cut back drastically. He also cast a withering eye over the general curriculum, deciding that more room needed to be given to core subjects. Not only art but the humanities subjects in general, went through something of a make-over. What was now offered became much more traditional and conservative.

'The pupils are here to learn, not to indulge their interests.'

He also opted for the syllabuses, where projects and continual assessment work, were kept to the absolute minimum. He encouraged cramming, where all the teacher's efforts were to be focused on the final exams.

The result rates had always been good. The new head thought we could do a lot better, especially by cutting out the 'frivolities'. It began to feel like an exam factory. All the staff felt disgruntled by these sudden changes, and the various unions were involved. He simply rode rough-shod over them.

'If you are displeased with the present management style, you know where the door is,' he would say in his high-pitched voice. 'It will not affect your references from me. I want a staff that are behind me and fully committed to my new methods, or really what is the point?'

I had always loved my teaching and especially since moving to Leeds a year before. Now it became drudgery. The pupils hated it also. All of their creativity had gone. All of their spontaneous curiosity was gone too. And how I missed their laughter! No one laughed, no one smiled, and all heads were too busy faced downwards over their work. I felt reduced to ticking boxes, churning out the great works of English literature and the glories of the English language to a pattern, a set and rigid formula.

He was such a busy fellow, looking out for minor infractions to the rules. He lived his life, strictly by the rule book, without exception. He was all for the letter as opposed to the spirit of the law. He had decided to set a whole group of tests, in all subjects, for all age groups. He wanted to really know, what level of attainment the pupils were really at. The pupils in all subjects, of all ages, performed really badly. This served as proof to him that his methods needed to be brought in as quickly as possible, to stop the rot.

He would pace up and down the school corridors with his quick little steps, frowning at pupils as he went. He began to bring his various gripes, which were many, to the morning assembly. One morning after the hymn he stood up to address the school.

'Gum, yes gum,' he said, standing up, after the morning hymn. 'I find it everywhere I go,' he went on to say, 'and see pupils, especially boys, indulging in this disgusting habit! And what do they do when they have finished chewing the wretched stuff? I'll tell you what they do, they spit it out! During the weekend I'm having every school pavement and surface cleaned of all gum. If anyone is found chewing the stuff in this school, that pupil will be suspended after a sound thrashing. Do I make myself clear? I will not tolerate such behaviour in my school.'

And then at one assembly, he talked about the graffiti, behind the bike sheds. Most of this was fairly lurid stuff. He said the wall would be cleared of all graffiti and anyone discovered in the act of defacing that wall, or any wall in the school buildings, would be instantly expelled.

He had a phrase for the telling off of pupils. 'They have been counselled,' he would say. He would also instruct staff that such and such a pupil needed to be 'counselled'. He was also rather keen on 'counselling' the staff, usually from the humanities. He was also fond of standing outside a classroom, looking in through the small glass section in the door, whilst a class was in session. He would do this with all classes.

Some of the pupils were rather alarmed by it. They would turn to look at him with his staring eyes. He would gesture to them to concentrate on the teacher and the lesson. He often did it to my classes. One day I grew tired of it, and went to the door and invited him in. He had no option, but to come in. He was unrehearsed, so had nothing to say. He felt like a fool. He was red in the face, with ill-suppressed rage. I was severely 'counselled' by him, before the end of the day for my, fractious and insubordinate behaviour. I had started to fight back. Phyllis had simply refused to suddenly set a further series of tests for her tenth grade pupils in the middle set.

'I'm sorry, headmaster,' she said, 'but they have already been through one set of tests this term, all of which I regarded as completely unnecessary. I shall not put them through any more trauma.' By the end of the day, she found herself suspended on the charge of insubordination. We all became fearful of not only our jobs, but our entire teaching careers, which this odious man could ruin at a stroke.

It was the kids themselves who came to the rescue. Kids are the most natural of comics and would-be-clowns. They began to poke fun at him, though never to his face. They would mince around the playground with his quick, little walk, and older boys would parody his high-pitched voice saying, 'Gum, yes gum, I wish to discuss gum.' And crowds of kids during playtime were in fits of giggles. Laugher had returned to the school corridors, through delightful subversion. The kids had set us free.

He started avoiding assembly. I believe he thought, all the kids were laughing at him, behind ever so obedient blank and submissive faces. And then he went on sick leave, which became long term sick. He was off sick for the whole of the following month. He returned for a couple of weeks, and then was off sick for the remainder of the term. He tendered his formal resignation whilst off sick.

Phyllis was placed in as acting head. By the beginning of the new term, the post was made permanent.

22

That winter seemed to go on forever. It felt like everywhere I tried to turn, I could find no comfort. There had been a mad man at work, my best friends were no longer talking to me, and if I chose to think about, Tyrone, I felt a deep sorrow no words of any kind of self-talk, could mend. The house seemed like a crazy warren, much too big for one person. It was a lonely and desolate place, in need of Rory's and Callum's bitchy chatter and outrageous laughter! Even the things that usually caused me pleasure, such as my music, gave me little joy. I would often go to bed early and cry myself to sleep. And even my fitful slumbers, offered but scant relief. Now that Phyllis was safely in place as our new head, I felt able to concentrate, on my most immediate concern. I wanted my friends back, here living in the house with me. I wrote what seemed like endless letters to them both. There was never any reply.

Towards the end of March, there was a sudden cold snap, bringing with it a hard frost and the last flurry of snow. And then the snow was washed away by the early April showers. The frost began to soften and just occasionally, through the still foreboding clouds, the sun would show her face. I ventured out one early afternoon, during the Easter holidays, and took myself back up to the park. It was now full of people, and all the shops and pubs were open along the road leading up to the park.

There were still one or two places that were treacherous underfoot, with the residual frost. The swans were gliding peacefully out on the lake, and children with their parents were throwing pieces of stale bread to them. I turned much deeper into the park, where the by-ways and rustic paths were not so well-kept and the landscape was less cultivated. And down in the lower fields, it was then that I saw them.

The bluebells were out, their fragile heads dancing in the April breeze. They were there, wherever I chose to turn my gaze. And from behind a cloud the sun came out, caressing them with the favour of her gaze. The sight shivered and shook through me, like turning on the very quick of me, out of death and back to life. The sudden strangeness of new life, caused me to cry, but the tears that streamed down my cheeks, were surely the healing tears of better days ahead and an end, to all my sufferings. And so I gathered up hope, like a precious garland of wild flowers, as I wandered back out of the park and wended my way home. And when I arrived home, the afternoon post had already been. There was a letter on the mat, and I could tell by the handwriting, it was from Rory.

He wanted to have a meeting. He suggested that we meet in a pub in town, which was fairly neutral territory. He would be in the snug, at the front of the pub a little after eight, that Thursday evening. He had said in his letter, not to get my expectations up. He said it was a meeting to help clear the air, nothing more. And yet despite this, I still dared to feel hopeful. I turned up to the pub, about half an hour before. I needed some beer inside me first. Rory wandered in at about ten past eight. He wouldn't let me buy him a drink.

'No,' he said, 'I'll get my own and I suggest we buy our own drinks.'

This part of the pub was empty, apart from our selves. I ventured to ask him how he was.

'Middling,' he said. 'I managed to pass my hospital finals, but then if I hadn't we really wouldn't be having this conversation, because I would be back living with, my mother, in Tilbury.'

'I'm glad you've passed, I really am,' I said.

'Why are you glad?' he said, 'I mean what do me or, Callum,' he said, 'actually mean to you? All you are bothered about is getting your end away, and to hell with everyone else.'

'I'm sorry if that's how it feels. I'm glad; of course I'm glad, because I care about you as a friend. I care about you both,' I said.

'As I seem to remember saying back in November, you have a very funny way of showing it,' he said.

'I was blinded, silly and stupid. I'm really sorry for all that happened,' I said.

'You had already made up your mind, thinking that we would trick you and run up a phone bill like that. There was no discussion, no usual conferences around the kitchen table

'As far as you were concerned, we were both guilty as charged.'

I hung my head, unable to answer him, for everything he said was true.

'And as for Callum,' he said, 'I can't even begin to tell you how hurt he feels. It is that word; *allow* that really sticks in his craw.

'Oh, and he said to tell you, not to bother sending him

letters. He hasn't read them, he won't read them. They've all been shredded.'

Things seemed pretty hopeless from that initial meeting. There was no forgiveness in sight.

'Well, I suppose that's it,' I said before he left the pub.

'No, I think we should meet again,' he said, surprising me as he was about to leave the pub. 'I'll phone you when I feel ready to talk. But don't keep on pestering me with letters,' he said and then he left.

I had lots of things to distract me at school as it was coming up to exam season. My O-Level and CSE groups were well revised. They had been working hard and I was giving them lots of pointers on their revision. For English Language, we were doing lots of timed passed papers to get them used to actually sitting in a classroom, under exam conditions.

'Look guys, there really is no way of getting round this, I know it's scary. All you can do is your best.'

Phyllis was pouring the sweet balm of her encouragement over us in school assemblies. The hymn, 'Lord of all Hopefulness, Lord of all joy' seemed to me and I think the kids, particularly meaningful and somewhat poignant, at this time.

I would wander myself down to the scene, usually to one of the rougher gay bars, because I knew that this was Rory's least favourite gay pub. One night I happened to get chatting, to a very rough looking lad called Darren. He was a hospital porter from Leeds General Infirmary. We talked and smoked cheap cigarettes, from the pub vending machine. He wanted me to come back with him. I was working the next day, so he would have to come back with me.

'I'll drive you to work tomorrow if you like,' I said. He

smiled. The deal was done.

He was something of a wanton, unwashed, slut, very much from the wrong end of town. He suited the general tone of my mood. I took him fairly quickly. He moaned a lot. It irritated me. I remember removing his grubby once white socks, only to reveal filthy feet. Even I was finding his complete lack of any kind of personal hygiene, difficult to cope with. And yet, he was affectionate enough and cuddled himself into me afterwards. The rank smell of him, however, woke me before the alarm went off. I was rather glad when I let him out of my car the next morning, and drove myself up to school. The car still stank of him when I left for home, later that day. The infernal itch had been scratched, nothing more.

One Saturday in early June, the rain was bouncing off the pavements, outside the house. Callum had left his umbrella in the hat stand in the hall. He tended to use it as a fashion accessory, as opposed to stopping himself from getting wet. But then it was an outlandish scarlet! Though the bus stop was only, a mere fifty yards from the house, I would be utterly drenched before I got there. So I knew I had to either use his umbrella or, remain indoors. Before leaving the house, I picked it up. It still smelt of his aftershave. It caused a lump in my throat.

I decided to have a bar snack and a few pints in a real ale pub in town, and sit and read *The Guardian*. The previous evening, I had endured one of my stand-off, stony-faced meetings with Rory, in our local. We were still buying our own drinks. It was like talking to a stranger. This pub was a popular haunt for Rory, Callum and me. It was the only place where Callum would drink beer, as opposed to his inevitable gin and tonic. In those days, it usually had about fourteen bitters, ten milds, one or two porters, a couple of winter brews, a real cider and a delightful selection of single malts.

The ceilings in both bars were high. The smoke from our cigarettes drifted upwards, gathering and hovering a few yards above our heads, and somehow adding to the atmosphere of the place. The pub itself was not very old, and yet with its bare wooden floors and most basic interior, it felt like it had been there for time out of mind. We had all loved the place. I went into the bar on my left, on entering the pub. I walked up to the bar and ordered myself a pint. The place was nearly empty, as it was not quite twelve. There was a young man, reading a broadsheet newspaper. He looked up. It was Callum. I went across to him.

'Are you in the habit of taking, what does not belong to you?' he said.

I knew he was referring to the umbrella. I handed it to him.

'Thank you,' he said.

'So then, how are you doing?' I said, sitting down beside him.

'I don't wish to talk to you, so I'm afraid if you don't leave, I'll be forced to do so, which would be rather a shame as I've just started my pint,' he said.

'It's OK, I wouldn't want to deprive you of your pint,' I said. I got up and walked myself into the other bar. Somehow, this seemed to hurt me even more than my all too formal meetings with Rory, over the last six weeks. I tried to distract myself, as best I could by reading my newspaper. I was well into the arts section, when Callum walked in. He came across to me.

'Can I join you?' he said.

'Nothing would give me greater pleasure,' I said.

I could not hold back a very tearful smile.

He placed a soft packet of his French cigarettes on the table. 'Go on take one,' he said.

He lit it for me with his vintage lighter. We talked. Small talk had never been part of our conversation. It wasn't now. We chose, however, to keep to safer subjects at first. I had not spoken about Eric Byfield, the crazed Australian headmaster with Rory. Any kind of levity, would have felt awkward. I now did so with Callum. I loved to see him giggling and doing his best to not choke over his pint. He went up to the bar. 'Same again?' he said, 'or something else?' The action was not lost on me.

'I'll have a pint of something really strong,' I said.

'Make that two,' said Callum, 'and two beef sandwiches please.' He then came back with our pints and he was smiling.

'God, I've missed you,' I said.

'And I've missed you, you daft bugger,' he said. We both laughed nervously.

I told him about my frosty meetings with Rory.

'Good old, Rory,' he said. He laughed at my tale.

'Anyway,' he said, 'I'll *allow* you an audience for the rest of the afternoon.' I told him jokingly to sod-off. We were both in fits of laughter. We got rather wasted that afternoon, with countless pints of the good ale, and rather too many shots, of best single malt. The ashtray in front of us on the table was full of our spent tab-ends.

'God, I'd so love to go to bed with you,' I said. He became tearful.

'Sorry, have I said something I shouldn't?' I said.

'You really hurt me you know,' he said.

'Sorry, I'll try to be more gentle,' I said. He laughed, though tearfully.

'No, Robbie,' he said, 'I don't mean that. I don't care how rough and ready you are in the bedroom or over the kitchen sink, for that matter. I mean all of that stuff, with that dreadful, Jason,' he said. 'What on earth did you ever see in him?'

'Looking back at it all, I really haven't the foggiest idea,' I said.

When we finally left the pub, quite a while later, the rain was still hammering down all along the street. We shared his umbrella, rushing for a bus. I loved the way, he kind of lent against me, as we stood at the bus stop. There was no one else there.

'Ah, the old homestead,' he said, entering the front door.

We went upstairs to make love, which seemed for us both, the only logical way to end the conversation. It was ungentle but strangely tender. He was wearing a new scent, it kind of added to the natural musk of him. Our kisses were hungry. I was biting his shoulders with my desire, whilst he cut his nails all along my naked back. He faced me and I took him totally and completely. Afterwards, he cried in my arms. And I just held him and kissed the top of his head, telling him I was so very, very sorry. Recovering himself, we made love once more, caught up in the wonder of naked discovery and a friendship that would now endure. This time, when we had finished, we shared a cigarette. This had always been the way we had finished our love-making.

'So then,' I said, 'am I forgiven?'

He burst out laughing and we were both in complete and uncontrollable hysterics, there on the bed!

It was late on the Sunday afternoon, when there was a loud knock on the door. It was Callum and Rory. They burst into the house, carrying a hold-all each. 'We'll sort out the rest of our stuff, later in the week,' said a grinning Callum. And there the three of us were, standing in the hall, kissing, cuddling, weeping and whooping our joy, all kind of crazy and all kind of nice!

'Have you eaten yet?' said Rory. I told him I hadn't, and that I was strangely famished.

'Good,' he said, 'let's go to a certain favourite Italian restaurant for tea, and it's my treat,' he said.

I had just been paid, and they fortunately still had twelve bottles of the very special full-bodied red wine, we had drunk, at Trevor's leaving do. I asked them to put a couple of bottles of it, onto a separate bill. It felt like the best forty pounds I'd ever spent! And there we all were, sitting at one of our favourite tables. We ate, we drank, we smoked, we chatted and we laughed, all wanting to tell the others all that had happened, since the last time we had met. It was Callum who found the appropriate phrase, with which to describe Jason. He said he was the ferret in the woodpile. Before the sweet course, Rory stood up and made a formal toast.

'To friendship,' he said. Callum and I raised our glasses and hollered out our responses. It was really not until a few days later, when they had moved all of their stuff back in, that it felt like they were truly home. It was late evening, just before bedtime. I had been marking project and continuous assessment work for my CSE pupils. I joined the other two at the kitchen table, for coco and a last cigarette, before bedtime, with Callum and the gentle murmur of our voices. It was this I had missed, most of all.

'My God,' I said, 'you are really, really back.' The other two laughed, ruffled my hair and gave me a hug.

It was the beginning of the school summer holidays. Rory and Callum were both doing a spell of nights. I was feeling at a bit of a lose end, so I decided one evening, to take myself across to Manchester and the delights of Canal Street. It was mid-week, a glorious evening in late July and it was full of revellers. I was sitting overlooking the canal with a bottle of beer; someone sat themselves down opposite me.

'Hello there stranger,' he said. It was Mark, Tyrone's, boyfriend.

'Hello,' I said, delighted to see him.

'So where's the other half?' I said.

'I suppose you mean, Tyrone?' he said.

'Yes, I do,' I said.

'Well I really don't know. He's probably flirting away like crazy in The Manhattan Bar, in sleepy old Munford,' he said.

'Are you two still together?' I said.

'No, not anymore,' he said. 'Don't get me wrong, we're still the very best of friends. But it all just kind of fizzled out between us, after about four months.'

'I don't suppose he's with anyone at the moment?' I said to him.

'Well, I saw him about six weeks ago, and he was single then. But he does rather like to screw around a bit,' he said. 'Still, I think he would drop whoever he was with for you. He's nuts about you.'

'How do you know?' I said.

'He never stops going on about you, that's why.'

I soon realized why they had ended up going their separate

254

ways. They were not really each other's type. Mark was out with his most recent boyfriend. He introduced us and brought him over to the table. Anthony was black, about thirty five, very manly and muscular. I wondered if he spent most of his time, working out in a gym. I thought to myself, with a wry smile, that Rory would not be averse to a tussle with him between the sheets!

'And how are your housemates, Rory and Callum?' said Mark. I told him they were both doing fine.

'You're not still with that other guy are you, whose name I can't seem to even remember?' he said.

'No, we finished ages ago,' I said.

'Thank God for that, he gave me and, Tyrone, the creeps.'

'He used to give me the creeps,' I said.

They both laughed at this. Mark also seemed to think, I'd probably only ever ended up going out with him in the first place, to somehow spite my face, because I was no longer with Tyrone. I thought it was a strange kind of logic, though it made me wonder whether there was perhaps, more than a grain of truth, in what he had said.

They both wandered off after that, leaving me to my beer and my thoughts. I went to one of the nightclubs, though I wasn't in the mood for dancing. I enjoyed the sight of all those gorgeous looking young men, hot and sweaty, and semi-naked, gyrating across the dance floor. And all that music, seemed to set my soul on fire with its insistent, primeval beat. This was the land of gay. This was their hour. This brazen celebration of heady youth, and all that it meant to be young! Church, Cathedral and sacred space, were all summed up there and all were supplicants, at the pagan alter of gay desire, the ecstasy of this strange trespass!

Trevor was visiting for a few days. I decided it was best to keep my thoughts on hold as regards to Tyrone, until he went back to Liverpool. I also thought it would be better not to make any big thing, about Eric Byfield. I knew he would want to somehow take the blame for it all. 'If I hadn't left, none of this would have happened.' He would say. I warned the others, not to mention it. Rory had cooked a sumptuous four course meal at home. Callum had gone to get the flowers; I had nipped out for the wine. There was plenty to chat and laugh about, without bringing Eric Byfield into the conversation.

Alastair joined us as well. And later that night, Rory went to bed with Trevor and Callum, went to bed with Alastair. I stayed up until the small hours, listening through my headphones to some Mahler; it somehow suited my altogether lugubrious mood. Trevor, being lovely Trevor, was unable to leave the three of us empty-handed. He had departed baring gifts. For Rory, he had bought him some hallmark silver cuff-links. For Callum, he had bought some of his favourite aftershave. For me, he had managed to get hold of a copy of the altogether wonderful mono recording, of some vintage Elgar.

There was another kitchen table conference. It was about me. I had told them about bumping into Mark, Tyrone's ex, on Canal Street. 'You need to go to Munford and bring him back here to live,' said Rory.

'I agree,' said Callum.

'So you want me to go all the way back over to Munford, on a wild goose-chase I might add, to ask, Tyrone,' I said, ' to drop everything and come back here to live?'

'That about sums it up,' said Rory. They were both smiling.

'I just couldn't bear it if he went and turned me down again,' I said.

'So you are going to spend the rest of your life doubting and probably worrying yourself, into an early grave?' said Rory.

'Look guys, I know you mean well, but I've really got to think about this,' I said. I came down to breakfast the next morning. 'I'll phone, Mum,' I said, 'to tell her that I'm coming up for a few days.' Rory and Callum chinked their mugs of coffee together, smiled at each other and said, 'Job done!' And then the three of us burst out laughing.

I was sitting in The Manhattan Bar the following evening, hoping that Tyrone would show up and yet nervous as hell, just in case he actually did. The place seemed smaller somehow, as did the whole of Munford. I had outgrown it. Nevertheless, the bar still possessed that ambient soft lighting, blending with the cigarette smoke, which lent it a peculiar charm. I met two people that night, I knew very well. Arthur, my father's old lover, came across.

'I'm not disturbing you or cramping your style?' he said.

'No,' I told him, 'not at all.'

'I think I know why you're here,' he said. 'You've come back for him.'

'That's very perceptive of you,' I said.

'And I don't even know his name,' he said.

'Tyrone,' I said.

'Well, it's a good enough Irish name, I'll give you that,' he said. We both laughed.

'I know that look, you both had it in your eyes the last time I saw you. When your father walked out of my life, I was young and full of hormones and damn arrogance. When I went to live in Dublin, I took lots of lovers, from barrow-boys, to farm-hands and farriers. I loved then all. And yet throughout, your father was always with me. He remained as a living presence in my mind,' he said.

'Is it like that with, Tyrone?' he said. I nodded to him that it was so.

'Before I left for Leeds, I happened to see Dad getting into a car with you,' I said.

'Do you think it's wrong?' He said.

'Perhaps it was wrong of my dad to get married in the first place,' I said.

'I tried to stay away, and then we bumped into each other in a cash and carry on the outskirts of town. We've been meeting every Wednesday afternoon since then. How many so called respectable marriages are really like that?' he said.

The next familiar face I saw that evening was Billy Hardcastle, my previous lover who had helped me fulfil, my best man duties. It was great to see him. And yes, a part of me still fancied him, but my heart was somewhere else. I could see by the look in his eyes, he also knew it. 'The marriage to, Shona,' he said, 'was a complete disaster. I tried really hard to go straight. And then she caught me in bed with the apprentice plumber, and that was that. It was a very acrimonious divorce, and I'm shelling out half of my wages in child-maintenance, to a little boy I'll never get to see,' he said. I felt sorry for him and told him so. All of this seemed to be the matter of the times, a self-oppression that made gay men fly into marriage. God, I'd nearly done it myself. Tyrone didn't show that night. I left the bar, weary at heart and wandered myself back to my parents' place.

The conversation over the breakfast table was stilted. It

always would be now, since I had come out. There were certain subjects I knew I couldn't discuss. I said nothing about my intentions of taking Tyrone, back to Leeds with me. 'Well you seem to have your feet well under the table at your new school,' said Mum. She always seemed pleased to know I was getting on well at work.

And so I wandered myself down to The Manhattan Bar for a second night. Still, Tyrone didn't show. Maybe they sometimes worked odd shifts at the post office I thought. There must be workers who attended to all the night mail which came off the trains in the early hours of the morning. That would be it, I thought. The third night, there was still no sign of him. I was resolved to go and call on Maggie, his mum. Surely she would know of his whereabouts. Then I wondered what if she has moved out of the area? I steadied my nerves with a large scotch, before wandering back to my parents' place.

It was Sunday the next day. Being a good Catholic, Maggie rarely worked Sundays. I thought if I called during the early afternoon, a little after lunch, she was sure to be in. Yet, even although we had been friends, my nerves almost got the better of me, as I turned into the road and saw her carefully kept front garden, towards the end of the row of houses. I took a deep breath and walked quickly up to the house, and boldly rang the front door bell. The first thing I heard was a dog barking. They had never kept a dog. Perhaps she had moved and my worst fears were about to be realized. But then Maggie opened the door to me and instantly broke into a smile.

'What an altogether lovely surprise,' she said and bade me to come in.

She made us both a cup of tea and then was asking about my

life in Leeds. Eventually we got around to the subject of Tyrone.

'You've come back for him haven't you?' she said. I hung my head.

'I suppose I'm just being a crazy love-struck fool?' I said.

'Maybe, but somehow I don't think so,' she said. There was a rather lovely Border collie dog who wanted a fuss made of him.

'He's called, Ben,' she said. 'He is only two years old and he's completely devoted to, Tyrone,' she said. 'That bit of trouble he had a while back there, well he decided to pay off all of his debts and he moved back in with me. We decided to get a dog. He's back on his feet now,' she said.

'So where is he?' I said. She filled up my cup with some more tea.

'Now we come to the difficult bit,' she said. 'They were advertising for workers at the post office, to sit for the civil service entrance exam. He decided to take it. He went and passed it with distinction. So he could go and become a clerical officer, and able to go for other promotions. Well that was nearly six months ago. He kept waiting for a vacancy to come up, but as far as Munford was concerned, there was nothing doing. And then a job came up in Dundee. He went up for the interview and he got it. He's been living up there in digs, for the last month,' she said. I felt all hope disappearing as we spoke.

'No matter,' she said, 'I'll phone him.' I thought to myself, this was Tyrone's big chance, his lucky break, where he could finally break free from his succession of dead-end jobs.

'No, Maggie,' I said, 'don't phone him.' She looked at me puzzled. 'This is his big break. I don't want to spoil it. He has a chance in a new place, to start his life all over again.'

'Robbie,' she said, 'my dear, you love him.'

'Yes, I love him more than I could ever say,' I said feeling tearful, 'but sometimes when you really love someone, when you love them so much, it hurts like hell, you have to know when to let go.'

A little while later I left. We shook hands at the door and wished each other the best. She watched me as I walked up the path. She called me back.

'Come here, you daft bugger,' she said, giving me a tearful hug.

I told the gang what had taken place in Munford and that everything, as far as I was concerned, was all over between Tyrone and me. I had to let him get on with his new life. And there were lots of hugs around the kitchen table. They were particularly gentle with me, over the next few days.

Fortunately, I had something else to distract me. Maureen Stepplemen, the new head of my department, together with Phyllis and me, decided to thrash out some ideas for a new part of the entire English Language curriculum. We had been rather weak on our CSE oral examinations. Suddenly the pupils were just faced with it, without adequate preparation. We called our new idea, *The Spoken Word Project*.

So there we were in Phyllis's front room, with hot jazz blasting away on the turntable, heaps of nice nibbles supplied by Bob, lashings of wine, copious amounts of full ashtrays and loads of creative attitude and cheek, hammering out our ideas. We were having a great time. Pupil's interests and hobbies were to become paramount, and they would be encouraged to stand up in class and talk about them, with their friends asking them questions about them.

We wanted these ideas of spoken word English, to be taught right across the board, from eleven to sixteen. We also thought it just might unlock untold potential from the remedial department. It was still early August, and for once I was eager for the start of term. I couldn't wait to get going. And so with the beginning of term, I really threw myself into the new material. We were getting marvellous results straight away. The kids loved it, and the remedial kids felt like they were actually being listened to, for the first time in their lives!

I'd be sitting cross-legged on the floor in the front room at home, bits of paper everywhere, jotting down new ideas and absorbing myself in it all. I was much too busy for silly distractions like going out for a drink, meals at our favourite Italian restaurant and night-clubbing. This was what mattered. The other two were concerned.

'It's all terribly exciting and all of that, but I wonder if you are throwing yourself into all of this extra-curricular activity, as a means of escaping having to think about, Tyrone,' said Rory.

'Yes, Sigmund,' I replied.

It was a Saturday and it had been one of those most wonderful autumn days, in the middle of October. Rory had been able to get some last minute tickets for Leeds Town Hall. It was an all-Beethoven evening, with an East European orchestra. 'It's all very good for *the spoken word,* you know,' said a cheeky Callum.

'Yes, you can discuss your interests about it with your fellow peers over a pint afterwards,' said Rory.

He was also buying tea at our favourite Italian restaurant, so I decided not to put up any further objections to going out. As expected, the meal and the concert were rather sublime! You could tell that the orchestra and the soloist were having the time of their lives, making all of that glorious music. The usual ritual after the concert, was to go on to the traditional jazz and then catch last orders at a favourite gay bar, before dancing and whoring our young rocks off at the night club, into the early hours of Sunday morning. This we had decided to do.

When we came into the bar, heaving with Saturday night revellers, I went to get in a round of drinks. The taciturn landlady was serving behind the bar. 'There was this young man in here, a little while ago. He was asking for you,' she said. I asked her if he was still here. 'Now how on earth would I know that, with all the crowds I've had in here tonight?' I asked her what he looked like. 'Oh, I don't really know. But he looked very much like your type,' she said, smiling. I was going to dismiss it as probably no more than one of my many one-night-stands. But then Rory came to help me with the drinks.

'Oh, while you are at the bar, get an extra gin and tonic would you,' he said. He was smiling like crazy.

'What gives? I asked him.

'Hurry up with the drinks and you'll find out,' he said.

They'd somehow managed to squeeze themselves into a table space, over in the far corner. It was difficult to see at first, with all the smoke. When I arrived at our table, I nearly dropped the drinks. For sitting there with a great grin, plastered all over his face, was Tyrone. And then I had to come out with something really daft.

'Are you just up visiting then?' I said.

'No, Robbie,' he said, 'I'm here to spend the rest of my life with you, if that's what you want?'

'But, Tyrone,' I said, 'what about your job in Dundee and all of that?'

'I got a transfer, but we'll talk about all the boring details later,' he said. 'Do you want me or not?' he said.

'Come here,' I said.

He got up and came across to me; in fact he all but leaped into my arms. And then we were hugging and smothering each other with kisses. And the whole god-damn pub was clapping and applauding our reunion! Rory had his hanky out and Callum was just grinning away like crazy!

'My God,' said Rory, 'this is every bit as moving as when the captain asked Maria to marry him in *The Sound of Music*.' And then we were all granted the relief of laugher.

The four of us went on to the club. Tyrone and I wasted no time, getting ourselves onto the dance floor. And how I loved all of his innate grace, dancing before me wild and free. Every-so-often, we would stop to give each other a long amorous kiss. He decided to scream out his glee, and had me falling about laughing. Eventually the other two joined us on the dance floor. Callum was passing round the poppers, and we were all about as high as high could possibly be!

We got back home, a little after two in the morning. I smiled to see Tyrone's car, parked beside my own. I could see the back seat was filled up with all of his stuff. The four of us sat up drinking coffee and smoking, and then the other two went to bed, leaving me with him in the front room. We gave ourselves over to the moment, kissing long and hard. He was still all, 'Mr Romantic,' and it was with gentle wooing fingers that I slowly began to undress him. I'd almost forgotten how strange and wonderful, his nakedness was! We left our clothes, strewn across the living room floor, and then went upstairs to bed. At last, I entered the deep, warm space of him. We were both crying with the shared ecstasy. And cuddling into me afterwards he said; 'now I really feel like I've come home to you at last.'

And so Tyrone moved in and he became my life. The four of us got on famously and yet, there was one member of our little household still missing. Maggie phoned us one Sunday morning. 'Ben, is fretting himself away for, Tyrone,' she said, 'he just won't settle without him.' And so we were joined by Ben, his Border collie, who ended up being spoiled completely by four adoring young queens!

During the first week of the Christmas holidays of that year, I received a rather anxious phone call from Natalie. 'I've applied for the headship, of course I don't stand a chance in hell of getting it, and it's, Chris,' she said, ' who has kept nagging me to go for it, but there we are,' she said. 'Anyway, is there any way I can persuade you and, Tyrone,' she said, 'to come up and spend Christmas with us?'

Rory and Callum had both said they were spending Christmas, visiting their mothers. So there would be no one to look after Ben.

'Oh, you must bring him, I'm sure, Ryan,' she said, 'will love him.'

And I don't know why, but there is something so very camp about two gay men and a boisterous collie, driving up to Scotland in a sixties moggie! And somewhere in the distance, I could hear the echoing tickling laughter of the Shaman elders, for Ryan and Ben became the best of pals on that very first meeting!

We went back to that intimate back street Italian restaurant. Chris, Tyrone and I were anxiously waiting for Natalie to join us. She had been to her gruelling interview, the day before. The board of governors had called her to a meeting at five, the following evening. We could have all bored holes with our eyes, looking at the entrance to the restaurant, waiting for her arrival. And then she came in. She was smiling. She saw us and gave us all a thumbs up sign. Chris got up and went and gave her a hug. We ordered the champagne.

The following day, Tyrone and I decided to do a spot of last minute Christmas shopping. It felt like a place filled with ancient resonances for all lovers. Robert Burns' statue was standing tall and proud on Princes Street, the Kilmarnock bard and maverick who was always being fined, for not attending church and puncturing, all of the pomposity of his day. As I gazed up at him, I could have sworn he gave me a mischievous wink back, with a sort of playful knowing, not unlike the smile on Tyrone's face. I felt he was of our kith. As we walked down Princes Street, the air was fresh and crisp, the highland sky, an immense blue. A busker playing the pipes was standing by the subway. He was playing *The Flowers of the Forest*.

'What a bloody miserable thing ta be playing hen,' said an old woman to her friend, busy with her shopping, coming out of the subway.

'Aye,' said her friend, 'yad think he'd play something we a bit mare tune.'

I smiled, but I felt they did not understand. It was a battle anthem. It made me think of all we had been through. It spoke to me of all those who had fought the age-old battle against oppression. And yet too, it spoke of all the secret lovers, embracing in the shadows and all the tender places of the dark; for together, on this bright morning; we were all warriors under the sun.

THE END

ACKNOWLEDGEMENTS

I would like to thank my agent, publisher and editor; James Essinger, for his support, encouragement and keeping hold of the dream for me; even when I sometimes wasn't able to hold it for myself. Huge thanks. I'd also like to thank Charlotte Mouncey, for taking my wacky and disparate ideas and turning them into the beautiful book you are now holding in your hands. I'd like to thank Leo Creighton my very own 'happy-ever-after' husband and gay partner; for the last twenty years. I'd like to thank Liam O'Shea for thirty-five years of friendship and hell-raising, Simon Wellings for the Science Fiction and the laughter, Mike Wood for the opera, Heather Stacey for your friendship, wisdom and compassion, Joanna Moodie, my sister; for the last sixty years and for all of those rainy afternoons in Carlisle, when we were both teenagers; listening to Motown records. I'd like to give a huge thankyou to the city of Leeds, the place I've made my adopted home since 1985, its theatres, concert halls, smoky hidden away jazz venues, its parks and wild woodlands, its streets and its alleyways, its gay scene and its people. All of this has been a constant source of inspiration. I'd like to thank Anna and Kit, and all the folks from The Chemic Tavern; for all of the ale, the laughter and so much else. I'd like to thank my late parents, John and Mary, who encouraged me to dare to be myself in a world that wanted me to conform. And lastly I'd like to thank all of my gay brothers and sisters; both the wanton and the coy!